The Riddles of *The Hobbit*

Also by Adam Roberts

Fiction:

JACK GLASS
MARTIN CITYWIT
BY LIGHT ALONE
ANTICOPERNICUS
NEW MODEL ARMY

Non-Fiction:

FIFTY KEY FIGURES IN SCIENCE FICTION (*co-editor with Mark Bould, Andrew M. Butler and Sherryl Vint*)

THE ROUTLEDGE COMPANION TO SCIENCE FICTION (*co-editor with Mark Bould, Andrew M. Butler and Sherryl Vint*)

THE HISTORY OF SCIENCE FICTION

VICTORIAN CULTURE AND SOCIETY: The Essential Glossary

SCIENCE FICTION

The Riddles of *The Hobbit*

Adam Roberts

Professor of Nineteenth-Century Literature, Royal Holloway,
University of London, UK

First published 2013 by
PALGRAVE MACMILLAN

Palgrave Macmillan in the UK is an imprint of Macmillan Publishers Limited, registered in England, company number 785998, of Houndmills, Basingstoke, Hampshire RG21 6XS.

Palgrave Macmillan in the US is a division of St Martin's Press LLC, 175 Fifth Avenue, New York, NY 10010.

Palgrave Macmillan is the global academic imprint of the above companies and has companies and representatives throughout the world.

Palgrave® and Macmillan® are registered trademarks in the United States, the United Kingdom, Europe and other countries.

ISBN 978–1–137–37363–2

This book is printed on paper suitable for recycling and made from fully managed and sustained forest sources. Logging, pulping and manufacturing processes are expected to conform to the environmental regulations of the country of origin.

A catalogue record for this book is available from the British Library.

A catalog record for this book is available from the Library of Congress.

Typeset by MPS Limited, Chennai, India.

Contents

List of Illustrations

Introduction

The Hobbit was after all not as simple as it seemed.

(Tolkien, writing to Stanley Unwin, 31 July 1947)

We call it a riddle because it rids us of something—
and what it rids us of is precisely our investment in
the four-square, straightforwardness of comprehension. The world is not simple.

(Pierre Delalande)

Riddles have lost none of their power over us. There are many examples of this fact in our twenty-first century lives, from crossword and
Sudoku puzzles, to children's rhymes and Christmas cracker gags (and
'when is a door not a door?' is just as much a riddle as the door without
hinges, key or lid)—indeed, these are just the tip of the iceberg. Some
of the most popular modes of art today manifest the riddle as both
form and rationale. Crime novels, for instance, very rarely describe
crime as it actually occurs in the world—that is to say, crime writers
very rarely construe their stories as either obvious, or else incomprehensible, which are the two main ways that crime actually presents
itself (for social offences are either lamentably straightforward, or
else unsolved, estranging and deracinating). There are good dramatic
reasons for this, for stories that style crime as stupidly obvious or
randomly baffling are unlikely to engage a large audience. Crime in
the real world is about the disruption of order, but our appetite for
story is a desire for closure and so that is what crime fiction provides
us. To put it simply, crime fiction says: crime is a riddle. More, such

1

fiction invariably includes the solution to its riddle.[1] The classic puzzle-whodunit is one mode of this; a complex riddle in which we are given textual space and leisure (as the story unfolds) to ponder, before the surprising solution is revealed. So successful has this mode been it has spilled into other modes. A show like Fox Network's *House* (2008's globally most watched television show) tropes disease, and by extension health as a riddle to be solved. Sherlock Holmes, upon whom the 'House' character was based, continues to be prodigiously popular (an ongoing motion picture franchise and two big TV serials based upon a modern-day version of him)—and much of his appeal is that he treats everyday life as full of solvable riddles, riddles that other people do not even notice. A novel like Dan Brown's *The Da Vinci Code* (2001) has even larger ambitions, for it styles not just murder but *religion* as a riddle, and presents us with a protagonist who is a professional riddle-solver. The phenomenal commercial success of this title can in part be explained by the way it leavens its narrative with a string of riddles for the reader to solve as she goes along. I can not pretend I have the highest opinion of Brown's talents as a writer, but it seems to me that there is something more ambitious than simply crowd-pleasing in his novel: presenting for a mass audience not only religion as a riddle, but religion as a riddle *that can be solved*. Brown's immense commercial success, quite apart from anything else, suggests common ground between cryptic crossword puzzles and the most profound religious mysteries of men and women, life and death. Brown's talents as a writer are not able to match the grandeur of this connection, but some sense of it hangs about the creaky pulpisms of the novel and connected with enough readers to make it so colossal a bestseller.

Tolkien is another writer of quest narratives, and a man and an artist profoundly concerned with religious questions. This is one of the jumping-off points of this present study. Religious mysteries are, in a strict sense, riddles. That might look like a trivialising way of talking about faith, but I prefer to think of it the other way around— as a way of elevating the significance and dignity of riddles. Perhaps it would be better to say that even though they may seem trivial, riddles embody in a small way a very large observation about human existence. Life riddles us.

Saint Paul, in his letter to the Ephesians, puts it like this: 'If ye have heard of the dispensation of the grace of God which is given me to you-ward: how that by revelation he made known unto me the mystery; . . . which in other ages was not made known unto the sons of men, as it is now revealed unto his holy apostles and prophets by the Spirit' (Ephesians, 3:2–5). In other words, Paul says: existence is a riddle of which the solution has been unknown, until now. The solution he proposes is, in a word, Christ. But this answer folds back on itself in that the answer to this riddle is itself a riddle, what Paul calls 'the mystery of Christ'. Later in the letter Paul hopes that his readers 'may be able to comprehend and to know the love of Christ, which passeth knowledge' (Ephesians 3:18–19). That we can be assured of knowledge of something which passeth knowledge, and comprehension of the incomprehensible, speaks to the way the logic of the riddle goes deeper than simply 'question plus answer'. This, I think, is why it is worthwhile to work, as it were, *upwards* from the simple riddle to the largest questions of God and the universe. Such a trajectory is, a Christian might note, the gradient of Christ's own human incarnation as a gateway to the suprahuman divine. Besides, to come at it the other way around is to knock one's head against the very enormousness of the enquiry. 'There are certain questions', Thomas Hardy once said, 'which are made unimportant by their very magnitude. For example, the question whether we are moving in Space this way or that; the existence of God, etc.'[2] A very unHarydesque writer, Tolkien constructed his own art upon his faith, and therefore upon his belief that such questions are not only important but answerable, although the answers may be neither straightforward nor convenient.

Catholicism is one important context for Tolkien's writing. Another, more obvious one, is the culture and art of northern Europe and Scandinavia during the first millennium. Tolkien immersed himself, professionally and creatively, in the culture of the Anglo-Saxon, Norse and Icelandic Dark Age peoples. He was a medievalist too, and a philologist, but when it came to writing his greatest novels he drew on the myths, literature and culture of an earlier period, the Dark Ages. In this first chapter I will go on to argue that riddles are a central feature of the Anglo-Saxon world. Tolkien certainly had a taste for them himself. The fact that he put a very high premium upon truth (as he certainly did) fed rather than denatured his fascination with ironic, riddling and unstraightforward talk.

Asked whether the riddles in *The Hobbit* were his own original compositions, or else versions of traditional Anglo-Saxon riddles,

Tolkien wrote to one correspondent strongly implying the former, and to another strongly implying the latter. That he could do both without mendacity is a function, I think, not of evasion but on the contrary of an active delight in riddling and misdirection—for to read both letters (they are discussed below, pp. 68–9) is amongst other things to see how precise Tolkien's use of language was. His letters are full of ludic diversions, games, wit and puzzles, designed to divert and amuse his correspondents. Tom Shippey, the best critic to have devoted his attentions to Tolkien, records a letter he received from the man himself in 1970 responding to some of Shippey's criticism.

> I do turn back to the letter Professor Tolkien wrote to me on 13 April 1970, charmingly courteous and even flattering as it then was from one at the top of his profession to one at the bottom ('I don't like to fob people off with formal thanks . . . one of the nearest to my heart, or the nearest, of the many I have received . . . I am honoured to have received your attention'). And yet, and yet . . . What I should have realised—perhaps did half-realise, for I speak the dialect myself—was that this letter was written in the specialised politeness-language of Old Western Man, in which doubt and correction are in direct proportion to the obliquity of expression.[3]

I speak this dialect myself, or at any rate a debased twenty-first century version of it (dialects, like languages, tend to change over time); and whilst it would be distorting to describe it as a *riddling* mode of speech it is certainly one in which the relationship between the said and the meant is not straightforward. We might say that it is a mode in which the gap between courtesy and unvarnished truth is closed with irony, of a sort. And irony is the currency of the riddle, just as 'mimesis' is the currency of realist discourse. And there, in a nutshell, is the argument I am making in this book. *The Hobbit* appears to be a straightforward childrens' adventure tale; but it is actually much less simple, rather more ironic, than that. 'Irony rather than mimesis' also happens to be a fairly neat thumbnail for separating out the textual strategies of science fiction and fantasy from 'realist' works more generally conceived. That *The Hobbit* and *The Lord of the Rings* are foundational texts for the modern genre of 'Fantasy' does not seem to me coincidental. It ought not to surprise us that riddles are more than just occasional diversions in a novel like *The Hobbit*.

In fact, *The Hobbit* is a deeply riddling book. In saying so I am suggesting that 'the riddle' runs deeper through the novel than merely providing some of the matter for its fifth chapter 'Riddles in the Dark', in which Bilbo and Gollum swap riddles. There are, for one thing, other riddles in the book. When Bilbo encounters Smaug he talks to the beast in riddles, and the narrator assures us that riddling 'is of course the way to talk to dragons . . . no dragon can resist the fascination of riddling talk'. When Bilbo meets Gandalf for the first time, right at the start of the novel, the wizard treats the hobbit's simple greeting of 'Good Morning' *as* a riddle:

> What do you mean? Do you wish me a good morning, or mean that it is a good morning whether I want it or not, or that you feel good this morning, or that it is a morning to be good on?'

And throughout Tolkien styles his story as a series of problems to be solved, or riddles to be unriddled: obstacles, set-backs, mysteries and secrets structure the storytelling. This, I argue, is a way of embodying a larger vision; for it is not just that *The Hobbit* is a novel that *contains* riddles. It is a riddle in a larger, formal sense. It is a text that articulates a number of very big questions. In the pages that follow I try to unriddle some of these: the riddle of this novel's relationship to Tolkien's next novel, *The Lord of the Rings* (a more puzzling relationship than merely that of prequel and sequel); the riddle of the book's relationship to the 1930s, the troubled decade out of which is was produced; and the riddle of its enduring popularity. The ubiquity of *The Hobbit* perhaps occludes the oddity that a book so profoundly (and designedly) old-fashioned could somehow manage to capture the zeitgeist of that rather un-nostalgic century designated 'twentieth'. It has fed, as a river does an estuary, the profusion of 'Tolkienesque' books produced in the latter third of that century, and which continue being produced in this, our twenty-first (I touch on the riddle of Fantasy's commercial success in the ninth chapter here). And there is the central riddle, to which I return in the final chapter, that perhaps looks more straightforward than it is: what is a *hobbit*?

Setting out, as I do here, to read Tolkien's work under the aegis of 'the riddle' is, amongst other things, an attempt to explore something I take to be axiomatic of generic Fantasy, and of science fiction, too: that (to repeat myself) its relationship to reality is ironic rather than mimetic; an art not of closure but disclosure, asking questions and playfully problematising our attitudes to the objects of our life. This, as the first chapter sets out to argue, is something Tolkien draws from the Anglo-Saxon culture he admired so greatly. But there is more to it than that.

One of the things implicit in my approach in this book is that 'the riddle' is a trope for reading itself. Of course not all texts present themselves as riddles, and not all critical interpretations are best viewed as 'the right' answer to the questions the texts pose. But there are several reasons for taking *The Hobbit* as more than just an entertainment. It is full of riddles, but it also constellates 'riddling' in a larger sense; and this is because of its roots in Tolkien's understanding of, and love for, Anglo-Saxon culture, as well as his desire to story-forth lived-through solutions to the 'riddles' posed by fundamentally religious mystery.

Reading is inevitably an unriddling. It is just that sometimes the riddle is more obviously framed *as* a riddle. Since this is crucial to the argument I hope to go on to make in this book, and since an obvious objection presents itself, I shall say a little more about it. The obvious objection is that I am tendentiously eliding two only superficially similar things: the riddle as a specific, and minor, literary genre on the one hand, and 'the riddle' as a metaphorical mode of 'questioning, interpreting and reading' on the other. I hold up my hand. I am indeed doing this, not out of conceptual confusion but precisely because I believe the former takes force and life from the latter. The riddle in the strict sense focuses and intensifies the same impulses that inform literary studies and reading more generally.

To quote W. P. Ker, a scholar of the Dark Ages whose work directly influenced Tolkien's own academic work, the riddle as 'translation of ideas' is

> peculiarly fitted for literary exercises: it requires neatness, point, liveliness. Hence it is not surprising that enigmas of this sort, with nothing altered in their methods of fancy, should adapt themselves to all changes of literary expression.[4]

Ker's argument is not as far-reaching (he might say: not as overreaching) as is mine, here; he sees riddles as a minor part of the kingdom of letters, and is uninterested in their meta-textual or metaphorical application to the larger matters of reading, believing in God and living. Nevertheless his statement here rather neatly encapsulates the thesis of this study.

It also, usefully, directs the spotlight on pre-Conquest culture, something with which this study must be largely (though not exclusively) concerned. Ker notes that 'poetical riddles were produced in England more largely than anywhere else in the Dark Ages, both in Latin and the native tongue'. There is something in the riddling mode that the English find peculiarly fascinating. Indeed, insofar as riddles involve making familiar objects beautifully strange, describing things in de-familiarising ways, it is at the heart of 'poetry' in the largest sense.

To illustrate what I mean by this I am going to step away from Tolkien for a moment, and quote two poems by Rudyard Kipling, both written at the time Tolkien himself was a young man, and both concerning the war in which Tolkien fought (although, of course, Tolkien fought on land rather than at sea). The first is 1915's 'The Changelings':

> Or ever the battered liners sank
> With their passengers to the dark
> I was head of a Walworth Bank,
> And you were a grocer's clerk.
>
> I was a dealer in stocks and shares,
> And you in butters and teas;
> And we both abandoned our own affairs
> And took to the dreadful seas.
>
> Wet and worry about our ways—
> Panic, onset and flight—
> Had us in charge for a thousand days
> And thousand-year-long night.
>
> We saw more than the nights could hide—
> More than the waves could keep—
> And—certain faces over the side
> Which do not go from our sleep.
>
> We were more tired than words can tell
> While the pied craft fled by,

> And the swinging mounds of the Western swell
> Hoisted us Heavens-high . . .
>
> Now there is nothing—not even our rank—
> To witness what we have been;
> And I am returned to my Walworth Bank
> And you to your margarine!

To read this poem is to understand not only its specific referents—that these two men left civilian jobs to serve in the Royal Navy, and afterwards went back to civilian life—but also to comprehend that as much as it celebrates the more traditional martial values of bravery, persistence, duty and so on, it also heroises something more specific, a mode of English (we could say; Old English) *reticence*, or *understatement*. The rhetorical term for this is litotes, something of which Anglo-Saxon poets were extremely fond. When a man achieves something very large, for example heroic feats of battle (or in Kipling's case, heroic feats of sheer survival) it is not only more seemly, it is more rhetorically forceful and effective to understate rather than overstate the achievement. We could say: the banker and the clerk are no small heroes.

It would not be right to call this poem a riddle as such, of course, since it does not seek to hide its meaning, although *part* of its affect is generated in ways that are more riddling. I very much like, for instance, the way marine terminology haunts even the landlubber existences of these two characters: such that 'Walworth Bank' sounds like it belongs on a naval map alongside Dogger Bank, and 'margarine' sounds like a sea-y 'mar' word. Here is another Kipling poem, 'The Egg Shell' (originally written in 1904, but enlarged and republished in 1916):

> The wind took off with the sunset—
> The fog came up with the tide,
> When the Witch of the North took an Egg-shell
> With a little Blue Devil inside.
> 'Sink,' she said, 'or swim,' she said,
> 'It's all you will get from me.
> And that is the finish of him!' she said
> And the Egg-shell went to sea.

The wind fell dead with the midnight—
The fog shut down like a sheet,
When the Witch of the North heard the Egg-shell
Feeling by hand for a fleet.
'Get!' she said, 'or you're gone,' she said.
But the little Blue Devil said 'No!'
'The sights are just coming on,' he said,
And he let the Whitehead go.

The wind got up with the morning—
The fog blew off with the rain,
When the Witch of the North saw the Egg-shell
And the little Blue Devil again.
'Did you swim?' she said. 'Did you sink?' she said,
And the little Blue Devil replied:
'For myself I swam, but I think,' he said,
'There's somebody sinking outside.'

Roger Peppe recalls a family recital of this poem in which the poem was read both as 'a nice piece of nonsense' and a technically specific piece of naval realism.[5] The latter reading, I would suggest, enhances rather than annihilates the former. That is how riddles work. A 'whitehead' is a naval torpedo (named after its inventor, Robert Whitehead) and this is a poem that tropes the World War I war at sea as a sort of dark fairy tale. The eggshell submarine is a particularly nice notion; not just its fragility but the sense of it as *hatching something out*—death, in this case. Also neatly worked is the way the submarine's captain's name suggests not only his diabolic purpose, but some sense of his depression: his mood mimicking his physical descent through the waters. It can not be a jolly business, lurking through the waters and killing civilians. It is the sensitivity of Kipling's touch here that is the really remarkable thing; the way he balances the poem between a surface-meaning akin to the phantasmagoria of fairy tale and a deeper meaning tied to actual naval operations. It is something that gains force from precisely the tension between ships on the surface of the water and submarines below that surface.

It does this powerful poem no disservice to read it as a riddle. On the contrary, it is a literary work that points up how expressive and potent riddling can be as a textual strategy. Some poetry is more straightforwardly riddle-like than others. John Donne's 'A Valediction, Forbidding Mourning' (written 1611) tropes the situation of the lovers as like the two spars of a hinged compass or divider. Four centuries later Craig Raine wrote a poem called 'The Onion, Memory' (1978). In a sense both poems are built straightforwardly around riddles: 'how is love like the two limbs of a divider?'; 'why is memory an onion?' Donne's poem gains force from the oddity and novelty of its conceit, where Raine goes a step further, with a conceit that is not only strikingly odd and novel but cleverly wrongfooting too. My experience of teaching Raine's poems to students is that readers asked 'why is memory like an onion?' will tend to focus upon the physicality of the vegetable and say things like 'because it is layered?' or 'because it grows as it is buried?' Raine's solution to his own riddle is neater, and more moving (memory is like an onion because it makes me cry).

I should add that not all poetry works this way; perhaps not most poetry. Metaphysical and Martian poetry both tend to foreground riddling conceits, but I do not want to limit myself to those two modes only. If I tell you that 'any poem requires a sort of unriddling, even if it is merely the construction of a context that makes sense of the direct', you might object that this dilutes the meaning of the word 'riddling' to the point where it loses purchase. But to argue that is, tacitly, to imply that most poetry *can* be simply decoded—that the world itself is simple. This is not right. The world is not simple, at least in the things that matter the most. By troping reading as 'unriddling' I am talking about more than simply solving certain clues, or slotting a particular solution into place. I am, on the contrary, thinking of 'the riddle' as the idiom of all epistemological *process*. Here is a poem that can neither be described as 'Metaphysical' nor 'Martian', but which is nonetheless (I think) a kind of riddle.

> She tells her love while half asleep,
> In the dark hours,
> With half-words whispered low:
> As Earth stirs in her winter sleep.
> And puts out grass and flowers.
> Despite the snow
> Despite the falling snow.[6]

I quote this famous Robert Graves lyric in part because Graves (whom Tolkien met, and found interesting, 'though—an ass') was himself fascinated by the thought of poetry as in the largest sense a riddle.[7] He comes into my discussion below in Chapter 5. But I also quote it because it is, we might think, very far away from the surface opacities of a conventional riddle. The lines are clearly expressed, the sense seemingly straightforward. Yet engagement with the poem requires us at the very least to intuit who 'she' might be; what her circumstances are; whether she is alone. This is not to say very much, for of course all texts require this of us. But there is more to it. In this case, the 'solution' of the poem provided by a simple reading takes us to something— love—that is very far from simple. Indeed, the unsimpleness of love is what the poem is about, and Graves' obliqueness and suggestiveness are not incidentals, or steps on the path to a straightforward comprehension. What Wallace Stevens famously identified as 'the beauty of inflections' is one kind of poetic-semantic riddling, which in turn can be construed. The beauty of innuendoes is another, deeper kind.

Of course, the riddling note or tone is not always appropriate, even to poetry that sets out to address deep mysteries in a playful manner. When W. H. Auden was revising his *For the Time Being: A Christmas Oratorio* (1944) he cut out the following stanza—

> Mary the Modest was met in the lane
> By Someone or Something she couldn't explain.
> Joseph the Honest looked up and God's eye
> Was winking at him through a hole in the sky.[8]

We might ask: what is wrong with this, as poetry? It is not that far removed, tonally or in terms of its approach to the Christmas mysteries, from the other *For The Time Being* stanzas that Auden kept in the poem—although, having said that, it is obviously far *enough* away for Auden to ditch it. I wonder if the problem with these lines is not that they are riddling, but rather than they are flippantly so. This in turn points towards a more important point. Some riddles *are* flippant (some paradoxes are flat; some mysteries banal; some questions trivial). But some riddles are not, and amongst this latter category are the riddles in, and of, *The Hobbit*.

There is one further sense in which this sort of hermeneutic opens up the possibilities of reading Tolkien. After the success of *The Lord of the Rings*, many reviewers and readers became persuaded that the novel was an allegory for the Second World War, the large-scale historical trauma through which Tolkien lived as he wrote the novel. The 'ring', according to this reading, is an allegorical representation of 'the atomic bomb'; Sauron is Hitler, Frodo and Sam represent the humble British solider. Tolkien repudiated these sorts of readings, and took time in his preface to the novel to express himself as unambiguously as he could. 'I cordially dislike allegory in all its manifestations', he notes, 'and always have done so since I grew old and wary enough to detect its presence.'[9]

We need to take Tolkien's cordial dislike seriously, I think. It is more than just aesthetic eccentricity. Taking the characters of any story 'allegorically' is to subordinate their individuality to some larger scheme, a notion repellent to Tolkien on religious and ideological as well as artistic grounds: 'the actors', as he put it, 'are individuals'.[10] On one level, he is making a fundamentally religious point. For a Christian, Christ is not a 'symbol' of God; he does not (as it were) *allegorically represent* God in the mortal realm. Christ *is* God, incarnated in human form. And, to go down to the level of doctrinal disagreement, for a Catholic the communion wine and bread at mass do not 'symbolise' God's blood and body, they literally, if rather mysteriously, *are* those things. Part of Tolkien's approach to Fantasy, something to which he gave the Coleridgean name 'Subcreation', is a belief that the true artist's creations exist as a small-scale, secondary version of what God Himself did when he created the cosmos: its relationship to larger reality being that of a ratio inferior that draws its force from the superior creative context. This in turn means that Tolkien's vision of Middle-earth is profoundly sacramental. Something similar is true of his friend C. S. Lewis's creation, Narnia. Lewis was more comfortable with allegory than Tolkien, but it would be a mistake (though one commonly made) to read *The Lion, The Witch and the Wardrobe* as an allegory of the Christian passion. Lewis's Aslan does not *allegorise* Christ; he is the form Christ's incarnation would take in a world of talking animals. Perhaps this looks like a quibble, but I do not think it is. It goes to the heart of what Lewis and Tolkien are doing as a writers of Fantasy—indeed it goes to the heart of that genre, Modern Fantasy, that is so largely formed in their image.

A book such as mine takes seriously two things—Tolkien's *The Hobbit* and riddles more generally—that many critics do not take seriously. It would overstate things to say that there is a prejudice against *The Hobbit* in Tolkien scholarship, although most Tolkienists I know think of it as a lesser text when set alongside *The Lord of the Rings*—a children's story with little more to it than a desire to divert and entertain. That I do not share such a view should be obvious from the fact that I have set out to write this book at all, and the justification for my dissent should emerge from the pages that follow. *'The Hobbit'*, as Tolkien wrote to Stanley Unwin in 1947, in a letter quoted as one of the epigraphs to this chapter 'was after all not as simple as it seemed.' I have decided to take him at his word. As for riddles: it is the process of engaging them, rather than the determining of any one 'answer', that is where their capacity for illumination is located.

Light is the *fons et origo* of Tolkien's imaginary cosmos, as it is of *our* cosmos (according, at least, to Genesis); and most of Tolkien's art is concerned, in deep ways, with exploring the interactions between seeing and unseeing, visibility and invisibility, brightness and darkness. It is worth holding in mind that a riddle, formally speaking, is a small example of something unseen presenting itself to us and asking to be seen. It is, as it were, a thing wearing a ring of invisibility. Our wits are the mode by which it can be made visible again. 'Blessed are the eyes', Christ told his disciples, 'which see the things which ye see. For I tell you, that many prophets and kings have desired to see those things which ye see, and have not seen them' (Luke 10:23). To the extent that riddles are seen as a negligible, or even despicable, mode of poetry I have attempted, here, to take them much more seriously, as both examples of and tropes for the broader mystery of what is hidden and what revealed in literature.

There is a danger, of which I am of course aware, that a critic working on a theme or topic for any length of time may become Casaubonised—that, in other words, s/he may come to believe that her pet subject actually is the key to all mythologies. The problem with riddles, it seems to me, is not that they are a trivial and marginal manifestion of culture; but on the contrary that they are rather *too* far-reaching and profound.

In other words my argument is a little less banal than 'reading is deducing things from the clues provided by the text'; or at least I hope it is. It is that even in texts that seem straightforward, interpretation is much more ironic than mimetic; more a process of opening disclosure than a narrowing-down enclosure. One of the points of a poem like 'A Martian Sends A Postcard Home' is that it is only familiarity (or habitude) that stands between us and a vision of the world as a fascinating but baffling series of puzzles to be decoded. That, we could say, if the doors of perception were cleansed to a properly Martian cleanliness we should see the world as it truly is, *a riddle*.

This in turn connects with the larger sense that human subjectivity—mind, personality, soul—is itself a riddle. Put like that the sentiment may come over as windy, the tawdry vatic in specie. But I mean it in a particular way. It is, after all, one of Freud's key insights that human life is not simple or straightforward; that we do not know ourselves after the direct mimetic model of a photograph or a textbook, but rather that our self-knowledge is an ironic business, slant, full of obscurity and gaps. Freud proposes that we are a riddle unto ourselves, and sets up psychoanalysis as a means of unriddling the puzzle of psychosis, trauma, hysteria or plain old human unhappiness. A dream (say) may appear to be one thing, but it is in fact something else; it is, in short, a riddle to be decoded with access to the right sorts of reading competencies. In Chapter 9 below I say something about the complexities of our psychological fantasies, and the relation of the desire they encode to the body of writing that is called, largely for bookselling convenience, 'Fantasy'—the genre of course to which *The Hobbit* belongs.

The Hobbit is not only a 'Fantasy' book; it is a book for children. This is also relevant to what I want to try and argue. It is, it seems to me, not coincidental that so many childrens' and 'Young Adult' books are so full of puzzles and riddles, from the *Alice* books to the anagrams and spell-puzzles of Harry Potter. These are books about 'growing up'. *The Hobbit* is likewise about Bilbo 'growing up', or least growing into something more than he previously was. As a hobbit he combines a child's stature with a middle-aged man's set-in-his-ways mind, and his adventures challenge both aspects of him. The point is that the world is more of a riddle when we are growing up—indeed, 'growing up' is in large part (inevitable physiological changes aside) a process of unriddling the many puzzles, larger and small, that experience joyfully showers upon us. One of the ways the unexamined wisdom of children manifests in the world, one of the ways in which the child *is* father to the man, is the way kids ask riddles all the time: why is the sky blue? Why is water wet? Why is that man crying? Why are that woman and that man cuddling so close? You might object that these are simple questions, not riddles; and certainly children do ask a great many questions. But 'why is the sky blue?' is more than a question (after all: could *you* supply a 5-year old child with an answer in a way that did not merely baffle her?) It is a way of reaching out towards the way beauty and wonder overroof our mundane worlds. It is to take the step beyond merely registering the glory of a blue sky, into the realm of wanting to comprehend that glory. It is, that is to say, intensely human.

* * *

In what follows a great many riddles are cited, and to many of these I offer solutions—if possible, I try to offer more than one. This is in the nature of what I am doing, and for it I make no apology. Riddling is as much as anything about ingenuity, and I value ingenuity very highly—find it baffling, in fact, how little regard most people have for it as a human skill. At any rate, I take it that a mode that prizes invention and ingenuity is best discussed *ingeniously*. A reader may ask: 'ah, but is what you are arguing here *true*?' That is a valid and important question, but it is not, I submit, a *simple* question. Truth is a riddle whose premises may not be what you thought, at first, they were; and whose answer may only be another, further riddle. Kierkegaard once defined truth as a leap of faith, a subjective and paradoxical thing. I might prefer 'riddle' to 'paradox', because the former term implies a process—a launch pad for the leap of faith—where the latter makes me think of knots and blockages. But that is only a personal quirk. More to the point, Kierkegaard's famous subjectivised truth ('an objective uncertainty held fast in an appropriation-process of the most passionate inwardness is the truth, the highest truth attainable for the individual') famously distinguishes between approximation and appropriation, the former akin to the scientific approach to veracity, the latter necessarily personal and subjective. It would be fair to say that I appropriate Tolkien's great novel in this little book, and it may be worth noting that I do so from a position of love. I first read *The Hobbit* as a young child, and fell deeply for it from the beginning (I am hardly alone in that, of course). My account can hardly be other than subjective. I say so not to try and exculpate myself, but to draw attention to the sense in which the truth-claims contained between these covers are themselves both subjective and bounded by the rubrics of the riddle. Kierkegaard puts into the mouth of his sock-puppet Johannes Climacus the more extreme version of this idea: that 'the supreme paradox of all thought is the attempt to discover something that thought cannot think. This passion is at bottom present in all thinking, even in the thinking of the individual, in so far as in thinking he participates in something transcending himself. But habit dulls our sensibilities, and prevents us from perceiving it.'[11] Riddles force us to look again at those things dulled by the habit of our sensibilities. Intervening into the large body of academic criticism about Anglo-Saxon riddles, Patrick J. Murphy rehearses the various proffered solutions to 'Riddle 69' of the *Exeter Book* (I look at this riddle myself below). But then he takes a step too few academics do: he asks not only what the answer is, but what the answer *does*:

> We might then ask what this solution *does*. Among other things, the solution snaps the text into sudden focus and reveals the great wonder of a commonplace thing. This sense of the miraculous in the mundane is at the heart of Old English riddling.[12]

This is very well put, and gains in insightfulness when we apply it (as Murphy does not) to Tolkien, because for him the category of 'the miraculous' is so profound, and so central to his art. Riddles stimulate and empower us, and they do more than that. In the largest sense they attempt to think the things thought cannot think.

In what follows I quote from a variety of Old English texts, sometimes citing the Anglo-Saxon, more often, since my concern is only rarely specific to that language, in modern English translation. I have decided to quote from a variety of translations, including on occasion my own—Kevin Crossley Holland's version of the *Exeter Book* riddles (Penguin, revised edition 1993) is a marvel of graceful precision and poetic effect, but although I do cite it in the pages that follow it did not seem fair to cite only him. It felt a little like I was picking on him. Accordingly, I quote a variety of other translations, of the riddles and of other OE texts. I have sometimes quoted Seamus Heaney's celebrated translation of *Beowulf*; unattributed translations from the Old English (including *Beowulf*) are my own.

A book about *The Hobbit* can hardly avoid quoting from Tolkien's own works. The Tolkien estate is, quite properly, protective of its various copyrights, and one of the processes of revising this book during its various drafts has been the removal of too generous quotation from Tolkien's own words, replacing some passages with paraphrase—not an ideal compromise, from my point of view, but necessary. I have tried to keep quotation from Tolkien to a minimum, and certainly to keep it within the bounds of the provision for scholarly and critical 'fair use'. I would have liked to quote a lot more.

Irony can be serious, but even at its most serious there is something playful—something crooked, something riddling—in the nature of it. The present book is written in that spirit. Most of its ironies are serious ones, and I am genuinely attempting to get to the bottom of what seem to me serious questions about Tolkien, about fantasy and about riddling. But sometimes that seriousness finds expression in more deliberately ingenious and playful mode than at others. The first two chapters aim to contextualise Tolkien's own riddling practice by looking at the prevalence, and nature, of riddles in Anglo-Saxon culture. The two chapters that follow ('Riddles in the Dark' and 'The Riddles of the All-Wise') read the riddle-contest between Bilbo and Gollum from chapter 8 of *The Hobbit* in some detail. There follows a chapter on The Hobbit as a whole, and another that considers how puzzling it is that a character inhabiting a pre-modern, medieval or Dark-Age world has *pockets*. Chapters 7 and 8 ('The Riddle of the Ring' and 'The *Lord of the Rings* and the Riddle of Writing') move into a broader discussion of *The Lord of the Rings*; and Chapters 9 and 10 ('The Volsung Riddle: Character in Tolkien' and 'The Enigma of Genre Fantasy') range more widely still, looking at the genre of 'Tolkienian' fantasy as a whole in an attempt to suggest reasons why it has proved so popular and enduring. For the final chapter I return to *The Hobbit*, and suggest a new answer to the most obvious riddle of all: 'what is a hobbit'?

1

The Anglo-Saxon Riddleworld

> Riddles are in origin a folk-art, ancient and
> worldwide . . . [Anglo-Saxon] riddles, therefore,
> enjoyable for their wit and its poetic expression, are
> also of crucial importance for the insight they offer
> into the intellectual structure of the Anglo-Saxon lit-
> erary mind. The mentality that can engage with the
> sense of the *literal* statement and with the *implicit*
> and 'truer' import of the concealed meaning is a
> mentality alert to symbolism and allegory; and not
> surprisingly techniques of the riddle may be traced
> in poetry of other genres where ambiguity and
> systematic symbolism or allegory are deliberately
> cultivated.[1]

Anglo-Saxon was a riddling culture. By this I do not just mean that
the Norse, the Icelanders and the Old English loved riddles—although
they certainly did. Old English culture was threaded through with
riddles, cryptograms, gnomic verses, charms and riddling modes of
speech such as litotes, just as *Modern* English culture is (if you will
forgive me) riddled with jokes and catch-phrases, crosswords and
quizzes, irony and sarcasm. But there is more to it than that. I mean
that the orientation of the Anglo-Saxons towards their world was
ironic, often wittily or sardonically so. They were more minded than
moderns to view life as a puzzle and a mystery. Anglo-Saxons tended
to prize a particular combination of strength *and* wit. It was good to
be brave, to fight fiercely, to stay true to your friends and your lord;

but it was better still to do all these things *lightly*, with humour, gaily. This is not a matter of modesty. On the contrary, *boasting* was a valued skill. Boasting, such as those contests in which warriors traded insults called 'flytings', were opportunities to show your cleverness as well as your forcefulness. What was particularly admired was *good* boasting— boasts that were witty and clever, as well as boasts you were prepared to expend your life, if necessary, making true. In all this there is something of the riddle, but on a grander, more existential scale. Riddles are more than mere pastimes; they speak to the puzzling circumstances in which we find ourselves. Threading through all this is the sense of the riddle, the joke, the ironic understatement, as all modes of *extravagance* of speech. They are, in modern parlance, the bling of words.

If this sounds as if I am granting riddles a more profound significance than mere word-games and children's rhymes might merit, then indeed I am. In the introduction to their translation of the riddling legend-poetry of *The Elder Edda*, (itself a key source for Tolkien's own imaginarium) Peter Salus and Paul Taylor begin with scholarly circumspection:

> Poetic composition of riddles was principally an exercise of scholastic wit throughout the Middle Ages. Hundreds of Latin riddles in poetic form have survived. In general they are puzzles in which some object of phenomenon is described; the reader or listener is expected to 'solve' the puzzle and state the object. Riddle making was equally popular in the vernacular. In Old English, for example, almost a hundred survive.

But they go on to suggest that, for the Norse mind, riddles were much more than just this:

> Riddles suggest the Nordic fascination with the apparent relationship between the structure of language and the structure of the cosmos. For the Scandinavians the wisest man—he who knows most of the structure of the cosmos—is also the most skilful poet . . . there is in the Nordic mind a subtle relationship, and a necessary one, between an event and the language with which it is described or anticipated. [2]

That the nature of this relationship is *ironic* in a profound way is one of the starting premises of this book. I aim to trace the place of 'the riddle' in Tolkien's fiction not just for the sake of it, and not because I consider such riddles as appear in *The Hobbit* to be diverting entertainments, but rather because it seems to me that riddling in this existential sense is crucial to Tolkien's whole artistic project. In a nutshell we could put it like this: for Tolkien the connection between words and the world is a deep one, not to be gainsaid or ignored. Riddles are a truer representation of the nature of reality than simple declarative statements. This is because, putting it simply, the world is not a simple or transparent business, but a mystery to be plumbed. Riddles themselves talk about ordinary objects or phenomena in an ironic way: they are sly, allusive, misleading. 'The point', in Carolyne Larrington's words, 'is not what is being said, but what is being concealed.'[3] And this in turn embodies the subtle, necessary link, between anything in-the-world and the language with which it is described.

This speaks, in the largest way, to the way the Old Northmen lived their lives. Irony is a way of expressing a sense that there is a gap between oneself and one's world, a mismatch between will and thing. This idea shaped Norse culture in ways from small to large. Take, for example, death. The Old English approach to this existential universal was a grim sort of acceptance that we must inevitably die, combined with a wry sense of the ironic mismatch between how much life we have in our doomed hearts. For the Anglo-Saxons the crucial thing was that death be met bravely. Their gods were capricious, puzzling creatures, because life is often that way; and those same Norse gods were themselves doomed to die (at the impending apocalypse the Northmen called Ragnarokr) because human life is so doomed. The question as to why that is poses one of the most profound riddles of all.

Take Tolkien's posthumously published tale *The Children of Húrin* (2006), perhaps the most uncompromisingly tragic thing he ever wrote. The story is set in the First Age of Middle Earth, thousands of years before the events of *The Lord of the Rings*. There are no hobbits, wizards, ents or Tom Bombadils in this book, although there are elves, men and orcs. Sauron appears as a minor character, for at this point in Tolkien's imaginary history Sauron was only the lieutenant of a far greater evil, Morgoth (also known as Melkor), a character of positively Satanic scope and wickedness. The tale opens with Húrin, a man from Mithrim, who fights in the battle of Nirnaeth Arnoediad, in which elves and men confront Morgoth, a very large number of orcs, and various assorted meanies such as Balrogs. The bad guys win. Captured by Morgoth Húrin is tormented by having his whole family cursed, and then being placed in a magic chair that not only preserves him from death but compels him to watch as this curse works its malign influence over his wife, son and daughter. This functions as a prologue to the rest of the tale; the bulk of the book is given over to Húrin's son Túrin, with a little bit to his daughter Niënor. In fact, Tolkien adapts his narrative from two celebrated mythic precedents—the story of Kullervo from the Finnish epic cycle known as the *Kalevala* on the one hand, and the better known Sigfried legend from the Nibilungen epic on the other.

That story traces the increasingly terrible lives of Húrin's children under the withering curse of Morgoth. Túrin is high-minded, noble, taciturn, and darkly charismatic. His sister Niënor is beautiful and virtuous and nothing more (something that does little to counter the idea that Tolkien was not skilled at portraying complex women in his writing). Túrin flees his northern home and takes refuge for a time with the elves, who love him; but his haughty manner and his disinclination to speak up for himself leads to him being—unjustly—banished. Armed with a terrible and magical black sword he takes up with some outlaws, leads men, becomes a prince of the hidden city of Nargothrond, and finally, in some very powerful chapters given added heft by the sheer density and momentum accumulated by Tolkien's lean prose, fights and kills the terrible dragon Glaurung.

But despite his strength and bravery, Túrin's destiny is consistently infelicitous. His pride contributes to the fall of the city of which he is prince; he inadvertently kills his best friend (who had just rescued him from orcs); and later he inadvertently marries and impregnates his sister who, when she learns what has happened, drowns herself in remorse. At various moments in the narrative Túrin comprehends what he has done, and is driven from his wits; but he always recovers them, propelled as he is by the ferocity of his will-to-revenge against Morgoth. But this last incestuous transgression is too great for him. The dragon Glaurung, dying, reveals Túrin's incest to him, and Túrin can bear no more. He draws his sword, addressing it ('what lord or loyalty do you know, save the hand that wields you? Will you slay me swiftly?') and the sword replies with cold certainty: 'yes'. Then Túrin sets the hilt of the sword upon the ground and throws himself upon the blade.

The Children of Húrin is a tragedy not in the Aristotelian sense, for there is precious little catharsis here; but rather in the northern-European sense of humans encountering an overwhelming fate with unyielding defiance. And that is at the heart of Tolkien's conception of heroism: precisely not achievement, but a particular and noble-hearted encounter with failure. Success in Túrin's world is always local and short-term, and always happens within the larger context of inevitable failure. What matters is not how one triumphs, but the spirit with which one resists the terrible fate one knows to be unavoidable. The mismatch between will and thing is, here, at its most biting. Death cannot be avoided, or bought off, or conquered; it can only be defied. And defiance is the properly heroic response to that inevitability. This is a dramatisation of Freud's famous 'riddle', 'the painful riddle of death, against which no medicine has yet been found, nor probably will be'.[4]

In his fiction Tolkien proposes two complementary solutions to Freud's deep riddle. *The Children of Húrin* embodies what we could call an Anglo-Saxon solution—that defiance in the teeth of an inevitable doom is the strength give to humans. But there is a Christian answer to this riddle too, that the riddle of death is 'solved' in Christ. Indeed, the extent to which Tolkien was able to constellate his deep fellow-feeling for the Anglo-Saxon code with his heartfelt Christianity is perhaps the key index to the success of his art overall. The Tolkienian notion of the eucatastrophe attaches a last-minute-reprieve happy-ending to the darker, older trajectory of inevitable loss heroically encountered; and, more, takes force and unexpectedness precisely from the fact that the preceding tale so unremittingly follows its Anglo-Saxon trajectory.

There are riddles in Christianity too, although communicants usually refer to them by the less trivial-sounding term 'mysteries'. I discuss some of those below as well; but for the moment I am interested in the pre-Christian, or early-Christian, ground upon which Tolkien's fantasies erect their eventual moments of consolation.

Not everybody shares Tolkien's view of the Anglo-Saxons. John M. Hill deplores (though courteously) the sense of Old English culture found in the work of scholars such as Ker, Raymond Wilson Chambers (a friend of Tolkien) and Tolkien himself, with their stress upon 'the angst of Germanic heroes caught in the chains of circumstance or their own character, torn between duties equally sacred, dying with their backs to the wall'. These perspectives, Hill suggests, 'endure without apparent half-life . . . well into the last decades of the twentieth-century', and quotes Bruce Mitchell and Fred C. Robinson by way of illustration:

A pagan warrior brought up in this tradition would show a reckless disregard for his life. When he was doomed or not, courage was best, for the brave man could win *lof* ['glory'] whilst the coward might die before his time. This is the spirit which inspired the code of the *comitatus*. While his lord lived, the warrior owed him loyalty unto death. If his lord were killed, the warrior had to avenge him or die in the attempt (and in extreme cases, perhaps, die with him). The lord had in his turn the duty of protecting his warriors. He had to be a great fighter to attract men, a man of noble character and a generous giver of feasts and treasures to hold them.[5]

Hill's point is not that this view is false, but that there is more 'artful variation' and 'situational irony' in the way it actually manifested; that the Anglo-Saxon warrior lived through the riddle of matching pagan belligerence with Christian pacifism in a way more than merely self-contradictory. This strikes me as right; but it also strikes me that Tolkien's own fiction advances a much more ironic ethos than is sometimes thought.

The Anglo-Saxon view of life is that it is a riddle not because it can be in some sense 'solved', but because there is an ironic relationship between what is presented and what is meant—between what is to-hand and how things really are. 'Riddling' is the best way to apprehend this irony, because the mismatch is something to be encountered playfully, joyfully, not surlily or resentfully. When you have fought bravely in battle and still lost, when your army is smashed and your lord killed beside you, the obvious (we might say: the *logical*) thing to do would be to concede defeat and surrender oneself to grief and despair. But the Anglo-Saxon response to such a situation is to *celebrate*, to fight harder. At the end of 'The Battle of Maldon', Byrhtwold addresses his exhausted comrades in some of the most famous words in the entire Anglo-Saxon canon (words Tolkien adapted for the speech of Theoden before the battle of Minas Tirith, in *The Return of the King*):

The will shall be harder, the courage shall be keener
Spirit shall grow great, as our strength falls away.[6]

On a cosmic scale, this exultant irony, this counter-intuitive, riddling manner of being-in-the-world, finds expression in the Norse myth of *ragnarök*—the twilight of the gods. According to this story the impending end of the world will not be a righteous last judgement that shall reward the virtuous and punish the wicked, as in Christian traditions, but rather a glorious defeat in the battle between the gods and the forces of chaos. W. P. Ker thought *ragnarök* a kind of answer, proposed by the Anglo-Saxons to themselves, to the riddle of existence: 'their last independent guess at the secret of the universe'.

As far as it goes, and as a working theory, it is absolutely impregnable. It is the assertion of the individual freedom against all the terrors and temptations of the world. It is absolutely resistance, perfect because without hope. The Northern gods are on the right side, though it is not the side that wins. The winning side is Chaos and Unreason; but the gods, who are defeated, think that defeat is not refutation.[7]

'What is a defeat that is not a refutation?' takes the form of a riddle; and it has more than one answer. For Christians, like Tolkien himself, it is a description of the death of Christ, an individual extinction that is paradoxically eternal life for him and all his followers. Many critics have discussed the way Tolkien reconciled his own devoutly-held Catholic beliefs with this pre-Christian, very different answer to the puzzle. What is a defeat but not a refutation for the northmen? *Ragnarök*, 'an allegory' (to quote Ker again) 'of the Teutonic self-will, carried to its noblest terms, deified by men for whom all religion was coming to be meaningless except "trust in one's own might and main"—the creed of Kjartan Olafson (from the *Laxdœla Saga*) and Sigmundur Brestisson (in the *Færeyinga Saga*) before they accepted Christianity.'

I suppose the danger is that this hefty, belligerent self-will may strike modern sensibilities as merely lunkish; or worse, as quasi-fascistic. What redeems it, I think, is the wit with which it is carried off: very far removed from the ponderous, deadening seriousness of those repellent twentieth-century political ideologies that styled themselves 'Nordic' in order to terrorise the world and destroy millions. A large part of the difference has precisely to do with the relationship of this ideology to truth. Truth for the fascist is something linear, forceful and strong. Truth in the sense this book discusses it is something more fundamentally oblique. Truth is not a swordstroke. Truth is a riddle. 'The riddle' also solves one of the problems of storytelling, what we could call the problem of fiction itself. It has occurred to many readers, as it certainly occurred to Tolkien—indeed, it has been one of the great ethical debates surrounding the novel in English since at least the eighteenth-century—that fiction is not true. I hardly need remind you that telling untruths, which we call 'lying', is a moral wrong. Storytelling is a special kind of lie, of course. It is marked, quite apart from anything else, by the reluctance of its auditors to call the teller on his or her mendacity. When a storyteller starts a story with 'Emma Woodhouse, handsome clever and rich . . . ' we do not immediately shout out 'there never was such a person! You just made her up!'

A news report (assuming it be truthful) or a person relating the day's events to a friend (assuming she has no desire to distort or mislead) are both stories that have a straightforward relationship to the reality they describe. Critics call this 'mimetic', a word with an rather complex semantic field, but which is the basis of the English words 'imitation', 'mimic' and 'mimeograph'. It means that the stories copy reality, in much the way that a mimic copies somebody else, or a mimeograph copies whatever is written on a piece of paper. Mimesis does not mean that we are liable to confuse the imitation *with* reality. We are usually clever enough to tell that a mimic is only imitating somebody, not actually becoming that person; and we are almost always clever enough to know that we are hearing a story about the world, rather than somehow seeing the world itself through a magic casement. Irony, though, is different. An ironic story does not seek to reproduce or mimic the reality it represents; it goes about the business of representing reality in a more complicated, even a more twisted, manner. This, though, does not make the ironic worldview *untrue*. On the contrary, and for the reasons I discuss above, I tend to consider it a truer mode of art than simple mimesis.

There are various sorts of ironic storytelling. One goes by the name Postmodernism, something with which I personally have a great deal of sympathy, but which we can be fairly sure that Tolkien himself (had he lived long enough to see its coming into vogue in the 1980s and 1990s) would have cordially disliked to an even greater degree than he disliked allegory. Then again there is another mode of 'ironic' art, more elegant and more widely celebrated than Postmodernism, although we might think equally removed from Tolkien's own storytelling instincts. This is embodied in the novels of writers such as Jane Austen or Henry James, both of whom were fascinated by the ironies life throws up, and who framed their stories via a series of beautifully judged formal and stylistic ironic moves. Tolkien's irony is of a different sort to this. His Catholicism was a genuine, deep part of his being. That meant that he thought of the world as simultaneously mundane *and* divine; as a realm in which all the ordinary obviousnesses obtain but also as an arena in which the sometimes puzzling grace of God works itself out.

Readers often note that Middle-earth, although rendered in extraordinarily vivid detail and breadth, contains no temples or churches, no priests or holy men. This was a deliberate choice by Tolkien, not because he wanted to repudiate his religious beliefs in his writing, but for exactly the opposite reason—because the whole world was intended to embody the religion. Tolkien wrote to a Jesuit friend in 1953 '*The Lord of the Rings* is of course a fundamentally religious and Catholic work . . . that is why I have not put in, or have cut out, practically all references to anything like "religion", to cults or practices, in the imaginary world. For the religious element is absorbed into the story and the symbolism.'[8] To read Tolkien's published letters is to be struck, time and again, how deeply he meditated the incarnation as the central mystery of Christianity. That God became man, that the immortal died (to be born again), that the divine realm and the material realm intersected in this unique occurrence—all this, for Tolkien, is a riddle of the profoundest and most reverent sort.

I want to dilate upon this point for a moment by pointing to a particular riddle of incarnation that occurs in *The Lord of the Rings*. The ents, who appear in *The Lord of the Rings*, are one of many strange beings that populate Tolkien's landscape, but they are also a riddle. 'Ent' is an Anglo-Saxon word. It occurs, for instance, several times in *Beowulf* where it means 'giant' in the particular sense of malign, pagan creatures stalking the wilds, a menace to men. Indeed, the Beowulf-poet suggests that 'ents' are descendants of the Biblical Cain—like Grendl himself:

> From Cain's bloodline   all wickedness was woken,
> all ents and elves   and all of the orcs too,

> also those giants   that grappled with God
> for a long time;   but at last they were paid off!
>
> (*Beowulf*, 112–15)

Tolkien takes orcs to be wicked creatures, of course; but he has different ideas regarding the moral alignment of elves and ents. And, although Tolkien appropriated the name 'ent', there is nothing in Old English or Norse culture to approximate walking, slow-talking trees of deep wisdom and majestic virtue. This, it seems, is Tolkien's own invention, one that perhaps elaborates the important role trees played in Anglo-Saxon and Norse culture, from specific holy trees to the great cosmic Yggdrasil tree that structured the universe.[9] Nonetheless, Tolkien's ents *are* a riddle.[10]

What are the ents? Commentators, wondering whence the idea might have come, sometimes pick up a clue from Tolkien's own correspondence and cite Shakespeare's *Macbeth* as a source. The wicked Macbeth is abandoned by his army but is safe in his tower (like Saruman in Orthanc). He falls back upon the magic charm that he believes will keep him safe. He cannot fall until Birnam wood should march against him. As Malcolm's army passes through the forest, each man takes up a branch or sprig as a ruse to hide their numbers. Watching from the battlements, Macbeth can see the forest begin to come towards him. Speaking for myself, I have never been entirely happy with this turn of events, howsoever dramatically effective it is (and it is, of course, a famously effective *coup de théâtre*). The problem is its vagueness. One feature of magic spells and charms in old culture is how *precise* their terms are. The fact that a crowd of men have chopped the branches from a number of trees and carried them a certain distance does not mean that Birnam forest has moved. The trunk and roots of the trees, as well as such boughs and branches as remain, are still where they ever were—a mapmaker (say) would surely still put Birnam wood in the same place.[11] If supernatural magic guaranteed me life until a forest actually came to my castle, then I should insist upon the terms of the agreement until the forest actually came.

So, here we have one possible solution to the 'riddle' of Tolkien ents, a solution that contextualises them in terms of Macbeth's famous charm. Like Macbeth, Saruman from his tower sees a forest literally moving against him, and his downfall is assured. But actually

I want to argue that Tolkien's ents literalise a deeper, older riddle than Shakespeare's. I want to suggest their solution is to be found in the New Testament:

> He took the blind man by the hand and led him outside the village. When he had spit on the man's eyes and put his hands on him, Jesus asked, 'Do you see anything?' And he looked up, and said, I see men as trees, walking. (Mark 8:23–4)

Commentary upon this passage tends to stress its mimesis, its closeness to our sense of the way the world actually works. Cures for impaired sight take time to work. The blind man's sight does not return immediately, but rather by a process of indistinct strengthening and gradual improvement (the next verse is: 'once more Jesus put his hands on the man's eyes. Then his eyes were opened, his sight was restored, and he saw everything clearly.') In other words the passage might mean 'I see men; for I see [them] as trees [except that, unlike trees, they are] walking'. The man miraculously cured could distinguish them from trees only by their motion. On the other hand it is clear enough that a typological reading is available to us here too. For Christ is the tree of life; the dead wood of his cross, and his own dead body, become vivid and full of motion again at the resurrection, to spread across the world. It is characteristic of Tolkien's literalising creative imagination—what we might think of as his mode of sub-incarnating—that he feeds this miraculous moment into his own writing as *actual* walking tree creatures. The passage in Mark is all about blindness and sight, about visibility and invisibility. It is about (to be a little more theologically specific) the way we can only *see* truly through Christ. It is easy to imagine that Tolkien, arbophile as he was, found peculiar resonance in the notion that the new sight of divine grace magically transforms ordinary men into fantastical walking trees. The destruction of Sauron's ring, at the end of *The Lord of the Rings*, is a way of destroying invisibility itself; in terms of a Christian logic, it is the global overcoming of 'blindness', of not-seeing; the making plain of God's grace in the world. It is in this, I think, that a solution to 'the ents' is to be found.

This unpacks into a larger thesis about Tolkien's approach to his art. In the ents, Tolkien imaginatively gifts an inanimate object with life, motion and personality. At the heart of *The Lord of the Rings* is a similar, though inverted and malign, process of reification: the ring itself—made of a substance more inert than the organic matter of arboreal life, yet somehow, mysteriously alive, possessed of volition and influence. 'Mysteriously', there, is meant in its fullest sense. How the One Ring is able to work its evil in the world is a riddle that is, in turn, one of the ways Tolkien articulates the riddle of evil more generally. In *The Hobbit* the Old English sense that treasure, though inanimate, can 'possess' living humans finds dramatic form in Smaug's hoard. The ring, at this stage in the story, gifts invisibility and nothing more. As the story grew in Tolkien's imagination, the heaps of treasure are replaced by a single golden ring. *The Hobbit* is a quest-narrative in which the object of the quest is to gain a quantity of golden treasure; *The Lord of the Rings*—this is one of the most frequently repeated critical aperçus about that novel—upends this venerable template, being the story of a quest not to find but specifically to *lose* one particular piece of golden treasure. But what links these two things is the quasi-animate power of the gold. When Saruman gives a kind of life to the inanimate by 'industrialising' the shire it entails the poisoning of the organic, and the scouring of the shire at the novel's end is precisely the undoing of this wickedness. Underlying this is a very profound riddle about life and nature, the riddle: how may inanimate matter become animate? In various versions this asks 'how can new life come into the world?' and 'from where did the first life come' and similar questions that continue to give philosophers and scientists matter for their enquiries. A Biblical version of the question is Ezekiel's 'can these bones live?' (Ezekiel 37:3)—a text read by Christians typologically as anticipating the resurrection. The inanimate object *is* brought alive. My point here, though, is that quite apart from its content the *form* of this conceit is riddling. In Daisy Elizabeth Martin-Clarke's words, 'the literary theme ascribing emotion to an inanimate object is characteristic of riddle literary traditions'.[12] *The Lord of the Rings* takes this literary convention and literalises it, building a monumental imaginative edifice about it.

Like scholars of the Anglo-Saxon age, the needful thing for readers of Tolkien is the ability to hold his quasi-pagan 'Old English' values and his immanent Christianity in harmonious relation. And there is a sense in which Tolkien's use of Anglo-Saxon models functions, formally—as it were, essentially—as a riddle. Maria Artamonova has discussed the ways that Tolkien, not content with writing *Lord of the Rings* and *The Silmarillion* in English, also composed Old English *Annals* or *Chronicles*-style texts relating important events in his imagined history. Here is an example:

> MMCCCCXCIX *Hér gefeaht Féanores fierd wiþ þam orcum / sige námon / þá orcas gefliemdon oþ Angband (þaet is Irenhelle); ac Goðmog, Morgoðes þegn, ofslóh Féanor, and Maegdros gewéold siþþan Féanores folc. Þis gefeoht hátte Tungolguð*

Here Fëanor's host fought with the Orcs and was victorious, and pursued them to Angband (that is Iron Hell); but Gothmog, servant of Morgoth, slew Fëanor, and Maedhros ruled Fëanor's folk after that. This battle was called the Battle-under-the-Stars.[13]

The composition of this kind of expert pastiche was more than a mere quirk or eccentricity on Tolkien's part. Nor, more interestingly, was it the equivalent to a 'method' actor immersing himself in his role prior to stepping on stage. Instead, it is best read as Tolkien deliberately part-obscuring or riddling his fictional material as part of a deliberate aesthetic strategy. Stepping outside one's linguistic comfort zone can have the effect of freshening or vivifying one's apprehension. Artamonova quotes Tolkien that 'seen through the distorting glass of our ignorance' our 'appreciation of the splendour of Homeric Greek in word-form is possibly keener, or more conscious, than it was to a Greek'. If our vernacular is deadened by the plainness born of over-familiarity, then learning—or better yet, *writing*—a language with which we are unfamiliar is a way of bringing alive the vividness inherent in poetry and story.

2
Cynewulf and the *Exeter Book*

I have started by arguing that riddles were important to Anglo-Saxon culture, important to Tolkien and that they remain important today. It is worth qualifying that judgement by noting that scholarship has not always seen things this way. For many people riddles are trivial and disposable, of only glancing relevance to larger questions of culture and art. Gwendolyn Morgan notes that the study of riddles and wisdom literature was 'almost entirely neglected through the 1800s. Late in that century and into the first quarter of the twentieth a flurry of interest in solving riddles occurred . . . [but] this interest soon petered out.' She adds that 'the same tends to hold true up to the present', although she does note that 'Gregory Jember has defended the riddles as essential expressions of Anglo-Saxon culture and its world view.'[1] This study thinks Jember is right.[2] In this chapter I will try to say something about specific Anglo-Saxon riddles themselves, and the significance of riddling more generally.

Many hundreds of riddles have come down to us from Anglo-Saxon times. How many hundreds remains unclear, for I do not believe there has ever been a complete tabulation. A good number of these riddles were written in the vernacular, and many more were written in Latin. Indeed, to a large extent these represent distinct riddling traditions.

The collection of riddles which exerted the largest influence . . . was that by Symphosius (an African writer of the fourth/fifth century), who was the author of one hundred *enigmata*, each one consisting of three hexameters. Aldheim, Eusebius, Tatwine and the authors of the Old English riddles of the *Exeter Book* all drew from Symphosius. The Anglo-Latin riddles are 'literary' riddles and are quite different from the 'popular' ones; they are provided with a title which gives the solution to the riddle, hence spoiling the ludic side of riddling and highlighting the erudite aspect of the compositions.[3]

It is the 'ludic' aspect that is relevant to my purposes here, and I shall have little to say about Latin riddles. The *Exeter Book* is a different matter.

One of the most celebrated collections of riddles, the *Exeter Book* is so called not because it is about Exeter, but because it lives there. It was bequeathed to the library of Exeter by Bishop Leofric after his death in 1072, '*.i. mycel englisc boc be gehwilcum pingum on leoðwisan geworht*', 'one big book written in English containing verse about many things'. Bound into this codex are various allegorical poems on Christian themes, some of the most famous elegies in Old English literature (amongst them *The Wanderer* and *The Seafarer*)— and ninety-six riddles. Some of the *Exeter Book*'s pages are missing, and scholars believe the original collection comprised a nice, round 100 riddles. It used to be thought that these riddles were written by the eighth-century poet Cynewulf. Modern scholarship considers this unlikely for a number of reasons, arguing instead that the riddles were originally written by various people or garnered from a wider folk tradition. This, in fact, has been the consensus for over a hundred years now. In 1910 Frederick Tupper wrote:

> The Riddles were not written by Cynewulf: all evidence of the least value speaks against his claim. It seems fairly certain that they are products of the North. Their place as literary compositions (not as folk-riddles) in one collection, and their homogeneous artistry, which finds abundant vindication in a hundred common traits, argue strongly for a single author, though a small group of problems brings convincing evidence against complete unity. That their period was the beginning of the eighth century, the hey-day of Anglo-Latin riddle-poetry, is an inviting surmise unsustained by proof.[4]

Cynewulf is most famous for two lines, riddle-like though not technically a riddle (in fact the lines are extracted from his poem *Crist*).

These lines, as it happens, had the most prodigious effect upon the imagination of J. R. R. Tolkien:

éala éarendel engla beorhtast
ofer middangeard monnum sended

Hail! Earendel of angels the brightest
Over Middle-earth to men sent down.

Tolkien wrote 'there was something very remote and strange and beautiful behind those words, if I could grasp it, far beyond ancient English'. The openness of his phrasing here is in its own way indicative of something important, as if it would miss the point to reframe the lines as a riddle posed in terms of content—for instance, 'who or what is Earendel?' Nonetheless, Cynewulf's powerful lines do riddle us, and they certainly riddled Tolkien. His proposed solution to this question was *The Silmarillion*, his earliest attempt at a systematic articulation of his fantasy legendarium, that in turn led to *The Hobbit* and *The Lord of the Rings*.

In *The Silmarillion* 'Eärendil' is a mariner descended from both elvish and mannish stock and therefore an individual who, in mythic form, mediates the 'immortal' and 'mortal' valences of Tolkien's own world-view. In 1967 Tolkien drafted a lengthy account of his reaction to Cynewulf's lines (and the role they played in sparking his own imaginative creativity). He wrote this as a letter to be sent to a man called Rang who had contacted Tolkien with queries about his invented nomenclature; although in the event the letter was never sent. In the letter he describes the Eärendil name as having an important connection with his own creative imagination. He notes how greatly he was struck, when studying Anglo-Saxon before the First World War, by 'the great beauty of this word (or name)'. It was consonant with conventional Anglo-Saxon, but also struck Tolkien's ear, he says, with unusual sweetness and euphony. In the letter he goes on to elaborate his theory that '*éarendel*', the OE original, is a name rather than a word, and that it referred to 'what we now call *Venus*: the morning star'.[5] His argument spills into a footnote, as Tolkien develops a thesis about Cynewulf's semantic signification: *éarendel* meaning 'ray of light' is etymologically connected with 'aurora', and also appears in the *Bickling Homilies* (a tenth-century collection of religious writing whose author or authors are unknown to us). Tolkien seems sure that Cynewulf's lines 'refer to a herald, a divine messenger', the morning star as 'herald of the rise of the true Sun in Christ'. Finally, and with a rather beautifully deflating final turn, he adds that this notion was 'completely alien to my use' in writing *The Hobbit* and *the Lord of the Rings*.

In adapting and re-appropriating, as he very often did, Old English words and names, Tolkien nonetheless insists 'the borrowing when it occurs' is 'simply that of sounds, that are then integrated into a new construction; and only in the one case of Eärendil will reference to its source cast any light on the legends or their "meaning".' The use of what we now call scare-quotes around 'meaning' in that quotation is revealing. The casting of light, on a name that *means* light, in a mythology whose deep past is about the holiness of light, may explain why Eärendil is excepted in this way from all the other names Tolkien coined. 'Light', he noted in 1951, 'is such a primeval symbol in the nature of the Universe, that it can hardly be analysed', although he makes the effort at least as far as his own invented mythology goes:

> The Light of Valinor (derived from light before any fall) is the light of art undivorced from reason, that sees things both scientifically (or philosophically) and imaginatively (or subcreatively) and 'says that they are good'—as beautiful.[6]

Tolkien hardly needs to make specific allusion to the opening of Genesis to make his point. 'Let there be light!' is, in one sense, behind the whole of Tolkien's imaginative enterprise. And a yearning to heal the breach between reason and imagination, between the auroral beauty of spiritual life and the practical necessity of the mundane, is exactly the role a figure such as Eärendil embodies. That God permits such a division to enter into existence—that he divided the light from the darkness before even creating human beings and giving them the power to choose the one or the other—is itself a very deep riddle.[7] Tolkien's appropriation of Eärendil's name to his made-up Elvish linguistic world, and his styling of his creation as specifically a *mariner*, takes us back, as it were, before the Genesis *fiat lux* to the primal waters of the deep. As he explains in his unsent letter to Rang, characteristically enclosing the word *poem* within the quotation marks of (I suppose) distancing modesty: 'before 1914

I wrote a "poem" upon Earendil who launched his ship like a bright spark from the havens of the Sun.' He notes that he adopted him into his personal mythology as 'a prime figure': a sailor, a guiding star and a 'sign' of mortal hope, adding that 'the name could not be adopted just like that: it had to be accommodated to the Elvish linguistic situation', something accomplished via a notional Elvish stem '*AYAR' meaning 'Sea', referring both to the great Western sea of Middle-earth and (*'Aman'*) to the Blessed Realm of the Valar.

'Earendil who launched his ship like a bright spark from the havens of the Sun . . . ' Heaven/haven is a linguistic riddle that fascinated Gerard Manley Hopkins, and which (of course) predates him as a word-quibble. More relevant to our purposes here is the sense in which it is the spiritual function 'Ayar'. For this is a word presented as meaning both sea and (Aiya!) 'hail' or 'greeting'; and as specifically intervening between the immortal and the mortal realm. In all this we are being given the answer to a riddle—'who is Eärendil'?—that reveals itself to be another riddle: broadly 'how is there a divide between the divine and the mortal?' and more practically speaking 'how can the breach be overcome?' The sea greets us; it welcomes us. But Middle-earth is bordered by a western, not an eastern ocean: a place of sunsets not sunrises.

Sea is also where the *Exeter Book* starts, with three linked riddles that still puzzle scholars today. Here are the opening lines of the first:

> Who is so clever and quick-witted
> as to guess who goads me on my journey
> when I get up, angry, at times awesome;
> when I roar loudly and rampage over the land?[8]

The riddle goes on to talk about 'I with my roof of water', adding 'I carry on my back what once covered / every man, body and soul submerged / together in the water'; although confusingly the riddle also claims 'I burn houses and ransack palaces'. It concludes: 'Say what conceals me / or what I, who bear this burden, am called.' Scholars gloss this as 'a storm on land', but we cannot be sure, for none of the *Exeter Book* riddles include their own solution. Conceivably lightning from a storm might set light to buildings, although the situation described in the riddle is surely far too wet to permit the sort of conflagration described ('smoke rises, ashen over roofs').

The riddle hinges, we could say, on the deliberate crashing together of two quantities (sea, land) more usually kept apart. One of Tolkien's more eccentric views was that 'the Atlantis tradition' was 'so fundamental to mythical history' that it must have 'some kind of basis in real history'; although this in turn (as he wrote to Christopher Bretherton, 16 July 1964) speaks more forcefully to some important component in Tolkien's personal subconscious ('what I might call my Atlantis-haunting') than actual history. He tells Bretherton how the Atlantis myth, or some version of it, has given him nightmares throughout his life: a 'dreadful dream' of a great wave, emerging either from the still waters of the sea or else washing over the green landscape. He adds that converting this nightmare into stories has to some extent 'exorcized' the dream, but not to the point of banishing it altogether. 'It always ends by surrender', he writes; 'and I awake by gasping out of deep water.'[9]

The temptation to psychoanalyse Tolkien for this vividly-recalled dream experience, though strong, is worth resisting—as an impertinence quite apart from anything else. And anyway there is a level on which this first *Exeter Book* riddle is not so puzzling: it means death, as with Christian passing finally to the city of Zion at the end of *The Pilgrim's Progress*. Indeed, I suggest that constellating the first *Exeter Book* riddle with Tolkien's imaginarium draws up another possible solution to the former. In Norse mythology the world-ocean was inhabited by, and to an extent identified with, a dragon called Jörmungandr. In the *Prose Edda* Thor goes fishing for this great serpent, rowing out in a boat and baiting his hook with an ox's head. A great sea-dragon, rearing up apocalyptically over the land-habitations of humankind, could both blast with fire and drown with water; but what is most interesting about this is not its specific solution itself as the way it draws together (pentecostal) fire and (baptismal) water in a catastrophic overturning of the mortal world. Who *conceals* such a dragon? God, of course. More to the point, concealment, and unconcealment, are what riddles do, as do divine mysteries.

According to the *Oxford English Dictionary* (a project with which Tolkien was involved for a time, although I am not suggesting he worked on this particular entry) the English word 'dragon' derives from Greek δράκων (*drákōn*), 'dragon, serpent of huge size, water-snake', which in turn probably comes from the verb δρακεῖν (*drakeîn*) 'to see clearly'. The ironic force of this etymology is rather striking, for it names an imaginary, and therefore (strictly) invisible, beast as precisely *the clearly seen one*. But it is right, of course. Dragons *are* clearly seen, in our cultural imaginary at any rate. And Tolkien's own love for dragons is clearly connected with what can be seen and what cannot be seen, dramatised in *The Hobbit* with Bilbo's first encounter with Smaug wearing a ring of invisibility. As with the larger fascination Tolkien's work manifests with questions of visibility and invisibility, or seeing and blindness, this turns out to be a way of finding dramatic and emblematic mode of rendering the fundamentally evangelical truth—seeing past the epiphenomena of this world to the prime reality of God. 'Because thou hast seen me', Christ tells Thomas, 'thou hast believed; blessed are they that have not seen, and yet have believed' (John 20:29).

The second and third riddles of the *Exeter Book* do similar work in elaborating a mysterious connection between destroying oceanic water and saving divine grace. Indeed, the riddles are so closely linked, thematically, that some scholars think we should read all three as one long riddle. Here, again in Crossley-Holland's translation, is the opening of Riddle 2:

> Sometimes I plunge through the press of the waves,
> surprising men, delving into the earth,
> the ocean bed. The waters ferment,
> sea-horses foaming . . .
> The whale-mere roars, fiercely rages,
> waves beat upon the shore; stones
> and sand, seaweed and saltspray, are flung
> against the dunes when, wrestling
> far beneath the waves, I disturb the earth,
> the vast depths of the sea. Nor can I escape
> my ocean bed before he permits me who is my pilot
> on every journey.

The riddle concludes by asking 'tell me, wise man: / who separates me from the sea's embrace / when the waters become quiet once again?' The answer provided by scholars is 'an earthquake under the sea', or perhaps 'a storm at sea'. Either answer could be correct. I would suggest, though, that we can also read this riddle in the light of Tolkien's own 'Fastitocalon', a poem he published in *The Adventures of Tom Bombadil*. He took the peculiar name 'Fastitocalon' from an

Anglo-Saxon bestiary. He explained in a letter to Eileen Elgar (5 March 1964) that the name may have come from '*Aspido-chelone*', which means a round-shield-shaped turtle. Of this proper name '*astitocalon*' is a simple corruption, although the initial 'f', according to Tolkien, was an unwarranted addition to make the word alliterate with the rest of the line in which it appears 'as was compulsory for poets in his day'.[10] The actual line is: *þam is noma cenned / fyrnstreama geflotan Fastitocalon*, which means 'he is given a name / the first-stream floating one, Fastitocalon'. Tolkien goes on to consider the widely-used trope of the treacherous location at which sailors moor thinking it an island, but which is actually a semi-submerged ocean monster. He thinks this myth derives 'from the East', and that it may embody some exaggerated memories of actual marine turtles. But when this legend comes to Europe, Tolkien notes, the monster becomes less turtle-ish and more whale-like. He hardly needs to add, but does for clarity, 'in moralized bestiaries he is, of course, an allegory for the Devil, and is so used by Milton'. In amongst the many other things Tolkien's own 'Fastitocalon' poem is, it can be taken as an answer to the question asked by *Exeter Book* Riddle 2 ('who separates me from the sea's embrace?'), the answer being 'God', the pilot who steers this destructive marine force for His own reasons, the mystery of his grace. And the Anglo-Saxon sense of the sea as a monster, magnificent and wonderful but also alarming and terrifying is picked up in Riddle 3:

> Sometimes my Lord corners me;
> then He imprisons all that I am
> under fertile fields—He frustrates me,
> condemns me in my might to darkness,
> casts me in to a cave where my warden, earth,
> sits on my back. I cannot break out
> of that dungeon, but I shake halls
> and houses; the gabled homes of men
> tremble and totter; walls quake,
> then overhang. Air floats above earth,
> and the face of the ocean seems still
> until I burst out from my cramped cell
> at my Lord's bidding, He who in anger
> buried me before, so shackled me that I
> could not escape my Guardian, my Guide.

> Sometimes I swoop to whip up waves, rouse
> the water, drive the flint-grey rollers
> to the shore. Spuming crests crash
> against the cliff, dark precipice looming
> over deep water.

The riddle continues for many lines in this vein, before concluding with the demand: 'tell me my name, / and Who it is rouses me from my rest, / or Who restrains me when I remain silent.' 'God' is a very good answer to these latter two questions, just as this and the two preceding riddles are, in the final analysis 'about' the combined grace and anger of God, the way he structures mortal existence on the largest scale via both giving and taking away (to quote the resonant line from Job 1:21). But the proper response to the first demand, 'tell me my name', must be more than simply 'earthquake' or 'storm'—although that tends to be what the scholars offer by way of solution. Crossley-Holland notes that in line 50 of the riddle its subject is described as '*scripan*', an Old English word 'meaning a sinewy and sinister gliding movement; it is also used by the *Beowulf*-poet in describing both the monster Grendel and the dragon.'[11] Is this also a riddle about a dragon?

There is a celebrated story about dragons that exists in a number of variants. Two dragons, one red and one white, are engaged in a titantic struggle underground. It is possible these stories began as folk-explanations for earth tremors into which nationalistic significance was later read—as, for instance, that the Red Dragon was Wales and the White England. In the *Mabinogion* tale 'Lludd and Llefelys', the hero Lludd is faced with three riddling afflictions to the land, the second of which is a terrifying scream that comes every first of May and makes all the women in the kingdom miscarry. The solution to this conundrum is two battling dragons; and Lludd solves it by putting them both to sleep with mead and burying them in Dinas Emrys, in North Wales. Nennius' *Historia Brittonum* (written sometime in the 820s) takes up the story centuries later. King Vortigern's attempts to build a castle at Dinas Emrys are thwarted, for the earth shakes his structures to pieces every time he tries. Eventually a soothsayer (according to Geoffrey of Monmouth's retelling in his *Historia Regum Britanniae* (c.1140), this soothsayer is Merlin himself) reveals that these earthquakes are being caused by the subterranean battling dragons, and shows how to subdue them.

Tolkien had some light-hearted fun with this myth himself, combining it with stories of the Norse world-girdling ocean-dragon Jörmungandr, in *Roverandom* (written 1925, though not published until 1998). This story is set at the seaside at Foley, but also encompasses the light side of the moon, where the Man in the Moon lives in a fine tower, and the dark side where sleeping children frolic in the valley of dreams and the undersea kingdom of the mer-king. The protagonist is a dog called Rover, who takes the name Roverandom to distinguish himself from two other dogs in the story (a moon-dog and mer-dog) also called Rover. These dogs get up to various larks, including teasing the Great White Dragon of the moon ('white with green eyes and leaking green fire at every joint, and snorting black smoke like a steamer . . . the mountains rocked and echoed, and the snow dried up; avalanches tumbled down') and rousing up the undersea serpent ('when he undid a curl or two [of his tail] in his sleep, the water heaved and shook and bent people's houses and spoilt their repose for miles and miles around.')[12] It is certainly possible that Tolkien had the *Exeter Book* riddles at the back of his mind when writing this.

Dragons are huge and destructive forces, as likely to appear on land as at sea. But which dragon? One possible answer to Riddle 3 is Niðhöggr, the vast dragon who lies under the ground gnawing at the roots of the world tree and making the earth and oceans shake. The creature's name means either 'malice-striker' or 'striker in the dark' and he is controlled by one figure only, the Norse god Hel, who rules the underworld. In the *Poetic Edda* Niðhöggr is described devouring the corpses of the dead, but also as coming out from time to time into the open air:

> There comes the dark dragon flying,
> the shining serpent, up from Niðafjöll
> Niðhöggr flies over the plain, in his wings
> he carries corpses.[13]

'Niðafjöll' means 'the Mountains of the Dark of the Moon'; another detail which feeds into Tolkien's *Roverandom* story.

To take stock for a moment: we have, then, three possible solutions for these famous Anglo-Saxon riddles. In setting out these three I am following a Tolkienian lead—not in the specific answers I propose, for as far as I know he himself offered no solutions to these riddles, but in a broader sense, the one outlined in his celebrated lecture 'The Monsters and the Critics'. In that work Tolkien insisted that although scholarship tends to want to downplay the fantastical and monstrous aspect of Old English literature in favour of rationalised, historical or social explanations, in fact the heart and soul of the literature is *in* the monsters. (I discuss Tolkien's lecture in more detail below). So: let's entertain the possibility that the answers to all three riddles are 'dragon'.[14]

Tolkien's imagination was strongly drawn to Dragons. 'I find "dragons" a fascinating product of imagination', he wrote to Naomi Mitchison in 1949. At the same time he noted that 'the whole problem of the intrusion of the "dragon" into northern imagination' was, in effect, a riddle to which he had not yet found a solution. Another letter, written to Walter Hooper on 20 February 1968, may be relevant here. In this letter Tolkien confirms that he has never himself seen a dragon, and that he has no wish to. He then relates a story he heard from C. S. Lewis concerning an individual named Brightman, an ecclesiastical scholar of some repute, who sat in the Common Room of Magdalen College Oxford saying very little for many years. One night there was a discussion of dragons, and according to Lewis:

> Brightman's voice was heard to say, 'I have seen a dragon.' Silence. 'Where was that?' he was asked. 'On the Mount of Olives,' he said. He relapsed into silence and never before his death explained what he meant.[15]

The riddle of Brightman's gnomic comment is not *so* very hard to unravel, except that it answers a riddle with another riddle, or perhaps it would be better to say: answers it with a religious mystery. The dragon he has seen presumably has to do with his personal encounter with Christ. The mystery here (which also, I think, galvanises Tolkien's own creative imagination) is that the fabulous type of Satan can also function as a type of Christ—that evil and good can be reconciled on the largest, spiritual scale. The dragon of which, despite all its instinct towards destruction, only good ultimately comes. The dragon, we might say, as a manifestation of what Graham Greene, in resonant phrase, once called the appalling strangeness of the mercy of God.

* * *

To broaden the discussion a little: in addition to specific poems set out as riddles, Anglo-Saxon poetry is threaded through with *kennings*: a distinctive, circumlocutionary trope that uses figurative and riddling phrases in place of simple indicatives. The *Beowulf*-poet for instance sometimes refers to the sea as 'the sea', and sometimes as 'the whale-road' or 'the gannets'-bath'. A kenning might be easily unriddled, particularly if predicated upon the object's use—an example would be a sword described as 'a wound-hoe'. Alternatively it might be more oblique and baffling: in *Beowulf* 1032 a sword is *fela lafe*, presumably 'that which the *file left* behind' when the smith was sharpening it.

The word kenning is originally Old Norse, and comes from the word *kenna*, which means 'knowledge'. The Modern English verb *to ken* does survives, although in a marginal and dialectic sense (although the phrase *beyond one's ken*, 'beyond the scope of one's knowledge', contains the word, like a bug in amber, preserved in its original sense). In other words, 'kennings' like full riddles are games of knowledge: they ask, in the first sense, 'do you know what this is?' and more broadly they open more puzzling questions about the certainty, ground and transparency of all knowledge. Since the pleasure of a kenning is proportionate to its complexity it does not surprise us that Old Norse texts are replete not only with the *kenning* but the *tvíkenning*—the double-kenning. To unpack *'grennir gunn-más'* from the Norse *Glymdrápa* (the phrase means 'feeder of the war-gull') we need first to understand that 'war-gull' is itself a kenning for 'raven'. 'Feeder of ravens' is a sardonic way of describing a warrior, somebody destined to end up a corpse on the battlefield and eaten by carrion birds. The modern 'cannon-fodder' is a similar kenning, although since it has become a phrasal cliché it is likely that few who hear it are moved to decode it *as* a kenning. How far Anglo-Saxon culture similarly took kennings as mere clichés, and how far they functioned as actually estranging mini-riddles, can only be a matter of conjecture. But at least *some* kennings engage the mind in the process of unriddling. When I first learned to ride a motorcycle a medical student friend of mine noticed my crash-helmet in the hallway of the flat we shared and said to me: 'I see you have become an organ donor.' This—although I did not then know the word—*was* a kenning, a distant cousin of the 'feeder of ravens' sort; for motorcyclists are much more likely to be involved in fatal accidents, and their corpses therefore are more likely to supply hospital surgeries with young, healthy organs for transplant.

It is a striking thing that, whilst scholars describe kennings as a characteristically common-Germanic business, only Old Norse and Old English poetry contain actual kennings. For our purposes, since these are the two literary and cultural traditions that most directly fed into Tolkien's own imaginative work, this is relevant; although it raises questions as to why kennings did not appeal more broadly. More, Old English writers do not seem to have been interested in the Norse *tvíkenning*: all Anglo-Saxon kennings are all of the simple two-term form like 'file-left' or 'whale-road'. But we can say that, on the level of word and form, the simple kenning is the bringing together of two terms that generates a third. This is, in other words, the action of metaphor, the leap into comprehension. The kenning mimics the process by which the mundane thing and the mundane thing can combine together to make something transcendent: meaning.[16]

* * *

Anglo-Saxon culture was fascinated by the intersection of the divine and the mundane, as was Tolkien. We can go further and suggest that it is in its *riddles* that this great mystery is most often given voice. By way of small example here, in Chris McGully's elegant translation, is Riddle 85 from the *Exeter Book*:

> My home's noisy.   I'm not. I'm mute
> in this dwelling place.   A deity shaped
> our twinning journey.   I'm more turbulent than he,
> At times stronger.   He's tougher—durable.
> Sometimes I come to rest. He always runs on ahead.
> For as long as I shall live I shall live in him.
> If we undo ourselves   death's due claims me.[17]

Scholars tend to agree that the solution to *this* riddle must be 'a fish in the river'; although I think we can be more precise, and say 'a turbot in the Thames'. Of all the rivers in England, only the Thames was worshipped in the Dark Ages as a god—archaeologists have recovered, only from this waterway, large numbers of swords and other valuable metalware from this period that had once been offered up to the god of the river. The point of this riddle, it seems to me, is to do more than pose a puzzle. It is to suggest the ways in which the river is continually pouring its life out into the ocean and yet is continually renewing itself. The river is both living and immortal, a deity: and the fish, who is always in motion, is its holy inhabitant. It is puzzling and yet it is *right* that the mundane and the divine are twined round one another. (In the 'Riddles in the Dark' chapter of *The Hobbit*, not one but two of the riddles have the answer 'fish'). Nor is this confined to a pagan sense of the world. Here is riddle 51, once again in McCully's version:

> Four wondrous things   fall through my eyes,
> travelling together.   Their tracks were black,
> but pale their path.   Among these planing birds
> swift was strongest: swooped up through air,
> dove under water.   He worked restless,
> this pioneer   pointing the journey
> all four must make   over filigreed gold.[18]

McCully himself follows conventional scholarly wisdom in proposing the solution: 'four fingers holding a quill'. Personally, I do not see that this is a terribly good solution to the riddle. One holds a pen with two fingers and a thumb, not with 'four fingers'; the digits of a writing hand can hardly be said to 'fall through the eyes' and it is not usual to plunge one's hand under water before writing. As a kenning for 'writing' *black tracks over a pale path* has a certain loveliness to it, I concede; but the filigreed gold at the end suggests to me that we are talking not about mundane writing but rather an elaborate, expensive illuminated manuscript. In other words I am suggesting that the answer to this riddle is not writing as such, but *the Gospels*. Producing beautifully illustrated versions of these texts was, of course, one of the main occupations of monks. Here, the four saints Matthew, Mark, Luke and John make their journey via the writing of black ink on white page, but their work is also illuminated by gold, and other colours too. And each gospel author had his own animal: the eagle for St John, an ox for Luke, a winged lion for Mark and a winged man (or angel) for Matthew. That is to say, Matthew, Mark and John could all fly, and could be described as 'planing birds'; but only St John, the eagle, is 'the strongest' bird, capable of swooping up through the air and diving down into the water—as both sea eagles and fish eagles do. John leads, 'pointing the journey' because he is the author of the prophetic Revelation with which the Bible concludes.

But these two specific readings are a roundabout way of making a larger and I believe fairly uncontentious point. One of the things riddles do is close the ground between mundane puzzle and divine mystery. There are several ways in which this is made manifest in Dark Age culture. Here is an example of what I mean: one way this culture tried to understand the puzzling nature of divine–mortal interaction was by having a god actually pose riddles to a mortal, in a contest. Indeed, riddle contests were an important part of Dark Age culture. This might be by way of passing the time and having fun; but they also had a deeper significance.

One example of this latter is the field of law. However counter-intuitive it might seem to modern sensibilities, Dark Age culture closely connected legal process and riddles. Perhaps this had to do with a sense that the law was rarely simple or straightforward; for the law, after all, tends to highlight puzzling or counter-intuitive aspects of human existence. In Dark Age and early medieval Ireland and Wales the riddle was thought an essential means of both teaching and practising law.[19] Where the latter is concerned, Judges in early Irish law courts were expected to base their judgment on five grounds, bringing to bear natural justice, Scripture, legal analogy as well as two riddle-like elements: the *fásach* (a group of legal maxims that can be thought of part of wisdom literature more generally) and the *roscad*. This last is a mode of gnomic verse jurists were taught, and which Fergus Kelly argues can best be thought of as riddles.[20] Riddles are a mode of wisdom, and wisdom should inform legal judgment. To quote Christopher Guy Yocum:

> While judges were not valued as highly as poets, possibly because of the view that they were artisans, the cultivation of wisdom literature was apparently entrusted to judges as part of their duties in regard to the law.[21]

We have evidence that the riddle was used as an instructional tool in Welsh and Irish law schools; and can assume it was used elsewhere in the northern world. The *Gúbretha Caratniad* ('False Judgments of Caratnia') is an Early Irish legal dialogue that foregrounds how important riddles were to Early Irish and Welsh jurisprudence. It is found in a manuscript dating from the mid twelfth century—Oxford, Bodleian Library, Rawlinson MS B 502—though the work itself is considerably older. It details a question and answer to-and-fro between a Judge called Caratnia and his king Conn Cétchathach. The Judge makes a series of 'false' legal judgments, and the king points out that these judgments contravene Irish law. The judge then explains the particular circumstances that make these superficially 'false' judgments actually true. As Robin Chapman Stacey points out, 'the genre to which these conversations belong' is the riddle. He adds that the fact that riddles formed part of a legal education 'is not surprising'.

> As Joan Radner has demonstrated, the genre [of riddles] itself is used frequently, in Irish and other world traditions, to underscore the limitations of human knowledge and categorizing techniques. 'Riddling,' she writes, 'reminds people of the unknown, of the limitations of what they regard as sensible and logical, of the inadequacy of their understanding. They are "manipulations of the power of knowledge," that implicitly render ambiguous or paradoxical that which might otherwise seem to be predictable and secure.'[22]

One reason riddles were treated with such judicial respect by the Northmen is that the gods love them. To meet a stranger, particularly a hooded-stranger with one eye and a mysterious manner, might well mean that you have met Odin himself, the father of the gods. And if Odin asked you a riddle, you had better know the answer. Indeed, riddle-contests like this—in which a supernatural creature asks a riddle to be solved by a mortal on pain of death—appear all over world-culture. We can hardly avoid thinking of the Sphinx testing Oedipus ('what walks on four legs in the morning, two legs at noon and three legs in the evening?') and of Samson's riddle in the Bible ('out of the strong came forth sweetness'). These puzzles encode the human sense that the divine is a mystery with which we must wrestle if we hope to do more than die like a beast.

The Old English poem *Solomon and Saturn* (possibly composed during King Alfred's reign, in the later ninth-century) includes a riddle contest between the pagan king called Saturn and the Christianised figure of the Biblical Solomon. It is a text in two parts, and although the second is most relevant to my purpose here—largely consisting, as it does, of an exchange of riddles between the two deuteragonists— the first has its place too. In part 1 Saturn, having searched through Libya, Greece and India hoping to find 'truth' has come back disappointed. He asks for Solomon's help, and is accordingly given a detailed account of the *Pater Noster*, going in detail through the individual letters that make up the prayer. He does this because these letters, represented as richly ornamented runes, individually contain divine power. I will come back to this sense of the power of the individual letter in my next chapter. The longer *Solomon and Saturn II* (327 lines, as compared to part I's 169) is a straightforward riddle contest.[23] In the words of Dieter Bitterli: 'the two interlocutors pose and answer several enigmatic questions, including at least two proper riddles whose subjects appear to be "book" and "old age".'[24] Another perhaps more directly pertinent example is the Icelandic saga of King Heidrek—Old Norse rather than Old English, a favourite of Tolkien's, and a book later translated into English by Tolkien's son, Christopher.[25] King Heidrek, a powerful king of men, happens to have a grievance against a fellow called 'Gestumblindi'. The king sends him word 'to come and be reconciled, if he cared for his life'; and Gestumblindi, doing so, proposes a riddle-contest.

But this fellow's name ought to alert us straight away that all is not as it seems: for 'Gestum Blindi' means 'Guest (who is) blind'—*guest* in the old sense of the word, 'stranger'. The blind stranger, if we know our Norse myth, puts us in mind of Odin: one-eyed, a wanderer, fond of riddles. At any rate, rather than face the judgment of Heidrek's counsellors, 'Gestumblindi' enters into a riddle contest with the king, and asks him:

> If only I still had
> what I had yesterday!
> discover what it was;
> it hurts mankind
> it hinders speech
> yet speech is inspired by it
> Ponder this riddle.

The king replies 'Góð er gáta þín, Gestumblindi, getit er þessar'—'Good are (these) *gáta* of thine, Gestumblindi; guessed them I have'; or in less

Yoda-like English, 'your riddle is a good one, Gestumblindi; but I have guessed it!' This is a line of verse, presumably the stock way of saying that you have solved a riddle, and the king repeats it after almost all the riddles he is asked. (The answer to the 'if only I still had' riddle is: 'ale')

> I travelled from my home
> And from my home I went
> I saw the road of road;
> There was a road underneath
> And a road overhead,
> And on every sides there were roads.
> Ponder this riddle,
> O prince Heidrek!

Góð er gáta þín, Gestumblindi, getit er þessar! 'You passed over a bridge across a river, and the road of the river was beneath you, but birds flew above your head and flew past on your either side, and that was their road.'

> What was the drink
> That I drank yesterday?
> Neither wine nor water,
> Neither mead nor ale,
> It wasn't any kind of food,
> Yet I came away thirstless.
> Ponder this riddle,
> O prince Heidrek!

Góð er gáta þín, Gestumblindi, getit er þessar! 'You lay down in shade where dew had collected on the grass, and with this you cooled your lips and satisfied your thirst.'

> Who is that shrill one
> on hard ways walking,
> paths he has passed before;
> many are his kisses
> for of mouths he has two,
> and on gold alone he goes?

Ponder this riddle,
O prince Heidrek!

Góð er gáta þín, Gestumblindi, getit er þessar! 'That is the hammer, which is used in the goldsmith's art; it screams shrilly when it beats on the hard anvil, and the anvil is its path.' And so it goes on: twenty-eight riddles in quick succession are asked and answered one after the other. A number of them are similar enough to some of the riddles of the contest between Bilbo and Gollum to excite scholars.

A cask of ale:
no hand shaped it,
no hammer built it,
yet outside the islands
its maker sits straight-up.
Ponder this riddle,
O Prince Heidrek!

'Your riddle is a good one', the king replies; 'but I have guessed it.' It is, of course, 'egg' ('the egg-shell is not made by hand nor is it formed by hammer; and the swan that produces it carries himself erect, outside the islands'). Another riddle familiar to readers of *The Hobbit* is:

Who is the mighty one
That passes over the ground
Swallowing water and forest?
He fears the wind
But flees no man
And wages war on the sun!
Ponder this riddle,
O Prince Heidrek!

The answer to this riddle is a particular sort of darkness, 'fog'; and Tom Shippey argues that this riddle is behind the 'dark' riddle that Bilbo answers 'without even scratching his head' because 'he had heard that sort of thing before'. We might want to pause and consider whether 'a cask of ale' is the same thing as 'a box without hinges'; or whether 'fog' means quite the same thing as 'darkness'; I discuss these near-analogues, or perhaps deliberate riddling swerves, in the next chapter.

Each riddle is a doddle for Heidrek (*Góð er gáta þín, Gestumblindi, getit er þessar!*) until the last one. Finally Gestumblindi asks this:

> What did Odin say
> Into Balder's ear
> Before he was carried off to the fire?

Of course Heidrek does not know the answer to this. Nor is it a riddle, or at least a riddle after the manner of the others; for it is not possible to guess or intuit it from the information given. Either one knows the answer or one does not; and in fact only two beings (Balder and Odin himself) can possibly know the answer to this one. In a rage, the king shouts that he has seen through Gestumblindi's disguise ('you alone know the answer to that riddle!'), whips out his sword and attempts to stab the god. To escape harm, Odin changes himself into a hawk and flies away, but not before cursing the king: 'because you have attacked me with a sword, King Heidrek, you yourself shall die at the hands of the basest slaves!'

What is the answer to this last riddle? The honest answer is: we do not know. Perhaps this is its point: that it is unanswerable. Tolkien, in what looks very like an imitation of this contest, concludes his riddle-contest between Bilbo and Gollum, with a similarly unanswerable question. 'What have I got in my pocket' is not a riddle in the sense that we cannot work out what the answer is; either we know, or we do not. Gollum does not know, and guesswork does not help him.

And here we come back to the question of the riddle in the court of law. Asking an unanswerable riddle is a way of overmastering the questioned person. One of the things the *Gúbretha Caratniad* is interested in is the respective power rightfully due the law on the one hand and the king on the other. By acting out their riddling exchange, the Judge Caratnia and his king Conn Cétchathach are jockeying for power and status, one with the other. In a much smaller sense, this is also what Bilbo and Gollum are doing. In the words of Robin Chapman Stacey: 'riddles function, in almost every culture in which they appear, as a means by which one person lays claim to power over another'.[26]

Like Bilbo and Gollum's contest, *The Saga of King Heidrek* ends on a debatable point. As Tom Shippey notes, Tolkien's mind was particularly drawn to the grey areas of scholarship—that is, his creative imagination was sparked by debatable points. Thus the cup-stealing episode in *Beowulf*, which inspired the chapter 'Inside Information', is based on a scholarly reconstruction of a badly-damaged section of the manuscript. Similarly the name *Eomer* in *The Lord of the Rings* is borrowed, not from *Beowulf*, but from a scholar's emendation of the word which actually occurs in the *Beowulf* manuscript. While *The Saga of King Heidrek the Wise* and its riddle-contest are well known among Norse scholars, 'this particular riddle ("alive without breath") is found in only one of the three main versions of the saga . . . Furthermore, the page containing this riddle is lost from the original manuscript.'[27] It is the very debatableness of riddles that makes them so imaginatively powerful.

* * *

One notion I am setting myself against, here—I may as well be plain—is that any given riddle has one right or correct answer. I take seriously the urge a riddle raises in us to 'solve' it, and I do not underestimate the extent to which the going from sifting through possible but unsatisfactory answers to any given riddle to lighting upon an answer that fits, like a key sliding in a lock, is a notable human pleasure. I do not repudiate this pleasure; but neither do I think it a simple thing. The thesis of this study (to repeat myself) is that riddles are, amongst other things, ways of *ironising* the world; and adding an answer to an unsolved riddle does not dissolve away such irony.

I need to tread carefully here, because I am not talking about *ambiguity*, either in the simple or even in the more complicated Empsonian sense of the word. To read through the *Exeter Book* riddles is to be struck that some of the answers seem obvious where for others the answer is hard to decide. Indeed, many people from specialist scholars to enthusiastic amateurs have proposed sometimes contradictory solutions. But I want to suggest that this contradictoriness is not an index of muddle, or confusion, but of something more radically ironic in the nature of the text itself.

I am going to look at one more *Exeter Book* riddle, the brief but lovely Riddle 69, by way of thinking what it means to 'answer' an Anglo-Saxon riddle. Here it is:

Wundor wearð on wege: wæter wearð to bane.

On the way, a wonder: water becomes bone.

Scholars agree that answer to this riddle is: *ice*. Scholars do not
always agree on the answer to any given riddle. For example, various
Old English riddle experts have looked at Riddle 74 ('I was once a
young woman, / a glorious warrior, a grey-haired queen. / I soared
with birds, stepped on the earth, / swam in the sea—dived under
the waves, languid amongst fishes. I had a living spirit') and suggested variously *cuttlefish*, *water*, *siren* and *swan* as the answer. By
comparison, and remembering that the answers to these riddles are
nowhere written down or officially tabulated, 'on the way, a miracle:
water becomes bone . . . *ice*' looks relatively straightforward. It is a
nicely satisfying and poetic image, too. But here is another answer
to the riddle:

> Climbing Cooper's Hill, and looking back at the curve of the Thames
> in the bright, cloudy light: the afternoon sun polishing away all grey
> or blue from the water until it is white, its edges sharpened by the
> angle of illumination, looking like nothing so much as a mighty
> rib-bone gleaming, set in the flesh of the land . . . and I thought to
> myself *yes, water becomes bone.*[28]

The answer *ice* identifies two points of similarity (hardness, colour)
with bone; but this vision of the Thames identifies three (colour,
shape, setting). Does that make it a 'better' answer to the *Exeter Book*
riddle? I suppose there are not many people who would say so. But
stop a bit. Here is a third possible answer to the riddle:

> The company said the decision to produce a calcium water had
> been made after the US Health Department highlighted calcium
> deficiency as a major problem in the US. SWG claims to be the
> first US bottled water company to directly address the growing
> consumer awareness of the benefits of calcium for healthier bones
> and teeth.[29]

Or, if you prefer: 'Milk, rich in calcium, builds strong bones!'
Now I would hazard that I would not find many Old English scholars
who could so much as give either of the above 'answers' the time of
day, much less a mention in a critical edition of the *Exeter Book*. As
far as I can see, the unwritten rules of scholarly investigation into OE
riddles goes something like this: the point of the exercise is not really,

ingeniously or otherwise, *to answer these riddles*. Rather the point is one of imaginative entry into the mind of an Anglo-Saxon. That is to say, the modern-day scholar sets out to answer them in a way that is consistent with the world-view of an Anglo-Saxon mind. The first answer (ice) is the sort of answer a ninth-century Middlesaxon might think of. The second (the Thames seen from a hill under certain conditions of light) is an answer that, although it probably wouldn't occur to Mr Ninth-Century, would at least be comprehensible to him. But the third answer ('milk') would make no sense to him at all. The fact that it makes perfect sense to a twenty-first-century dweller in Middlesex, like me, is not relevant. These, after all, are Anglo-Saxon, not modern English, riddles.[30]

But why do we conceive of riddles in this way? A 'riddle' (from *rædan*, to counsel, advise or teach), like a kenning, is a mode of knowing. Riddles are about giving the commonplace a conceptual shake to enable us to see it anew. Thinking of milk as a way in which water becomes bone is a perfectly good way of knowing. If Bilbo Baggins asks 'what have I got in my pocket?' and Gollum answers 'molecules of air', then Gollum has answered the question asked. Would it be fair for Bilbo to say 'no . . . although I *do* have molecules of air on my pocket, *that's not what was in my mind when I posed the question*'—? Surely, if Bilbo were minded to say such a thing, then he ought to have cut straight to the chase and asked a different question, along the lines of 'I'm thinking of something: guess what it is'. But that sort of question would make a very poor riddle indeed. Or:

SPHINX: You must answer my question or die! What walks on four legs in the morning, two legs at noon and three legs in the evening?

OEDIPUS: Samuel Johnson's well-trained dog.

SPHINX: No! The answer is man, who crawls as a babe, walks tall in youth, and uses a stick in his dotage!

OEDIPUS: You said morning, noon and evening; not infancy, youth and dotage.

SPHINX: It's metaphorical!

OEDIPUS: Besides, a baby doesn't walk on four legs. It crawls on its legs and arms. Arms aren't legs.

SPHINX: [*Utters a howling, glass-shattering shriek*] Metaphorical legs! Not literal legs! Legs in a *man-ner of speak-ing!*

OEDIPUS:	Well, it's half metaphor and half literal, isn't it, since the baby uses two legs and two arms. So of the four legs stipulated, two are literally legs and two are only metaphorically legs.
SPHINX:	Git!
OEDIPUS:	So, which is it to be, literal or metaphorical?
SPHINX:	I'm not listening! I'm putting my wings over my ears! La! La! La!
OEDIPUS:	And the noontime walking on two legs is literal, not metaphorical. So your riddle mixes metaphor and literal application in an inconsistent manner.
SPHINX:	Shut up! Shut up!
OEDIPUS:	Of these two answers to the riddle, mine better fits the terms of the question.
SPHINX:	That's not the point. When I asked the question I was not inviting you to answer it; I was demanding that you guess what was in my mind! I was thinking of man, not Samuel Johnson's dog; you didn't guess that. So you must die!
OEDIPUS:	That's hardly fair. Call your supervisor; I want to have a word with her.
	[*There's a great deal of squawking and shrieking. The Over-Sphinx comes in.*]
OVER-SPHINX:	Can I help you?
OEDIPUS:	Yes. I'm far from happy with the level of service I'm getting from this Sphinx. In the first place she asked a thoroughly misleading question, and now she's trying to palm me off with an illogical and internally inconsistent answer, even though I provided, as I was requested to do, a perfectly reasonable riddle-solution.
OVER-SPHINX:	I do apologise sir. Might I offer you a replacement riddle? I can offer you 'Is the present king of France bald?' or 'how many roads must a man walk down?'
OEDIPUS:	No, I think I'd like my money back.

Surely it is legitimate to argue that the purpose of asking a question is not to try and guess what is in the mind of the questioner, but *to answer the question.* Which is to say, the point of interpreting text is not to try and retrieve what was in the mind of the author but, you know, to read the text. So I am going to stick with *milk*.

Another way of putting this would be to stress the *playful* aspect of riddling. It is a game; stimulating as well as diverting, but of necessity open-ended, an art of disclosure rather than enclosure. The name for the sort of person who would close down the possibilities of the game is *kill-joy*. But perhaps that looks merely petulant; so I shall close this chapter with a quotation from one of the most respected contemporary academic scholars of the OE riddle-form, Patrick J. Murphy. Murphy is less interested in simple 'solutions' to riddles (although he is also interested in those) because he is more interested in the way riddles work. In a word he is intrigued by what they *do*. He insists, helpfully, upon 'the distinction between a riddle's solution and its interpretation', and he is open to the role of play in riddling. Riddles, he argues, 'draw intricate links between disparate things, as birds become letters, bright riders shift into suns and stars, and onions strip away layers of allusion and mordant metaphor'.[31] Riddling is a bringing-together; and in the 'Riddles in the Dark' chapter of *The Hobbit*, riddles bring together two creatures, seemingly very different, but (we eventually discover) very alike.

3
Riddles in the Dark

Bilbo, fleeing goblins through the subterranean chambers of the Misty Mountains, chances upon a golden ring. Later, groping about in the dark, he meets Gollum, a murky creature who dwells in the gloom catching fish in the underground lakes and eating them raw. The ring, it seems, is his. Bilbo needs a guide to help him out of the labyrinth of caves. Gollum wants to eat Bilbo. These desires, clearly, are incompatible. The two decide to settle the matter with a riddle contest.

This may, if we stop to think about it, strike us as a puzzling way of mediating their opposing needs. This is a serious matter: life-or-death to Bilbo, and staving off starvation to Gollum. A game of riddles seems, perhaps, an infantile mode of settling the dispute. But Tolkien was drawing on a rich Old English tradition that saw riddles not as infantile or trivial. Riddles were more than simple word-games; they had binding power. Riddles for the Anglo-Saxons were not any old word-game or puzzling question; they were rituals, poems, a canon of questions about the world and ways of seeing that world. This in turn has a bearing on the legitimacy of the last 'riddle' Bilbo asks ('what have I got in my pocket'; this, as Gollum rightly notes, is 'not fair'). But before we get there let us look at the contest itself.

It seems uncontentious to call the 'riddles in the dark' chapter one of the best loved sections of the novel. This reflects both the intrinsic appeal of riddles, and the brilliant characterisation of Gollum himself, one of Tolkien's—and Fantasy's—most iconic figures. It is worth reflecting for a moment on this, for in this first iteration there is very little *to* Gollum. We know he is a hobbit-sized creature, who lives in the dark. His gulping throat-noise (from which he gets his name) speaks to a degree of de-socialisation that combines the intimation of horrible appetites—after all, he does hope to eat Bilbo—with a kind of internalised nervousness or uncertainty. He has his habit of referring to himself both in the first and third person ('I' and 'my precious') which suggests the mild schizophrenia of the long isolated. More strikingly he also refers to himself in the second person plural, as 'us', as if folding both halves of his split personality into one. The first thing he says upon seeing Bilbo is a self-address to 'us': 'bless us and splash us, my precioussss!'—a nice oath: clean (for a family audience) and with plenty of opportunity to show off the hissing sibilance of Gollum's trademark phrasing. More, it hovers nicely between a positive, even pious sense—the baptismal splashing of water, the religious blessing—and something darker: 'bless' also means wound, and the splashing might be blood.

The conversation between Bilbo and Gollum that follows is predicated upon that ancient courtesy by which not even a troll, or a sphinx, will devour a person until a riddle has been asked and answered. (The courtesy of this circumstance is helped by the fact that Bilbo has a sword, which he does not forget to brandish.) The riddles themselves are presented to the reader as a series of poems, the verse in each case being Tolkien's own.[1] We are given the answer to each riddle immediately. The first riddle is Gollum's:

> What has roots as nobody sees,
> Is taller than trees,
> Up, up it goes,
> And yet never grows?

Bilbo announces this one to be easy. And since the answer is literally all around them, so it is: *mountain*. Nonetheless, it is in the nature of riddles to encourage a pedantic, even legalistic frame of mind in the riddled. Is the answer correct in all its particulars? For if not it will be straightforwardly misleading. The geological knowledge that tectonic activity results in mountains *actually* growing (Mount Everest is growing at a rate of several centimetres a year) postdates Tolkien's novel, and certainly postdates the Anglo-Saxon culture out of which these riddles are drawn; so we can perhaps forgive the riddle for that inaccuracy. But in what sense, even for the Anglo-Saxons, do mountains have 'roots'?

This answer may perhaps puzzle us, for of course, unlike trees, mountains are not rooted in the earth. I used to assume that it was a common Norse belief that mountains were supplied with stony roots; that, in other words, the subterranea of mountain ranges (which, after all, nobody can see) were *like* the subterranea of forests. In fact the truth is otherwise. In the *Prose Edda*, an anthology of Norse myths composed (probably) by Icelandic king Snorri Sturluson we find the story of the terrible wolf Fenrir, a beast so powerful and monstrous it threatens the whole world. The gods try to restrain this being with increasingly strong fetters, but Fenrir breaks them easily. Finally though they manage to trap the beast with 'a fetter called Gleipnir'.

It was constructed from six elements: the noise of a cat's footsteps, the beard of a woman, the roots of a mountain, the sinews of a bear, the breath of a fish and the spittle of a bird.[2]

This fetter, being both insubstantial as a fish's breath and strong as a bear's sinews, is beyond the power of Fenrir to break. What of the other four elements? One section of the 'prose Edda' (the *Gylfaginning*, or 'the Gulling of Gylfi') is styled as a conversation between a mortal called Gangleri and the god Odin. Having told him the story of the fetter called Gleipnir, Odin tells Gangleri: 'though previously you had no knowledge of these matters, you now can quickly see the proof that you were not deluded. You must have noticed that a woman has no beard, a cat's movement makes no loud noise and mountains have no roots.' So there we have it; straight from the Norse's mouth— the roots of mountains do not exist.[3] Whether we prefer to take '*as nobody sees*' to be periphrasis for '*as do not exist*', or whether we would rather take the riddle at face value and come up with an alternate answer ('Yggdrasil', for example) is up to us. Gollum, at any rate, is satisfied with the answer Bilbo gives him.

The second riddle is asked by Bilbo of Gollum:

> *Thirty white horses on a red hill,*
> *First they champ,*
> *Then they stamp,*
> *Then they stand still.*

When I was a boy, not yet a decade old, I received for a birthday present an audio-book version of *The Hobbit*, on four cassette tapes, read by the great Scots actor Nicol Williamson. I listened to those tapes over and over. Indeed, I listened to this recording so many times that, even today as I read *The Hobbit*, Williamson's lovely, cawing cadences still hover over my sense of the words. The audiobook text was abridged, and indeed would hardly have fitted onto only four cassette tapes otherwise. Mostly the abridgement was sensitively done, but at one point in the book—this one—the anonymous abridger made a mistake. The answer to this riddle is 'teeth'; but the exchange that precedes the answer goes as follows:

> That was all [Bilbo] could think of to ask—the idea of eating was rather on his mind. It was rather an old one, too, and Gollum knew the answer as well as you do. 'Chestnuts, chestnuts,' he hissed. 'Teeth! teeth!'

'Chestnuts', here, is idiomatic for 'that's easy!' But the audiobook abridger, in haste or perhaps in simple misunderstanding, omitted the last two words of this passage. As a result, in my puzzled 8-year old brain, I tried to work out in the answer to a riddle about *Thirty white horses on a red hill, champing, stamping, standing still* could possibly be that type of nut popular at Christmastime. But we are entitled to wonder whether there is not more to this riddle than simply Bilbo's anxiety that Gollum will shortly be sinking *his* teeth into hobbit flesh.

Teeth were important to the Anglo-Saxons; which is to say, they were important when they went wrong. The three *Leechbooks of Bald*—and *what* a superb name for a medical textbook that is—were written in Old English at Winchester, possibly in the ninth century, making them our oldest extant vernacular medical works. The third volume contains a variety of remedies for dental malaises. Here, for example, is the prescription 'for a mouth broken inside':

> *Take a plum* (Prunus domestica) *tree's leaf, boil it in wine, let him swill his mouth with it*[4]

Unlikely to help the dental pathology, although the alcohol in the wine would perhaps sterilise the mouth against the spread of infection. If an Anglo-Saxon complained of 'hollow teeth' (presumably cavities), this is what they were advised to do:

> *Chew bothen's root with vinegar on that side.*

Nobody seems to know what 'bothen's root' is, so this may not be of use to any present-day cavity-afflicted readers. But the longest and weirdest prescription in the *Leechbooks of Bald* is for a 'crooked or deficient' mouth—either a specific medical diagnosis of something like cleft-palate, or else a description so general as to encompass pretty much the whole of the British Isles, tooth-wise:

> *Take coriander* (Coriandrum sativum), *dry it out, make it into dust, mix the dust with the milk of a woman who is feeding a boy-child, wring it out through a blue cloth and smear the healthy cheek with it, and drip it into the ear carefully. Make a bathing, then: take bramble* (Rubus fruti-cosus) *bark and elm* (Ulmus campestris) *bark, ash* (Fraxinus excel-sior) *bark, blackthorn* (Prunus spinosus) *bark, apple tree* (Pyrus malus) *bark, ivy* (Hedera helix) *bark—the lower parts of all of these—and cucumber, smearwort* (Aristolochia rotunda), *boarfern* (Polypodium vulgare), *elecampane* (Inula helenium), *elfthon* (Circaea lutetiana), *betony* (Stachys betonica), *horehound* (Marrubium vulgare), *radish* (Raphanus sativus), *agrimony* (Potentilla anserina), *scrape the plant into a cauldron and boil them thoroughly. Once it is thoroughly boiled, take it off the fire and let it stand and make the man a seat over the cauldron and cover the man so that the vapour cannot get out anywhere except that he might breathe it in. Bathe him with this bathing for as long as he can bear it. Have another bathe ready for him then, take an entire anthill—of those that sometimes fly, it will be red—boil it in water, bathe him with it, with excessive heat. Then make him a salve: take some plants of each of those kinds, boil in butter, smear the sore parts with it, they will soon come back to life. Make him a lye from elder* (Sambucus niger) *ashes, wash his head with it cold, it will soon be better for him; and let the man's blood each month on a five-night-old moon, and on a fifteen, and on a twenty.*

The sheer complexity of this speaks to a world in which tooth-pain was a genuine problem. Untreated dental abscesses can kill, and even if they do not the prolonged intensity of pain the sufferer experiences is rarely equalled in life. Still, treating a patient not only with herbs but *boiled anthill vapour* strikes a strange, even riddling note to modern ears.

Here is another interpretation. The riddle suggests a heraldic bla-zon of a white horse, or several white horses, against a red field: to use the technical phrasing, horses argent against a gules field. The white horse is (amongst other things) the animal used to represent Tolkien's home county, Oxfordshire, usually in conjunction with an ox. For example, the Oxfordshire coat of arms is a horse argent and an ox gules; the coat of arms of Deddington (a village a little way north of Oxford) includes a horse argent holding a gules shield, and the coat of arms of Wallingford (south-east of Oxford, and not far from Tolkien's house in Headington) includes two horses argent and a gules field. The gules field suggests martial or royal qualities: the arms of the kingdom of England are three or lions rampant (we might almost say: champing and stamping) upon a gules field. Perhaps this riddle invites the reader to reflect the answer back home, to Tolkien's nation and county: that the riddle evokes a sort of visual rebus of the thirty towns of Oxfordshire.

This leads us back towards landscape. Bilbo's riddle is simultaneously interiorising and exteriorising, the former since it invites us, imaginatively, inside his mouth; the latter because it calls to mind a landscape—not anthills but actual hills. It is not hard to picture a hill topped with thirty as-it-were 'horses', because the landscape of southern England is supplied with many such sites. The most famous of these, Stonehenge in Wiltshire, predates the Anglo-Saxon period by a great stretch of time. Still, features of the pre-Dark-Age English landscape, such as barrows and hills and stone circles, are worked into Tolkien's Middle-Earth as well. To picture a stone circle is to see landscape arranged with giant stone teeth, sticking upward.

The *Oxford English Dictionary* derives the word 'stonehenge' from stone + 'henge', reading the latter as a word etymologically connected with the modern 'hanging' or 'suspended'. Since the lintels are indeed suspended above the earth (although the standing stones are not) the idea that Stonehenge means 'hanging stones' is widely accepted. Indeed, it has been for centuries. Nonetheless, there are other theories—for instance, that 'henge' derives not from *hangian*, to hang, but *hencg*, hinge, because the main stones were hinged up into position, or else because the lintels 'hinge' upon the upright stones. I want to suggest another possibility, one suggested by Bilbo's riddle, although not one ever advanced (as far as I know) by Tolkien himself. It is the suggestion that 'henge' is linked etymologically with *hengist* or *hengst*, 'stallion, steed, horse, gelding'. It does not require a great stretch of imagination to see the teeth-like protrusions of 'stonehenge' as a circle of stone horses, *stān hengsten*, having champed and stamped their way in a circle, and now standing still. There is something undeniably equine about the Π-shape, after all.

Gollum then asks Bilbo the third riddle:

> *Voiceless it cries,*
> *Wingless flutters,*
> *Toothless bites,*
> *Mouthless mutters.*

Bilbo has heard this one before, however, and it does not trouble him. This riddle's answer—wind—is mimicked in the sibilant onomatopoeia of the ninefold 's' tucked into these four brief lines. The alternating masculine and feminine line-endings, and the half-rhyme of 'cries/bites' are unusually effective. It is likely that Tolkien was aware of the following Norse riddling question and answer:

> What is the source of wind that wanders
> The waves unseen?
> The Corpse-Eater Hraesvelg sits in the skin
> Of an eagle at the end of heaven.
> When his wings beat, wind moves
> Over the world of men.[5]

This brief exchange sets up an inversion of the specified qualities of Bilbo's riddle: sightless, lifeless instead of voiceless and mouthless; toothed ('Hraesvelg' means 'chewer of corpses') and winged instead if toothless and wingless. But the riddles share a sense of the uncanny, death-linked force of the wind. Gollum's eerie riddle seems to me about mouths and words ('winged words', Homer calls them)—about speech and the impossibilities of speech. All speech ends when breath ends.

The next riddle is, we are told, made up by Bilbo on the spot:

> *An eye in a blue face*
> *Saw an eye in a green face.*
> *'That eye is like to this eye'*
> *Said the first eye,*
> *'But in low place,*
> *Not in high place.'*

The answer comes to Gollum easily: 'daisy'. The 'day's eye' finds a parallel for itself in the humble flower; but this riddle takes on added resonance when *The Hobbit* is put in the context of *The Lord of the Rings*, and the lidless eye of Sauron—an eye, we might say, in a black face, nightsy rather than daisy in nature. This eye foully mimics and inverts the brightness and wholeness of the sun. The fourth riddle is asked by Gollum:

> *It cannot be seen, cannot be felt,*
> *Cannot be heard, cannot be smelt.*
> *It lies behind stars and under hills,*
> *And empty holes it fills.*
> *It comes first and follows after,*
> *Ends life, kills laughter.*

The answer ('dark') comes to Bilbo because he happens to be sitting in the dark. There is a logic of opposition that determines the way this riddle, about unlight, follows a riddle about light. In the last chapter I quoted the lines from the *Saga of King Heidrek* that several scholars consider behind the 'dark' riddle.

> Who is the mighty one
> That passes over the ground
> Swallowing water and forest?
> He fears the wind
> But flees no man
> And wages war on the sun!
> Ponder this riddle,
> O Prince Heidrek!

But the answer to this, given in the original text, is 'fog', not 'dark'. Despite the fact that both of these are modes of visual obscurity, they really do not mean the same thing. Indeed, the experience of being inside a daytime fog is that of being surrounded by an opaque *brightness*, and not a darkness at all. If we think Tolkien's *Hobbit* riddle a version of the Old Norse original, then we must also concede that the process of adaptation has, again, involved a sort of inversion, such that a riddle to which the answer is 'opaque brightness' has become one in which the answer is 'opaque darkness'. This sort of tricksiness is not uncharacteristic of the way riddling works in this volume, something discussed in the next chapter. Indeed, tricksiness is the whole point of riddles.

The fifth is asked by Bilbo:

> *A box without hinges, key or lid,*
> *Yet golden treasure inside is hid.*

This riddle (to which the answer is 'egg') is taken by some scholars to be a version of one found in the *Saga of King Heidrek*. I discuss it in more detail in the tenth, and final, chapter of this present book. The sixth is Gollum's:

> *Alive without breath,*
> *As cold as death;*
> *Never thirsty, ever drinking,*
> *All in mail never clinking.*

One striking aspect of the answer to this riddle—'fish'—is that it is also the answer to the seventh riddle, Bilbo's:

> *No-legs lay on one-leg, two legs sat near on three-legs, four-legs got*
> *some.*

'Fish on a little table, man at table sitting on a stool, the cat has the bones.' The reduplication of answers seems to me a puzzling thing, not least because it in effect gifts the answer to Gollum ('as it was', the narrator notes, 'talking of fish [it] was not so very difficult'). I have a theory as to why Tolkien includes two riddles next to one another with, in effect, the same answer; and I elaborate it in the next chapter. For the moment I will confine myself to noting that there are many riddles that have a similar form to this one of Bilbo's—I do not mean in the sense that they are about fish, but in the sense that they stack up numbers in the service of trying to baffle the listener. For example, a riddle collected in a seventeenth century collection called *Holme Riddles*:

> Q. ther is a thing that doth both goe sit & stand hath eight legs &
> lives 3 reed this ridle i pray thee

Or in modern English: *there is a thing that all at once goes, sits and stands; it has eight legs and three lives. Read this riddle I pray you!* The answer is 'a man on horse-back with a hawk on his fist'. Gollum asks the eighth riddle:

> *This thing all things devours:*
> *Birds, beasts, trees, flowers;*
> *Gnaws iron, bites steel;*
> *Grinds hard stones to meal;*
> *Slays king, ruins town,*
> *And beats high mountain down.*

The answer to this riddle ('time') comes to Bilbo in a fluke: he means to ask for more time to work out the solution, but can only gasp out 'time! time!' But it may occur to readers of *The Hobbit* that there is a more straightforward answer to this puzzle lurking, underneath a different mountain to the one in which the riddle contest is being held, at the end of the novel. For Smaug has turned Erebor into a wasted land, denuded all the countryside of life, slain kings, destroyed towns, and smashed all the iron and stone weapons sent against him. But Bilbo, I suppose, can be forgiven for not yet knowing about him. Critics compare one of the Solomon and Saturn riddles:

> Ac hwæt is ðæt wundor ðe geond ðas worold færeð
> styrnenga gæð, staðolas beateð,
> aweceð wopdropan winneð oft hider?

> But what is that wondrous thing that travels around the world
> going sternly beating at the foundations
> awakens weeping often works his way in here?

The answer to this is *yldo*, old-age. It is hard to avoid the sense that this provides a poor fit to Tolkien's riddle; for whilst age is a function of time, time is not the same thing as old age. The two have a non-commutative relationship (the one causes the other, but the other does not cause the one). What this does, I think, is put into question that approach to Tolkien's riddles that likes to parse the riddles only as variants of pre-existing originals. Bilbo and Gollum trade 'old chesnuts' and new-minted riddles both; but, as John Rateliff notes, the riddle contest as a whole is more remarkable for Tolkien's creative input: 'it should be stressed however that, whatever Tolkien's sources and inspiration, this striking scene and the riddles it is built around are almost entirely Tolkien's own creation. Both frame (back and forth interaction of the two contestants) and content (the riddles themselves) differ greatly from their precursors.'[6]

And finally Bilbo asks the ninth riddle: 'What have I got in my pocket?' We shall come back to this tricky question later.

The answers, then, to the riddles are as follows:

> *Mountain; teeth; wind; daisy; dark; egg; a fish; a fish being eaten; time; the ring.*

In miniature this reproduces the balance of good and evil construed, symbolically, by the novel itself. On the one hand we have the things of the above-ground, the open-air and sunlight (wind, daisies, eggs); on the other, we have things hidden away, inside (as teeth are inside your mouth, or fish inside water—these two things are combined in the seventh riddle, as teeth mash-up the fish and deliver it inside the body). The mountain is defined by its roots—where Bilbo and Gollum are—and its dark. Time devours. The ring is a vacancy that, we go on to learn, unites all that is dark, and hidden, and destructive.

Why did Tolkien choose these ten riddles, and put them into his story in this order? Mountain; teeth; wind; daisy; dark; egg; a fish; a fish being eaten; time; a golden ring. It works, almost, as string of rebuses encapsulating the narrative of the novel itself: the Misty Mountains, the teeth of the various creatures that seek to devour our heroes (trolls, Gollum, orcs, wolves and dragons); the day's-eye of the sun revealing Bilbo's invisibility; the dark under the mountains, or within Mirkwood, both standing for the evil against which good must fight; the box and its treasures that is the subject of this quest; the various times Bilbo and the dwarves fall into water; the time of the narrative itself; the ring—and its larger significances. Here is an Old English 'gnomic' poem:

> A stream must mingle with the sea
> And a mast stand tight when winds are free;
> A sword be dear to humans still
> And the wise serpent live in a hill;

A fish in water spread its race
And a king give gold from his lofty place;
An old hungry bear walk out on a heath
And a river fall over a hill without death.
An army united by unity stand
And truth be in man, and wisdom in his hand.
A wood cover the land with its courtly green boughs
And a hill be fresh green; and God in His house
The judger of deeds; and a door in a hall
Shall still be the wide mouth that opens to all,
And the shield have a bow where the fingers can lock.
Birds shall speed up to heaven from every tall rock,
The salmon shall leap like the shot of a bow
And showers bring discomfort on worldlings below.
A thief still steal out on the darkest of nights
And the fiend live in fens full of misleading lights.[7]

We might recognise elements of this in *The Hobbit* too, the Anglo-Saxon text being filtered through Tolkien's creative imagination. The road that goes ever on; Bilbo's 'sting'—and Smaug in his cave; the fish upon which Gollum feeds, and which the dwarves, enclosed in their barrels, sort-of become in order to escape the wood-elves; Thorin granting his followers treasure, Beorn; the waterfall at Lothlorien; the battle of the five armies; Mirkwood—courtly, to the elves, in its eastern reaches—and Bilbo's own underhill home ('the door in a hall shall still be the wide mouth that opens to all' could hardly be bettered as a description of Bilbo's round front door). The birds in the tall rock will make us think of the ravens at the Lonely Mountain; and the thief stealing out is of course Bilbo. We could put it this way: that these 'Gnomic Verses' construe a riddle to which the answer is—the book called *The Hobbit*.

* * *

Are the riddles in chapter 8 Tolkien's adaptations or versions of traditional riddles, or did he invent them all himself? This looks like a simple question, but in fact it leads us into debatable, even riddling territory. You would not think so, mind, from what the scholars say. The consensus there is that the riddles are all, in one form or another, traditional. Tom Shippey notes that 'Gollum's riddles, unlike Bilbo's, tend to be ancient ones.'[8] Two of them—'this thing all things devours' riddle and 'it cannot be seen, cannot be felt'—are both adapted from an Old English riddle poem 'Solomon and Saturn'; his 'alive without breath' fish-riddle is from the Old Norse *Saga of King Heidrek* the Wise. Bilbo's riddles, on the other hand, are mostly versions of nursery-rhyme traditions—Douglas Anderson, for instance, prints three such rhymes that he suggests stand behind Tolkien's versions of the 'teeth', 'eggs' and 'no-legs' riddles.[9]

I am not sure it is quite as clear cut as this. True, there *are* riddles in English or Latin, nursery rhymes or other folk poetry to which all these answers apply—mountains; teeth; wind; daisy; dark; egg; fish; time. This ought not to surprise us, for the answers are none of them unusual, abstruse or unique. All are simple nouns, concrete or abstract, all familiar features of Old English culture (there are no riddles about such non-Anglo-Saxon pastimes as smoking a pipe or wearing a waistcoat, for example). This fact alone might give us pause, actually; for often Old English and medieval riddles have bizarrely specific answers—a few paragraphs back we encountered 'a man on horse-back with a hawk on his fist' as an answer to an actual OE riddle, for example.

Nonetheless, it *is* odd, if they are all adaptations of OE and Nursery Rhyme originals, that scholarship has been unable to find analogues for all Tolkien' Bilbo–Gollum riddles. Conversely, if they were all invented by Tolkien it is odd that this fact has not been established. Broadly speaking, critics simply start from the premise that these the Bilbo–Gollum riddles *must* have analogues in OE riddle culture. For some of the riddles they have found near-analogues, and declared them to be sources. For others they have been unable to discover anything at all, and have suggested that the search must continue. I have an alternative theory.

Tolkien himself, asked about this matter, replied variously. In a letter published in *The Observer*, 16 January 1938, he expatiated upon various sources for *The Hobbit*, stressing the importance of *Beowulf* in particular ('*Beowulf* is among my most valued sources') and talking a little about the then-unpublished *Silmarillion*. The penultimate paragraph of this letter mentions the riddles:

> And what about the Riddles? There is work to be done here on the
> sources and analogues. I should not be at all surprised to learn that

both the hobbit and Gollum will find their claim to have invented any of them disallowed.[10]

This seems, at first blush, to support the idea that Tolkien adapted all his riddles from traditional sources. But this is not actually what the passage says. In fact it is couched in a rather elegantly riddling idiom. It asserts nothing, but rather intimates ('there is work to be done here . . . I should not be at all surprised to learn') in a manner precisely designed to lead the unwary reader astray. We might answer: of course these riddles were not invented by Gollum and Bilbo—for Gollum, and Bilbo themselves were 'invented' by somebody else, the writer of the present letter. But to say so gets us no closer to the 'sources' of the riddles.

If this letter implies that the Bilbo–Gollum riddles are all variants of traditional sources, another letter *denies* precisely this. Writing to Allen & Unwin on 20 September 1947 Tolkien declared:

> As for the Riddles: they are 'all my own work' except for 'Thirty White Horses' which is traditional, and 'No-legs'. The remainder, though their style and method is that of old literary (but not 'folklore') riddles, have *no models* as far as I am aware, save only the egg-riddle, which is a reduction to a couplet (my own) of a longer literary riddle which appears in some 'Nursery Rhyme' books, notably American ones.[11]

In other words, Tolkien is asked twice whether these riddles are versions of traditional examples, or all his own work. The first time he answers the former, or at least strongly implies that; the second time he answers the latter, although with a raft of exceptions. It is hard to avoid the sense that, whatever else is going on in these letters, Tolkien is being playfully mystifying about his riddles.

In the next chapter I suggest that Tolkien's selection of riddles in this chapter was not random, and that one of the things that this chapter does is reveal 'riddling' to be a more self-reflexive mode than a simple sequence of questions-and-answers. But before I do that, I want to explore the notion that Tolkien's apparently contradictory approach to the question of 'sources' for his riddles is actually itself a sort of riddle.

The Hobbit is full of rhymes and songs. Ten of these (in chapter 8) are specifically called 'riddles'. But in fact not only do these various

verse texts draw broadly on OE riddle traditions, but that the poems
that are *not* specifically identified as riddles are the ones with the
most readily identifiable sources in Anglo-Saxon riddle literature.
This perhaps looks counter-intuitive, but that of course would be
precisely the point: for a riddle works exactly by being counter-
intuitive. To play such a game over the length of a novel would be
evidence of a ludic slyness certainly not incompatible with Tolkien's
imagination. 'There is', as he put it, 'work to be done here on the
sources and analogues.'
    A few examples will give a sense of what I mean. Here is 'Riddle 28'
from the *Exeter Book*:

> Biþ foldan dæl   fægre gegierwed
> mid þy heardestan   ond mid þy scearpestan
> ond mid þy grymmestan   gumena gestreona,
> corfen, sworfen,   cyrred, þyrred,
> bunden, wunden,   blæced, wæced,
> frætwed, geatwed,   feorran læded
> to durum dryhta.   Dream bið in innan
> cwicra wihta,   clengeð, lengeð,
> þara þe ær lifgende   longe hwile
> wilna bruceð   ond no wið spriceð,
> ond þonne æfter deaþe   deman onginneð,
> meldan mislice.   Micel is to hycganne
> wisfæstum menn,   hwæt seo wiht sy.

Crossley-Holland translates as follows:

> Some acres of this middle-earth
> are adorned with the hardest and the sharpest,
> most bitter of man's fine belongings;
> it is cut, threshed, couched, kilned,
> mashed, strained, sparged, yeasted,
> covered, racked, and carried far
> to the doors of men. A quickening delight
> lies in this treasure, lingers and lasts
> for men who, from experience, indulge
> their inclinations and don't rail against them;
> and then after death it begins to gab,

to gossip recklessly. Even clever people
must think carefully what this creature is.[12]

His translation, as he himself notes, is slanted towards the solution
he considers the most likely: 'the evidence is overwhelmingly in
favour of *John Barleycorn* or *ale'*. But he concedes:

> My version of lines 4–6 to some extent simplify the original . . .
> there is unfortunately no way in which a translator can echo the
> remarkable music (achieved by adding rhyming pairs to the usual
> alliteration and four-stress lines) of this same passage:

> *corfen, sworfen,   cyrred, þyrred,*
> *bunden, wunden,   blæced, wæced,*
> *frætwed, geatwed,   feorran læded*
> *to durum dryhta.*. . . *clengeð, lengeð,*

I think this piece of rousing Old English verse is behind the song
the goblins sing as they carry Bilbo and the dwarves underground as
their prisoners:

> Clash, crash! Crush smash!
> Hammer and tongs! Knocker and gongs!
> Pound, pound, far underground!
> . . .
> Swish smack! Whip crack!
> Batter and bleat! Yammer and bleat!
> Work, work! Nor dare to shirk!
> While Goblins quaff and Goblins laugh,
> Round and round far underground!

> (*Hobbit*, 68)

We read this as a simple, if cruel hearted, song of goblin triumph. I am
proposing that, like many riddles, it has a double meaning—it celebrates the capture of dwarves and a hobbit; but it also asks us to *solve*
it as a puzzle. What is smacked, cracked, couched and kilned, battered
and beaten, mashed and strained, covered and racked, and finally
carried far from the doors of men—such that goblins can quaff and
laugh? I am with Crossley-Holland: the answer would seem to be: *ale*.

Later in the story the goblins trap the party up some fir trees, which are then set on fire. They sing a characteristically cruel song:

> Fifteen birds in five firtrees,
> their feathers were fanned in a fiery breeze!
> But, funny little birds, they had no wings!
> O what shall we do with the funny little things?
> Roast 'em alive, or stew them in a pot;
> fry them, boil them and eat them hot?

(*Hobbit*, 107)

'Fifteen birds in five firtrees' straightforwardly describes the situation the dwarves, wizard and Bilbo have found themselves in, of course. But the rhyme has something in common with the tradition of number riddles. Crossley-Holland notes a Brahman riddle from the *Rig Veda* that describes a wheel with twelve spokes upon which stand 720 sons, all from one father—the year ('720' sums the days and nights). In the *Exeter Book* Riddle 22 plays similar number games:

> Sixty men in company came
> riding down to the estuary. Eleven
> of those mounted men had horses
> of peace, and four had pale great horses.
> They could not cross the water
> as they wished for the channel was too deep,
> the shelf too abrupt, the current too strong
> the choppy waves thronging. Then the men
> and their horses climbed on to a wagon—a burden
> under the cross-bar.

The riddle continues, describing how 'a single horse' pulls the wagon over the estuary, 'no ox, nor carthorse, nor muscular men / dragged it with him' and 'he did not swim, / nor muddy the water, nor ride on the wind, nor double back.' Scholars suggest two possible solutions to this riddle. One is that the sixty men in company are the stars surrounding the pole star, circling through the sky during the course of the night; and the fifteen mounted on horses are the specific constellation of the Great Bear, or 'the Great Wain' (sometimes called Charles' Wain), that 'crosses the estuary' in the sense of being reflected in its waters. The four 'great pale horses' are the four stars marking out the rectangular component of the constellation, which are visibily of a different intensity to the others.

A second answer, quite incompatible with the first, is that the sixty men are the half-days of the month of December (it was a common Anglo-Saxon habit to calculate by half-days, or half-years). The eleven riders on 'horses of peace' stand-in for the holy days— the month's four Sundays and seven feast days. The 'estuary' is then taken as the divide between the old year and the new. As to whether we are supposed to take the 'four' as part of the eleven, or to add them *to* the eleven (the latter seems to me to make more sense), the question remains moot. And the fact that there are two possible answers seems to me a strength of the riddle rather than a weakness.

In Tolkien's riddle, 'fifteen' crops up again, this time disposed into 'five' groups. Tolkien was attentive to the dates over which his fictional narrative was disposed, dates which can be calculated with reference to the descriptions of full, half and new moons. As Douglas Wilhelm Harder shows, the events of *The Hobbit* begin in April 2941; and Bilbo returns home in June 2942 (3rd Age): fifteen months.[13] The 'five' may refer to the five stages of the journey: from Bag-End to Rivendell, Rivendell to Erebor, Erebor back to Beorn's house (Harder shows that on the return journey they stay 'approximately four months', time for the snows to melt), then to Rivendell again and finally back home.[14]

I want to close this chapter with the suitably riddling suggestion that the answers to the nine Bilbo–Gollum riddles—mountain; teeth; wind; daisy; dark; egg; a fish; a fish being eaten; time; a golden ring—are bodied forth into the verse that surrounds the 'Riddles in the Dark' chapter, and all occur elsewhere in *The Hobbit*. We might take this a number of ways: as mere coincidence (of course); as a sign that the answers to the Bilbo–Gollum riddles are so generalised and appropriate to the cultural idiom of a reinvented 'Dark Age' fantasy as to be ubiquitous; or—perhaps—as design.

Mountain: The song the dwarves sing as they come to Laketown (chapter. 10):

> The King beneath the mountains
> The King of carven stone,
> The lord of the silver fountains
> Shall come into his own!

This refers, in terms of its apparent reference or surface meaning, to Thorin coming home; he is 'king of carven stone' in the sense of having rule *over* the carven stones of the halls of Erebor. But I am proposing an alternate solution to this verse, taken as a riddle: that it is the mountain itself that is being described in royal terms.

Teeth: Here I propose 'teeth' as an alternate answer to the Goblin song, quoted a few pages above, taken as a riddle:

> Clash, crash! Crush smash!
> Hammer and tongs! Knocker and gongs!
> Pound, pound . . .
> . . .
> Swish smack! Whip crack!
> Batter and bleat! Yammer and bleat!
> Work, work! Nor dare to shirk!
> While Goblins quaff and Goblins laugh,

We might want to say that teeth, in the action of crushing, mashing, laughing and speaking, are constantly in motion in these lines.

Wind: The song sung by the dwarves in Beorn's house, begins:

> The wind was on the withered heath,
> but in the forest stirred no leaf:
> there shadows lay by night and day,
> and dark things silent crept beneath.
>
> The wind came down from the mountains cold
> And like a tide it roared and rolled.

Daisy: Amongst the songs sung by the rejoicing elves in the last chapter is one that describes stars as flowers scattered in the lawn: 'the stars are in blossom, the moon is in flower . . . Dance all ye joyful, now dance all together! / Soft is the grass, and let foot be like feather!' (*Hobbit*, 279).

Dark: The dwarves' song from the first chapter seems to describe them:

> Far over the misty mountains cold
> To dungeons deep and caverns old
> We must away ere break of day.

But we could also ask; what lives over the mountains before the break of day, and dwells in deep dungeons and old caverns? Dark.

Egg: The song the wood-elves sing as they roll the barrels through the hatch and into the river:

> Roll—roll—roll—roll,
> Roll-roll-rolling down the hole!
> Heave ho! Splash plump!
> Down they go, down they bump!

Read as a riddle, this invites the answer: eggs being boiled in a pan of water.

The two **Fish** riddles are particularly interesting. The second song the wood-elves sing seems to refer as well to spawning salmon as to barrels:

> Down the swift dark stream you go
> Back to the lands you once did know!

But I wonder if the two little rhymes Bilbo sings to taunt the giant spiders have more to them than meets the eye:

> Old fat spider spinning in a tree!
> Old fat spider can't see me!
>   Attercop! Attercop!
>   Won't you stop,
> Stop your spinning and look for me?

> Lazy Lob and Crazy Cob
> Are weaving webs to wind me.
> I am far more sweet than other meat
> but still they cannot find me!

Each of these could be recontextualised as riddles spoken by fish mocking fishermen who are either spooling their line (spinning in a tree) or weaving a net. Both 'lob' and 'cob' are names for fish—the saltwater pollack and and freshwater gudgeon (sometimes called 'The Miller's Thumb') respectively. Of course, 'lob', 'attercop' and 'cob' are all ancient names for spiders as well—the latter survives in the word *cobweb*. Indeed, 'attercop' is an interesting word: a disparaging way of referring to a spider of great antiquity: *attor* or *ater* is the OE for 'poison', and *cop* means cup.

A golden ring: This, I think, is the answer to the riddle enclosed in the last rhyme in the book; Bilbo's rhyme—'Roads go ever ever on' (which he reprises in *The Lord of the Rings* as 'the road goes ever on and on'). The rhyme describes Bilbo's journey, a round-trip away from home through danger and adventure and back again to home. But the answer to a riddle 'what road goes on for ever and for ever?' is, of course, *a circle*.

4

The Riddles of the All-Wise

Bilbo and Gollum's exchange takes place in the chapter called 'Riddles in the Dark'. It is an appropriate location for a riddling game, since the point of riddles is precisely to leave you 'in the dark'. In this chapter I intend taking the answers to these nine Bilbo and Gollum riddles as a sort of meta-riddle, a larger, darker puzzle, to which I propose an answer. I do so in the spirit of riddling proposed at the end of the last chapter. I am proceeding, in other words, from the notion that riddles are more than simple puzzles, mapping one answer onto one question; that riddles, on the contrary, are rebuses that open larger and more profound questions about the mysteries of story, art, life and afterlife. I can only ask you to bear with me.

To recap: the answers to the ten riddles Gollum and Bilbo asked one another are: mountain; teeth; wind; daisy; dark; egg; a fish; a fish being eaten; time; a golden ring. We may wish to believe, of course, that Tolkien simply selected riddles at random, either recalling riddles from his wide reading, or perhaps making them up himself, and that this list of items has no further significance.[1] Or we might want to go a little further that the riddles, over and above posing interesting questions for the reader to answer, do extra work in the text by characterising Gollum and Bilbo. Tom Shippey makes this case, and persuasively too, pointing out that Gollum's riddles tend to be more ancient, darker, about hidden or more terrifying things like darkness, all-devouring time and the roots of mountains. The answers to Bilbo's riddles, on the other hand, tend to be more quotidian, above-ground, cheery (daisies, eating a fish-supper sitting at a table and so on). And perhaps that is as far as it goes: the riddles

work as entertainments in their own right, and as ways of obliquely
characterising the two speakers, and nothing more.

At the end of the previous chapter I suggested that these answers—
mountains, fish, wind, flowers, dark and so on—were important
enough symbols to Tolkien's imagination to figure not only in
the riddles themselves, but in the majority of other pieces of verse
included in the book—as well (of course) as props and settings in
the novel itself: the misty mountain (and Erebor); the fish Gollum
catches and so on. I also pointed up the curious, rather beguiling
unclarity of Tolkien's responses to the question whether he invented
the riddles himself or adapted them from ancient sources: claiming
both the former and the latter. This in itself seems to me a significant
thing. In effect, it is Tolkien riddling about the riddles. Taking my cue
from this, I hope in this chapter to advance an argument about, as it
were, the meta-riddling aspect of Tolkien's novel.

We might begin by noting that the answers to the nine, or ten,
questions Bilbo and Gollum swap—depending on whether we wish
to take 'what have I got in my pocket?' as a 'proper' riddle, or not—
take the form of a sort of riddle in their own right. We could write
it out this way:

> I am a mountain;
> I am teeth;
> I am the wind;
> I am a daisy;
> I am the dark;
> I am an egg;
> I am a fish;
> I am a fish;
> I am time;
> I am a golden ring.
> What am I?

There are plenty of ancient riddles that take this form; 'The Song of
Amairgen' from the eleventh-century old Celtic *Book of Leinster* is one;
supposed spoken by Amairgen Glúngel son of Míl as he first arrived in
Ireland.

> *I am a wind in the sea*
> *I am a sea-wave upon the land*

> *I am the sound of the sea*
> *I am a stag of seven combats*
> *I am a hawk upon a cliff*
> *I am a tear-drop of the sun*
> *I am fair*
> *I am a boar for valour*
> *I am a salmon in a pool*
> *I am a lake in a plain*
> *I am the excellence of arts*
> *I am a spear that wages battle with plunder.*
> *I am a god who forms subjects for a ruler*
> *Who explains the stones of the mountains?*
> *Who invokes the ages of the moon?*
> *Where lies the setting of the sun?*
> *Who bears cattle from the house of Tethra?*
> *Who are the cattle of Tethra who laugh?*
> *What man, what god forms weapons?*[2]

This ancient Celtic riddle enjoyed a vogue during the early years of the twentieth century (Yeats's Lady Gregory translated it, amongst others) although its answer or answers are the subject of some debate. Robert Graves spends a good portion of his monumental study of poetry and myth *The White Goddess* (1946) trying to solve it. Here is his 'reconstruction' of the poem:

> I am a stag: *of seven tines,*
> I am a flood: *across a plain,*
> I am a wind: *on a deep lake,*
> I am a tear: *the Sun lets fall,*
> I am a hawk: *above the cliff,*
> I am a thorn: *beneath the nail,*
> I am a wonder: *among flowers,*
> I am a wizard: *who but I*
> *Sets the cool head aflame with smoke?*
>
> I am a spear: *that roars for blood,*
> I am a salmon: *in a pool,*
> I am a lure: *from paradise,*
> I am a hill: *where poets walk,*
> I am a boar: *ruthless and red,*

I am a breaker: *threatening doom,*
I am a tide: *that drags to death,*
I am an infant: *who but I*
Peeps from the unhewn dolmen, arch?

I am the womb: *of every holt,*
I am the blaze: *on every hill,*
I am the queen: *of every hive,*
I am the shield: *for every head,*
I am the tomb: *of every hope.*[3]

This is powerfully written stuff, certainly better poetry than James
Carey's duller rendering; but it brings us no closer to an answer. It
is true that Graves thought he had got to the bottom of it, although
the mournful truth Gravesphiles (and I would describe myself as one)
have to confront is that few professional scholars of Celtic literature
think that his speculations have any scholarly or intellectual merit
whatsoever. This does not dismay me, however, since one of the
things this book is trying to do is precisely to engage imaginative
ingenuity as the proper idiom of riddles—and *The White Goddess* is
certainly an ornately ingenious book. Graves takes his cue from
a number of other old Celtic riddles that encode alphabet solutions, and over many pages teases out his theory that 'The Song of
Amairgen' is a poetic expression of an ancient 'alphabet of the trees',
spelling out a particular message. The details of Graves 'solution'
need not concern us here. What is relevant is that he takes it as an
acrostic at all. This brings us to the large topic of Anglo-Saxon, Norse
and Celtic 'acrostic' riddles.

There are many examples of both acrostic and mesostic riddles
in Anglo-Saxon literature. An acrostic is a text in which the initial
letters of each line spell out a hidden message, usually (in the case of
Anglo-Saxon riddles), the solution. A mesostic is a form of acrostic
in which the embedded letters that spell out the solution is included
in the middle of the poem, usually after the caesura. I shall give you
some examples of what I mean. The late seventh-century priest and
author Aldheim wrote a book called the *Enigmata* comprising one
hundred riddles in Latin verse. This book was included in the letter
Aldheim wrote to the reigning King of Northumbria, the *Epistola
ad Acircium*, which begins with a Latin verse preface that is itself an

acrostic: cleverly, the first letters spell out the sentence, 'Aldhelmus cecinit millenis versibus odas', from both the initial and the final letters of the lines. Aldheim's *Enigmata* was modelled on a similar collection by an earlier writer called Symphosius, called the *Symposii Aenigmata*, which also includes acrostic riddles.

Old English riddlers had a similar predilection for acrostics. Riddle 19 from the *Exeter Book* contains not one but several acrostics, rune acrostics in this case, embedded into the Roman letters of the Anglo-Saxon poem. Here it is, and for ease of modern reading I have transliterated the original runes into their modern alphabetical equivalents, and put them in as capital letters:

> Ic on siþe seah SRO
> H hygewloncne, heafodbeorhtne,
> swiftne ofer saelwong swiþe þrægan.
> Hæfde him on hrycge hildeþryþe
> NOM naegledne rad
> AGEW Widlast ferede
> rynestrong on rade rofne CO
> FOAH For wæs þy beorhtre,
> swylcra siþfæt. Saga hwæt ic hatte.

Do not to be fooled by the line breaks. Here is a modern-English version:

> I saw one (S R O H) high-spirited, his head bright with ornaments, swiftly running over the pleasant plain; upon his back he had warlike strength; this (N O M) rode armourless; travelling far upon (A G E W), swiftly going on, he carried (C O F O A H). The journey was all the brighter, the expedition of these three. Say what I am called.

To solve the riddle you need to clock that its acrostics are included *backwards*, presumably because straightforwardly spelled out rune words would be too easy. Run the letter order in reverse and you have:

> HORS (the OE for 'horse')
> MON (= 'man')
> WEGA (= 'ways')
> HAOFOC (= 'hawk')

And the riddle is solved. There are a great many modern-English descendants of this particular form of riddle:

> My first is in blood and also in battle,
> My second in oak and acorn and apple
> My third and fourth are both the same
> And can be found twice in refrain,
> My second to last begins ending
> And my ending begins last. What am I?[4]

A related tribe of riddles presents the reader or listener with a series of descriptions, inviting us to visualise them as things in the world, only to reveal that the key is alphabetical. Here is an example from Alan Garner's 2004 novel *Thursbitch*. John Turner is trying to get his horses home through a snowstorm.

> The wind was full in their faces and the horses were trying to tuck into a bank for shelter, but Bryn kept them from shoving their panniers against the rocks. Now it was dark and the snow was swarming into his lanthorn and he could not see for the whiteness; but he knew the road. 'Eh. Jinney. Can you tell me this poser? "Luke had it in front. Paul had it behind. Phoebe Mellor had it twice in the middle afore she was wed. Lads have it. Wenches don't. Yon's in life, but not in death".'[5]

We are tempted to think that Turner is referring to the male member and its sexual potential. In fact the solution to the riddle (you have guessed it already, I am sure) is the letter 'L'.

In Chapter 2, above, I mentioned the idea that the *Exeter Book* riddles were all composed by one figure, the poet Cynewulf, two of whose lines ('Hail! Earendel brightest of angels / Over Middle-earth sent down to men') had such an important effect upon Tolkien's own imagination. The idea that Cynewulf composed the riddles was widespread in the nineteenth century, although scholarship today considers it unlikely. But Cynwulf wrote a great many other poems—indeed Cynewulf and Cædmon are the only two Anglo-Saxon poets whose names are known to us (which is to say: there are plenty of other OE poems, but all the authors' names have been lost).[6] And one thing for which Cynewulf is particularly famous is inserting runic acrostics, usually of his own name, into his verse.

Runes are interesting things in their own right, and are also of course a feature of Tolkien's particular creative strategy.[7] He inserts runes in *The Hobbit* (for instance, in the map of the Lonely Mountain), and the *Return of the King* includes amongst its appendices a key to these strange letters. More, Tolkien sometimes wrote letters in runic script: simple greetings, for instance at Christmas, made strange and riddling by the alphabet in which they are couched. Part of the appeal of runes is surely this—that they add glamour to otherwise straightforward communication precisely by *riddling* it. What cannot be denied is that Cynewulf used runes in exactly this way:

> Anglo-Saxon scribes made use of [runes] for purposes of shorthand, as happened also in Scandinavia, writing the rune where the meaning denoted by the name was required . . . Cynewulf uses the same device to conceal, or rather reveal his name in three of his four signed poems, and the same principle is also employed for acrostic purposes in some of the Riddles of the *Exeter Book*.[8]

Sometimes Cynewulf would add runes in a straightforward or consecutive manner, spelling out his name. Sometimes the elements would be rearranged, presumably to make the riddle more challenging.

> Cynewulf's method of inserting his runic acrostic is quite straightforward in *Christ II* and *Elene*. In both poems the runes occur in their right order, heralded as it were by the unmistakeable rune-name *cen*, and woven singly into the structure of the verse so as to further the narrative rather than in any way impede it. . . . [On the other hand] *Juliana* preserves the right order, but inserts the runes in three groups. CYN, EWU and LF, with points separating each run from the next and from the surrounding text in the MA. *Fates*, which like *Christ II* omits E as far as can be judged from the damaged MS, disturbs the position in the poet's name by the words *F þær on ende standeþ*, followed, as far as can be surmised, by the runes W, U, L, C, Y, N, again woven singly into the text.[9]

It is in this broader context of acrostic and letter-puzzles that I want to try and read the nine riddles of chapter 8. I am, in other words, taking these various riddles as kind of 'meta-riddle'. Indeed, in keeping with the theoretical approach of this study as a whole, I want to suggest two 'solutions' to this meta-riddle, both, I think, equally valid. One will bring us back to *The Hobbit* as a novel, via the slightly indirect route of *trolls*. The other will lead us out, into the larger world of Tolkien's Middle-Earth storytelling. In each case the approach to the business of solving the riddle will be different.

Let us put on one side (for a moment) the 'what have I got in my pocket?' riddle, and start from the premise that each item in the poem stands for a different letter, a conceit for which there is precedence in Anglo-Saxon and Celtic riddle-culture.

The first thing that leaps out is the duplication of fishes ('I am a fish / I am a fish') in the middle of the sequence. The relevant letter in this case is 'S', or 'Z'; embodying in its shape the sinuous curve of a fish swimming; and capturing sonically the splash and hiss of the motion it imparts to the water.[10] The initial word is suggestive, too: we can see the visual pun between the letter 'A' and a mountainous peak—in Tolkien's own invented script, the Tehtar vowel sign for 'A' is the shape, 'Λ'.[11] Although a number of Old English and Celtic words for 'mountain' (*munt, beorg, héahbeorg*) do not begin with A, others do. There is, for instance, the word *aran* (seen in the name of the Welsh mountain Aran Fawddwy, for instance), a word related to the Old English *aræran*, 'to raise, to stand-up, to be erect'. We might also think of the modern words such as the French 'aiguille' or the mountain range known as the Alps. Indeed, the name 'alps' derives from an Old Gaelic word 'alb', meaning 'mountain'.[12] The consonant 'ł', represented in modern Welsh by 'll', is formed by pressing the tongue against the teeth in a particular way; and writing it out in Roman script creates a little schematic of a tooth, LL. This provides us with a kind of visual rebus: as 'A' or 'Λ' resembles a mountain, so LL or Ц resembles a tooth. Now the OE for 'teeth' is *tēþ*, but there are a number of related words, to do with the sound teeth make, that begin with 'hl' (which approximates to 'ł' or an aspirated 'l', and which words are sometimes spelled without the 'h'). For instance there is *hlýdan*, which means amongst other things 'to chatter' or 'clatter' ones teeth; and *hleahtor*, which is the action of laughter—or showing one's teeth. There is also *læswian*, which means to feed, graze or chew. Then we have 'V', the first letter of 'wind' in many languages (the Latin *ventus*, the French 'vent'; and of course the German 'wind' is pronounced 'vind'). The Old Norse *Vindr* influenced the OE and the modern English word descends from it. 'I' takes the form of a plant (and the modern lower-case 'i', with its dot-like calyx sitting atop its stem, is even closer in this regard). But more relevantly, perhaps, is that this English letter, 'i', puns on 'eye', which is precisely the heart of the original riddle. The OE for 'eyes' is 'eáge'; although the *OED* records a number of variant spellings in early usage, amongst them 'iȝe' and 'yȝe'. Also relevant may be the OE íwan, which means 'to show, to bring before the eyes'. The OE for 'dark' is *mirk*, something Tolkien encodes into the name of the spider-infested forest through which Bilbo and the dwarves must travel. O is (obviously) a letter shaped like an egg; but we might also wish to consider the two-letter ligature known as 'ash', the Æ—because in Old English the word for 'egg' was 'æg' or 'ǽg'. Then we have our two *swimmers*—the relevant OE here being *swimman*: S, S. Finally there is 'time', a concept for which there are several Old English words that begin 'l': *læne*, which means 'a short time' or 'temporary, transitory'; and *lange*, which means 'a long time'.

To summarise, I am proposing a reading of Tolkien's string of riddle answers as a single acrostic. I suggest a simple re-ordering of one element in the resulting word (following the OE habit of reversing elements in their own acrostic riddles), such that the two swimmers migrate, as it were, upstream before the æg and mirk. This brings us to the following, tentative solution:

I am a mountain;	A
I am teeth;	Ł or L
I am the wind;	V
I am a daisy;	I
I am a fish;	S
I am a fish;	S
I am the dark;	M
I am an egg;	Æ
I am time;	L
What am I?	

In other words, the meta-riddle reveals itself, when read acronymically, as spelling out a word: *Alvissmæl* or *Alvissmǽl*. Now, the *Alvíssmál* (as the name is conventionally modernised) is the name of a poem with which Tolkien was very familiar, and one with an undeniable relationship with *The Hobbit*. It is part of the compendium of Norse mythological texts of which mention has already been made, the *Elder Edda*, The *all-viss* portion of the title is the same as

Figure 4.1   Thor protects his daughter as he riddles a rather egg-like Alvíss: illustration by W. G. Collingwood (1908)

the English 'all-wise'; it is the name of the dwarf who appears in the poem. The 'mal' part means 'sayings', or 'riddles'. So this poem is called the 'All-wise's Sayings'.

The *Alvíssmál* concerns a dwarf called Alvíss who claims that Thor's daughter has been promised to him in marriage; this is a match the hammerman is not keen to see go ahead. Thor makes the match conditional upon Alvíss correctly guessing a series of thirteen riddles, all taking the same form (see Figure 4.1). Indeed, we could say that these riddles have a kind of *reverse* structure to them. Thor provides what amounts to an answer, Alvíss replies with a number of riddling equivalents to the term. Here is the first two of Thor's questions, and the dwarf's answer:

> 'Tell me this, All-wise—I foresee, dwarf,
> that you have wisdom about all beings—

what the earth is called, which lies in front of men,
in each of the worlds.'

'Earth it's called among men, and ground by the Æsir,
the Vanir call it ways;
the giants evergreen, the elves the growing one,
the Powers above call it loam.'

And here is the second:

'Tell me this, All-wise—I foresee, dwarf,
that you have wisdom about all beings—
what the sky is called, known everywhere,
in each of the worlds.'

'Sky it's called among men, home of the planets by the gods,
wind-weaver the Vanir call it,
the giants call it the world above, the elves the lovely roof,
the dwarfs the dripping hall.'[13]

We can imagine inverting the process to generate more conventionally framed riddles ('I am the dripping hall, the lovely roof; I am wind-weaver. What am I?') One of the *Alvíssmál* riddles overlaps with the Bilbo–Gollum game more directly:

'Tell me this, All-wise—I foresee, dwarf,
that you know all the fates of men—
what the wind is called, which blows so widely,
in each of the worlds.'

'Wind it's called among men, the waverer by the gods,
the mighty Powers say neigher;
whooper the giants, din-journeyer the elves,
in hell they call it stormer.'

This provides an interesting contrast to Gollum's 'wind' riddle. Indeed, we might rewrite the *Alvíssmál* riddle this way:

> *Waveringly it always flows*
> *Horseless it neighs*

> *Whooping and dinning-down it goes*
> *To storm hell's ways.*

The riddles of the *Alvíssmál*, even though each starts with (as it were) the solution, contains one riddle that no modern scholar has yet solved. Thor asks All-wise what the ocean is called, and the dwarf replies:

> 'Sea it's called among men, and endless-lier by the gods,
> the Vanir call it rolling-one;
> home of the eel the giants, "lagastaf" the elves,
> the dwarfs the deep ocean.'

And a little later, Thor asks what 'seed' is called, to be answered:

> 'Barley it's called by men, and grain by the gods,
> the Vanir call it growth,
> eatable the giants, "lagastaf" the elves,
> in hell they call it head-hanger.'

The riddle here is that nobody, not even the professors of Anglo-Saxon, Norse and Celtic, know what the word 'lagastaf' means. It is hard to see how the same word could be applied both to the ocean and a seed—although we can set our riddle-solving imaginations to the task and suggest possible solutions.[14]

But there is another way in which the *Alvíssmál* relates to *The Hobbit*. We know that Tolkien quarried the *Elder Edda* to write his novel, and populate his imaginary world. For example, he took his names for the dwarfs, or dwarves, who visit Bilbo from the *Edda*'s opening poem, 'The Seeress's Prophesy' or *Voluspa*. But he took more than names from the Edda. From the *Alvíssmál* he took an important plot element.

You remember that Thor was quizzing Alviss the dwarf about his knowledge of the names of things for a reason—he wanted to prevent him from marrying his daughter. But Alvíss knows all the answers, so it looks as though Thor's plans are going to fail. It is only at the end of the *Alvíssmál* we realise the true cunning of Thor's plans. In the last stanza of the poem he compliments Alviss ('In one breast I've never seen / more ancient knowledge') adding:

> With much talking I say I've beguiled you;
> Day dawns on you now, dwarf.

It was all a trick: the rising sun turns Alviss into stone, and Thor is spared the indignity of having a dwarf for a son-in-law.

This, of course, is how Gandalf saves Thorin and company from the trolls in *The Hobbit*'s second chapter, 'Roast Mutton'. Having captured all thirteen dwarves, and Bilbo, three trolls are bickering amongst themselves how best to cook and eat them, when the sunrise surprises them and turns them to stone. After this lucky escape, Bilbo realises that Gandalf, in amongst the trees, has been provoking the fight by imitating the voices of each of the trolls in turn in order to say disobliging things about the *other* trolls. It is a clever strategy; worthy of Gandalf, and rather more than we might expect from the—usually, in Norse myth—rather slow-witted Thor.[15]

It is worth saying a little more, here, about trolls. Tolkien's three trolls are called William Huggins, Bert and Tom (we are not vouchsafed Bert and Tom's surnames): good, solid English names, all. They are a bit dim, a bit quarrelsome, small-c conservative and they like a bit of cooked meat washed down with beer—in other words they could hardly be *more* English, excepting only their propensity for cannibalism, something generally frowned upon in England. Bilbo introduces himself to them with an inadvertent riddle of his own:

'Blimey Bert, look what I've copped!' said William.
'What is it?' said the others coming up.
'Lumme if I knows! What are yer?'
'Bilbo Baggins, a bur—a hobbit,' said poor Bilbo.

(p. 44)

This puzzles the trolls, as well it might: 'what's a burrahobbit?' We know, of course, that Bilbo had been going to say 'Bilbo Baggins, a burglar' and has, wisely, thought better of it halfway through. But there are other ways of approaching this riddle. What *is* a burrahobbit?

One answer might be: the sort of a hobbit who lives in a burrow. Of course, as the opening of the novel makes clear, all hobbits live in such domiciles, so the distinction might seem superfluous. No: Bilbo is (or at this stage in the narrative, *will become*—for a Norse riddle is as likely to be a prophesy as a description of the world as is) a very special, indeed a unique sort of hobbit.

The word 'burr' or 'bur' means *ring*. It derives from the Middle English *burwhe* or *burwe* and can mean, variously, 'a circle', 'a ring', a protective ring (for instance, of a fence or wall), or a circle about the moon or a halo of moonlight—this latter is also called 'a brough', which is a variant of the same word. Another, related word is 'broch' or 'brogh', which is, to quote the *OED*, 'a sort of round tower, having an outer and an inner wall of dry stone'. The modern word 'brooch', for the round ornament that some people wear pinned to their lapels or dresses, is very likely etymologically related to this.

In other words, 'burrahobbit' might be an archaic way of saying 'ring-hobbit'. And that brings me to my second reading of the 'meta-riddle' of the 'Riddles in Dark' chapter, which in turn leads me on to discuss the relationship between Tolkien's *Hobbit* and its much longer, follow-up story, *The Lord of the Rings*.

> I am the mountains;
> I am teeth;
> I am the wind;
> I am a daisy;
> I am the dark;
> I am an egg;
> I am a fish;
> I am a fish;
> I am time;
> I am a golden ring.
> What am I?

A possible way of reading this, as a riddle, would be to see its constituent elements not as letters, but as separate items that all share one quality. Indeed, it would be to see the final item—since 'what have I got in my pocket?' is a question of a different sort to all the other riddle questions—as being not another riddle, but as the *answer*, included in the riddle itself. There are certainly many riddles that play this sort of game with the reader. One you may know is the riddle 'As I Was Going To St Ives':

> As I was going to St Ives
> I met a man with seven wives
> Every wife had seven sacks
> Every sack had seven cats
> Every cat had seven kits

> Kits, cats, sacks, wives
> How many were going to St Ives?

The answer is displayed in plain view in the first line of the poem, of course: only I was going to St Ives. All the other creatures were going in the opposite direction. Jonathan Wilcox notes that there are several Old English riddles that operate by the same logic.[16] He gives the example of riddle 86 from the *Exeter Book*, which I quote here in the original and Wilcox's translation.

> Wiht cwom gongan,   þær weras sæton
> monige on mæðle   mode snottre;
> hæfde an eage   ond earan twa,
> ond twegen fet,   twelf hund heafda
> hrycg ond wombe   ond honda twa,
> earmas ond eaxle,   anne sweoran
> ond sidan twa.   Saga hwæt ic hatte.

(A creature came walking where men sat, many in an assembly, wise in mind; it had one eye and two ears, and two feet, twelve hundred heads, a back and a belly and two hands, arms and shoulders, one neck and two sides. Say what it is called.)

'The survival of a partly analogous Latin riddle', Wilcox argues, 'has made possible a solution.' The later, Latin riddles is: 'now may you see what you scarcely may believe: one eye within, but many thousand heads. Whence shall he, who sells what he has, procure what he has not?' Unlike the riddles in the *Exeter Book* this puzzle includes its own answer ('a one-Eyed Seller of Garlic'). Wilcox comments: 'since the Old English riddle contains the same paradox, albeit in more bewildering form, this same answer has been universally (and gratefully) accepted by modern editors and commentators ever since the discovery of the analogy by Dietrich.' But Wilcox thinks this answer is wrong. Instead he proposes that the solution to the question 'say what I am' is *riddler*; and he brings in the 'As I Was Going To Saint Ives' rhyme as a comparison.

Following a similar logic, we might want to solve the Bilbo–Gollum meta-riddle by reading the final element 'what have I got in my pocket' as answer rather than question. All the things Bilbo and Gollum riddle one another about are *ring-like*. Some of the elements are obviously round or ring-shaped (egg, teeth, daisy); some are metaphorically so—time is marked by the circular reoccurrence of days, and seasons, and clocked so on the faces of our timepieces. The winds blow around the world, itself conceived as circular by the Anglo-Saxons and the Norse, which is to say as land circled by a great ring-shaped ocean. Darkness, whilst not in itself having any shape, signifies the absence or gap in the centre of a ring. 'Mountains' are harder to parse as ring—except that Tolkien's Middle-earth is surprisingly well-supplied with ring-shaped mountain ranges, and those mountains are hollow, bodies of matter around an absent centre. The original riddle, of course, describes mountains in terms of two features—roots and height—of which the latter is material and the former, as I discussed earlier, absent; which is in turn a way of describing the structure of a ring.

And what of fish? As I mentioned above, the Norse view of the world saw it as ring-shaped: a circular shield with a mass of land in the middle (itself a sort of ring around the hollow Mediterranean sea at its centre), in turn ringed-about by a great circular ocean. And in that ocean is Jörmungandr, a name that means 'enormous monster'—a sea-serpent or enormous fish, that lies encircling the world with its huge tail in its huge jaws. In the *Prose Edda* Thor goes fishing for this great serpent, rowing out in a boat and baiting his hook with an ox's head. Gollum, sitting in his little boat fishing for much smaller fish, seems trivial by comparison; but the comparison is interesting nonetheless. The entire world, for the Northmen, was ringed about with a gigantic fish, biting its own tail.[17]

So these things all speak to one thing: bands of solid matter around a central vacancy. The ring. And as Corey Olsen notes, the 'pocket' question signifies a particular sort of circling round from Gollum to Bilbo's experience.

> The Pocket question also prompts us to think about the fate from which Bilbo's luck is saving him. Throughout the riddle contest, Bilbo and Gollum have stood forth as spokesmen for opposing perspectives, for light and darkness, for wholesomeness and corruption, for contentment and despair. We end the game, however, with a question that serves not to separate the two, but to establish a link between them. Both of them have had the same ring

in their pockets, and we see Bilbo doing for the first time what Gollum has been doing for ages; fingering the ring in his pocket and talking aloud to it. . . . Tolkien shows us the connection between the two worlds, a connection that is embodied in the ring, Gollum's ring that turns out to be the answer to Bilbo's last and most personal riddle.[18]

The circularity of the ring embodies the tendency of evil to recirculate through our lives, passing from one generation to another. This is in turn leads us to consider the relationship between *The Hobbit* and Tolkien's great sequel, *The Lord of the Rings*. That relationship is more complicated than you might think. Indeed, it would not go too far to call it a riddle in its own right.

5
The Puzzle of the Two *Hobbits*

How many *The Hobbits* did Tolkien write?

The short answer is that Tolkien wrote two versions of the story. In the first, a troop of (to use what Tolkien insisted was the proper plural form of the word) dwarves are planning to trek to a distant mountain in order to steal a great pile of treasure guarded by a lethal, fire-breathing dragon—or more properly, to steal it *back*, since they claim it belongs to them. They are looking for a professional thief to help them in this dangerous business. The wizard Gandalf, for reasons that appear largely capricious, tricks the dwarves into hiring Bilbo Baggins, an ordinary, sedentary, unadventurous hobbit. He likewise tricks Bilbo into going along. This situation is played broadly for laughs, because Bilbo is so patently unfitted to the business of adventuring. Actually, 'unfitness' also seems to characterise the dwarves: the party stumbles from disaster to disaster as they journey, escaping death by hairs' breadths half a dozen times at the hands of trolls, goblins, wolves, spiders and hostile elves. They are saved from their early misadventures by Gandalf's interventions, for though eccentric he is considerably more competent than they. Later, though, Gandalf goes off on his own business, and the party has to get into the habit of rescuing itself. They stumble through a series of potentially fatal pickles, somehow managing, by a combination of luck and hobbit-judgement, always to get away. Indeed, tracing Bilbo's development from massively incompetent to marginally incompetent is one of the readerly pleasures of the narrative.

The titular hobbit happens to have picked up a magic ring during the course of his travels. Ownership of this ring, and a rather shallow learning curve, gradually make Bilbo better at thieving and sneak-ing about. When, against the odds, the party reaches the dragon's mountain, the quest *is* achieved, much more by luck than judge-ment. Bilbo uses the magic ring to creep into the dragon's lair and to steal one cup from the great hillocks of piled pelf; but that is as much as he can do. Luckily for all of them, the loss of this single piece hap-pens to enrage the dragon, causing him to leave the mountain with the furious intention of burning up the local town of men. One of the defenders there, warned by a talking bird, shoots a lucky arrow that kills the beast. After this there is a big battle: armies converging on the mountain and its now undragoned hoard. The leader of the dwarf-band is killed, but otherwise things work out well for every-body. Finally, having spent almost all the novel adumbrating the 'there' of the novel's subtitle, the story sprints through the 'and back again', hurrying the materially enriched Bilbo home in a few pages.

I stress the 'incompetence' angle in this retelling because, really, that is what characterises the main players. It is an endearing incompetence, used partly for comedy, partly for dramatic purposes (by way of racketing up the narrative tension and keeping things interesting) and partly to facilitate the readers'—our—engagement. Because we can be honest; we would be rubbish on a dangerous quest. We are hobbitish types ourselves, and *our* idea of fun is snug-gling into the sofa with a cup of cocoa and a good book, not fighting gigantic spiders with a sword. Or more precisely, we enjoy fighting giant spiders with a sword—in our imaginations only. *The Hobbit* has been as commercially successful as it has in part because the hobbits are able (textually-speaking) so brilliantly to mediate our modern, cosseted perspectives and the rather forbidding antique warrior code and the pitiless Northern-European Folk Tale world.

That there is something haphazard about the larger conception of this adventure is part of its point. Obviously, it makes for a jollier tale if a clearly unsuitable comic-foil is sent on a dangerous quest, and a less jolly tale if that protagonist is some super-competent swords-man alpha-male. The bumbling, homely qualities of Bilbo, and the pinball-ball bouncing trajectory from frying pan to fire to bigger fire of the narrative, are loveable aspects of the whole. It also expresses a larger truth. The motor of the story is the idea that *adventure will come and find you*, and winkle you out of your comfortable hidey-hole. It is a beguiling idea, in part because it literalises the action of story itself.

We settle ourselves to read, in physical comfort; but the story itself transports us imaginatively out of our cosy cubby and away, upon all manner of precarious, exciting, absorbing and diverting journeys.

This is *The Hobbit* that appeared in 1937, to both acclaim and commercial success. But there is another *The Hobbit*; a second *The Hobbit* written by Tolkien, comprising revisions to this first edition, additional material written for the *Lord of the Rings* and the appendices of *The Lord of the Rings*, plus other material. The most significant of these latter are two separate prose pieces, both called 'The Quest for Erebor' first collected in the posthumously-published *Unfinished Tales* (1980). Tolkien's first revisions were confined to the 'Riddles in the Dark' chapter. After writing the first *Hobbit* Tolkien came to the conclusion that 'the Ring' was more than just a magic ring conferring invisibility on its wearer—that it was indeed the most powerful artefact in the whole world, one with which people could become so besotted as to lose their souls. Gollum, he reasoned, would not freely give up such an item. So he rewrote the scene, and all subsequent editions of the novel treat the encounter in a less light-hearted manner. This is symptomatic of something larger, a reconceptualising (Tolkien purists might say: a distillation or focusing) of his now-celebrated legendarium. No longer a folk-story, it now becomes a grand sacramental drama of incarnation, atonement and redemption.

This is not a random observation. Tolkien's 1939 essay 'On Fairy Stories' celebrates two distinct modes of Fantasy, the homely and the transcendental. The former is epitomised by traditional fairy tales, which Tolkien sees as beautiful and profound narratives of escape and resacralisation. The latter is the New Testament, which Tolkien thinks shares those key qualities with fairy stories but which he also thinks exists on a higher, truer and more important plane. This is how he puts it:

> The Evangelium has not abrogated legends; it has hallowed them, especially the 'happy ending.' The Christian has still to work, with mind as well as body, to suffer, hope, and die; but he may now perceive that all his bents and faculties have a purpose, which can be redeemed. So great is the bounty with which he has been treated that he may now, perhaps, fairly dare to guess that in Fantasy he may actually assist in the effoliation and multiple enrichment of creation.[1]

My beef, if I may slip into a nonvegetarian idiom for a moment, is not with Tolkien's religious beliefs, which (although I do not share them) are clearly essential to the dynamic of his art. My beef is with the notion that *all our bents and faculties have a purpose*. In Tolkien's second version of *The Hobbit*, it is precisely the haphazardness, the intimations of glorious, human, comic incompetence, that must be sanded, smoothed and filed away. It is no longer enough for Gandalf to turn up on the doorstep of the world's least likely adventurer merely because that is the sort of thing batty old wizards do. Now he must do so because he has a larger plan. In the first version of the story it does not really matter why Gandalf chooses a hobbit, of all people; or more precisely, his whylessness of choice is actually the point of the story. ('I am looking for someone to share in an adventure that I am arranging', Gandalf says, with what could easily be read as desperation, 'and it's very difficult to find anyone.') This is because the novel is not about Gandalf's whys, it is about Bilbo's adventure. Why he is chosen matters less than the way he acquits himself on his journey, and the extent to which he sheds his unheroism to become a better fellow. That is what matters because we are he. That is how the reading experience goes.

But in Tolkien's second version of *The Hobbit* everything has to happen for a reason. Gandalf was not idly arranging an adventure; he was setting in motion one crucial play in a larger strategy of the grand war against Evil.

> I knew that Sauron had arisen again and would soon declare himself, and I knew that he was preparing for a great war. . . . The state of things in the North was very bad. The Kingdom under the Mountain and the strong Men of Dale were no more. To resist any force Sauron might send to regain the northern passes in the mountain and the old lands of Angmar there were only the Dwarves of the Iron Hills, and behind them lay a desolation and a Dragon. The Dragon Sauron might use with terrible effect. Often I said to myself: 'I must find some means of dealing with Smaug.'[2]

Just to be clear: I have no problem with what SF and Fantasy fans call 'retconning', the retrospective rewriting of a text to make it more coherent with the later iterations of that textual world. Not in the least, for I take 'text' to be fundamentally fluid and adaptable.

I can go further, and say that one of the things that gives Tolkien's art depth and resonance is precisely the way he layers medium and deep historical pasts into his present-set tale; and having this secondary perspective on the material of *The Hobbit* adds echoey, plangent splendour to the whole. But that is not to say that this particular piece of retconning makes sense. On the contrary: it compels us to believe that Gandalf, deciding that it was a strategic priority that Smaug be eliminated, thinks not of sending an army, and certainly not of going himself and tackling the dragon with his, you know, *magic*. Rather he thinks: 'I'll go to the *extreme other end of the continent*, recruit a number of dwarves, some of them manifestly not up to the task (Bombur?), plus a hobbit *without any experience or aptitude for a mission of this sort whatsoever*, and send them off travelling halfway across the world past unnumbered perils, most of the way unchaperoned, in the hope that somehow *they'll* do the old worm in.' Why the dwarves? Well, I suppose they can at least be persuaded to go, since they regard Erebor as rightfully theirs; although you have to wonder whether a competent military strategist might not think first of approaching the men of Dale. But there is no reason in this scenario why Bilbo would be anyone's first, or thousand-and-first choice. Actually, in this second version of the story Tolkien comes up with three reasons why it is a good idea to wager the entire success of the operation on Bilbo, a figure of whom Thorin rightly says 'he is soft, soft as the mud of the Shire, and silly', a judgement with which Gandalf concurs.[3] Those three reasons are:

1. That hobbits do not wear shoes, where Dwarfs do ('suddenly in my mind [I pictured] the sturdy, heavy-booted Dwarves . . . the quick, soft-footed hobbit'), a consideration, certainly, since Dragons have good hearing; although you might think that advising the Dwarves to *take off* their boots might be less precarious than hanging the success of the enterprise around the neck of a sort of Middle-earth fur-footed Homer Simpson.
2. That Smaug would not know Bilbo's scent, where he would recognise the smell of Dwarves, although apparently Tolkien added this as an afterthought to his MS (it is written in pencil: 'a scent that cannot be placed, at least not by Smaug, the enemy of Dwarves'). A scent that cannot be smelt *at all* by Smaug would make more sense, but fair enough. The fact that he smells a thief in his lair but

can not immediately place the thief's provenance might confuse him for . . . oh, six seconds or so. The third reason is the most arbitrary of all–

3. Gandalf just feels in his water that it would be a good idea: 'listen to me Thorin Oakenshield . . . if this hobbit goes with you, you will succeed. If not you will fail. A foresight is on me.' Hard not to see this as code for 'I've already written this story and know how it turns out', which in turn comes dangerously close to a cheat.

The story of *The Lord of the Rings* is that even 'the little people' (which is to say: people like you and me) have their part to play in the great historical and martial dramas of the age; and it is a potent and truthful story, well told. But *The Hobbit* is that story only in its second iteration. In its first *The Hobbit* is not about the great dramas of the age; it is about us-sized dramas of people being taken out of their comfort zone and whisked away by Story.

I am happy that there are two versions of *The Hobbit*, and feel no desire to try and force them into some notional procrustean 'coherence'. Only narrative fundamentalists, the textual Taliban, believe that all stories must be brought into that sort of rigid alignment. But of the two stories, really I prefer the one (homely, funny, a little bit slapstick and a little bit wondrous) over the other (grand-verging-on-grandiose, theological, epic and strenuously, to coin a phrase, *eutragic*). Although I do love them both. And I love the Dwarves vastly more than any number of elves. I love precisely their lack of graceful elegance. Thorin Oakenshield has some noble speeches in *The Hobbit* it is true; but his Dwarves are better at stuffing themselves with food and drink, and getting (with endearing incompetence) into ridiculous scrapes.

6
The Riddle of Bilbo's Pocket

'What', Bilbo asks Gollum, 'have I got in my pocket?' The answer turns out to be an item with the most profound importance for Tolkien's larger invented world. But for a moment I want to think about the content of this riddle rather than its solution.

'Pockets'—hand-sized pouches of cloth sewn inside trousers near the waist band and connected to the outside world via slits cut into the fabric of those trousers—are features of modern life. No mythic of Dark Age hero has them. Given how handy they are for keeping things in—money, keys, rings—they are a surprisingly recent development in the history of couture.[1] The Anglo-Saxon, and the medieval, way of keeping your portable property about as you travelled was to cache it in a separate bag or pouch, which you then either carried in your hand or else tied to the outside of your clothes. The old term for what we would nowadays call 'a pickpocket' was *cut-purse*: a perfectly straightforward descriptive name, for this sort of thief would use a surreptitiously held knife to sever the cord that attached the purse to the victim's clothes. Having your valuables dangling externally is clearly less secure than keeping the purse *inside* your clothes; although the best modern-day pickpockets are worryingly adept at getting hold of your stuff anyway.

We might expect, in a pre-Industrial, fundamentally 'medieval' or 'Anglo-Saxon' world like Tolkien's Middle-earth, for pockets to be unknown. That they are not is a feature of the creative *anachronism* that characterises the novel. Tolkien's hobbits, as many critics and readers have noted, are in effect nineteenth-century types. They wear waistcoats, smoke pipes, possess steam kettles and pop-guns, all of which are items unknown in the medieval world of Gondor or the more archaic Dark Age world of the Rohirrim. It is, after all, hard to imagine Beorn playing with a pop-gun, or Bard the Bowman wearing a three-piece suit. We might want to object that no Europe-sized world (as I take Middle-earth to be, or at least that portion of it portrayed in the *Lord of the Rings* map) could include such wide divergences of cultural development. But to insist upon this would be to miss the point. The relative modernity of the hobbits is one of Tolkien's ways of bridging the gap between our own, necessarily modern readerly sensibilities and the pre-modern matter that consti-tutes the bulk of his story.

This, moreover, is a problem faced by any writer who wishes to write about a pre-modern world. To explain what I mean, I lay my finger upon one of the most commercially successful of recent post-Tolkienian Fantasies, Patrick Rothfuss's *The Name of the Wind* (2006). Rothfuss' enjoyable narrative concerns a main character called Kvothe, who lives in a pre-Industrial, medievalised, magical world. Kvothe grows up as a neglected street-kid in a crime-riddled city, but manages to enrol in a legendary university of magic and learn the true names of all things so that he can control them. He has a variety of colourful adventures on his way to realising his destiny, to become 'the greatest magician the world has ever known'. But despite being set in a medieval world, *The Name of the Wind* is written in the bourgeois discursive style familiar from a thousand nineteenth- and twentieth-century novels. Here is a passage picked at random:

> I settled onto the stone bench under the pennant pole next to my two friends.
> 'So where were you last night?' Simmon asked too casually.
> It was only then that I remembered that the three of us had planned to meet up with Fenton and play corners last night. Seeing Denna had completely driven the plan from my mind. 'Oh God, I'm sorry Sim. How long did you wait for me?'
> He gave me a look.
> 'I'm sorry,' I repeated, hoping I looked as guilty as I felt. 'I forgot.'
> Sim grinned, shrugging it off. 'It's not a big deal.'[2]

This could be three pals from any twentieth- or twenty-first century-set novel; and hundreds and hundreds of similar passages serve only to show the author has not entered into the medieval pre-industrial mindset that his medieval pre-industrial world required—to, for example, understand the crucial point that not guilt ('I looked as guilty as I felt') but *shame* was the moral dynamic for the period. But to understand that would involve shifting about the psychological portraiture of the entire project; it would have meant writing characters less like, and therefore less appealing to, a twenty-first-century readership disinclined to make the effort to encounter the properly strange or unusual.

This speaks to a broader state of affairs in which style (the language and form of the novel) is seen by many writers and readers as an unimportant adjunct to the 'story'. It is not. A bourgeois discursive style constructs a bourgeois world. If it is used to describe a medieval environment it necessarily mismatches what it describes, creating a world that is only an anachronism, a theme park or a World-of-Warcraft gaming environment rather than actual place. This degrades the ability of the book properly to evoke its fictional setting, and therefore denies the book the higher heroic possibilities of its imaginative premise.

How to make a bridge between our modern sensibilities and the medieval matter is the problem that any modern writer of Fantasy must try to address. Rothfuss's solution, for good and ill, and mostly for ill, is simply to write the pre-modern as if it is modern. In the *Silmarillion* Tolkien was widely criticised for writing in an unadorned antique style ('like the Old Testament', reviewers complained; although actually it is rather unlike the Bible and more like the northern Sagas). Ordinary readers often could not stomach this, although Old English specialists and medievalists, who are used to reading this kind of thing, usually speak of the book in warmer terms.

The Lord of the Rings represents one solution to the problem of how to achieve this bridge. It is deliberately constructed by braiding modern perspectives (the cosy bourgeois hobbits) and pre-modern (the medieval Gondor, the Old English Rohan) together, not only in terms of story but style: the hobbit chapters are of course written with a kind of early-twentieth-century contemporaneity of narratorial voice, where the later sequences inhabit a more antiquated and high-flown idiom, full of inversions, dated vocabulary, invocative and rhetorical stiffness, although at the same time rather splendid and suitably heroic. But it is surprising how few writers have attempted to imitate Tolkien's stylistic strategy in this, although of course they have stolen plenty of other things from his writing. This takes us a little away from *pockets*. My point, before it gets away from me, is that the way Tolkien creates a Dark Age and medieval world and then sets a bourgeois, modern individual (Bilbo) loose in it is not undeliberate, or a problem, but part of the novel's design, a feature rather than a bug. This sort of anachronism, I am arguing, is part of the way the novel generates its unique effects. A better way of thinking about it would be to see it as a kind of conceptual riddle. Bilbo's pocket is a sort of emblem for this. We can imagine the final exchange between Bilbo and Gollum re-written this way:

BILBO: What have I got in my pocket?
GOLLUM: What's a *pocket*?

This brings me to *Beowulf*, the Old English epic that is both the longest and the most magnificent relict of Anglo-Saxon literature we have.

Beowulf tells the story of its titular hero; a warrior from 'Geat-land' (modern day southern Sweden) who travels to the court of Hrothgar in Denmark. The Danes are allies of the Geats; but Hrothgar's court in the splendid hall of Heotot is plagued by a murderous monster called Grendl, a creature man-shaped but of huge stature. The poem tells us that he is ultimately descended from the Biblical Cain. Every night Grendl breaks into Heorot and kills or carries off some of Hrothgar's warriors; swords are useless against the creature's magically-protected hide. Beowulf comes, wrestles with the monster and rips off its arm, whereupon it runs away into the night to die. Everyone is delighted at this, but celebrations are premature. Grendl's mother, an even more terrifying creature, comes out of her lair to pay back her son's death, and more Danish warriors are slain. Beowulf then tracks this she-devil to her home at the bottom of a lake. He swims down and fights her. His own sword Hrunting is useless against her, but luckily he finds, amongst her own spoils, a magic sword with which he cuts off her head. Once this is accomplished he finds the corpse of her son Grendl and decapitates it too, bringing the severed head back to Heorot. At last the threat has been overcome, and Beowulf returns a hero to Sweden. But the story is not over: we skip forward many years. Beowulf has acceded to the throne and ruled for many years as a wise king, but in his old age a great dragon afflicts his nation. So he rides out to fight this monster, succeeding in killing it, although at the cost of his own life. *Beowulf* the poem ends with elegiac praise of Beowulf the hero and all that he represented.

Now, *Beowulf* occupied a central position in Tolkien's imaginative and scholarly life; he taught it, wrote critical essays about it, delivered public lectures upon it, and left (at his death) an unfinished commentary upon the poem that, apparently, runs to some 2000 manuscript pages. Some of the ways in which this powerful poem directly informs *The Hobbit* have been covered by other commentators. Tolkien himself, in a letter he wrote to *The Times* and which has already been mentioned, pointed up the incident of the thief stealing the cup from the huge dragon as a starting point for the portion of *The Hobbit* when Bilbo steals the cup from Smaug.

And I have already had cause to mention Tolkien's celebrated 1936 lecture about *Beowulf*, 'The Monster and the Critics'. Published, and later reworked more than once, it remains a profoundly influential intervention into twentieth-century *Beowulf* studies, and has had a wider impact upon the criticism of Fantasy more broadly conceived. One of the main arguments that Tolkien makes in this lecture is that the Beowulf scholars have been too narrowly focused on the poem's linguistic, philological and historical interest—in what *Beowulf* tells us about the development of the language and about the society and culture of northern Europe in the later Dark Ages. For such critics, the monsters were embarrassments to be hurried past, gauche story-filler, unworthy of the noble, uplifting verse in which they were realised. Tolkien, eloquently and persuasively, disagreed. For him the monsters were not elements to be explained away; they were the *point* of the poem.

Actually, Tolkien was not the first to talk of the poem in these terms. A. J. Wyatt's 1914 standard edition, still widely used in the 1930s, starts with a prefatory note saying that whilst 'the editors of *Beowulf* have with rare exceptions concentrated their attempts upon the problem of fixing and interpreting the text and have avoided discussing the literary history of the poem', there *are* many critics ('in monographs such as those of ten Brink, Mullenhoff and Boer') who do precisely that, and Wyatt himself promises a volume entitled 'Introduction to the Study of Beowulf' which will take the poem *as* poetry.[3] Perhaps for our purposes what is more interesting is that

Tolkien's lecture expressly considers *Beowulf* to be a 'riddle': an 'enigmatic poem', constituted by the bringing together of two apparently incompatible things. He quotes from W. P. Ker's *The Dark Ages*:

> The fault of *Beowulf* is that there is nothing much in the story. The hero is occupied in killing monsters, like Hercules or Theseus. But there are other things in the lives of Hercules and Theseus besides the killing of the Hydra or of Procrustes. Beowulf has nothing else to do, when he has killed Grendl and Grendl's mother in Denmark: he goes home to his own Gautland, until at last the rolling years bring the Fire-drake and his last adventure. It is too simple. Yet the three chief episodes are well wrought and well diversified; they are not repetitions, exactly; there is a change of temper between the wrestling with Grendl in the night at Heorot and the descent under water to encounter Grendl's mother; while the sentiment of the Dragon is different again. But the great beauty, the real value, of *Beowulf* is in its dignity of style. In construction it is curiously weak, in a sense preposterous; for while the main story is simplicity itself, the merest commonplace of heroic legend, all about it, in the historic allusions, there are revelations of a whole world of tragedy, plots different in import from that of *Beowulf*, more like the tragic themes of Iceland. Yet with this radical defect, a disproportion that puts the irrelevances in the centre and the serious things on the outer edges, the poem of *Beowulf* is undeniably weighty. The thing itself is cheap; the moral and the spirit of it can only be matched among the noblest authors.

Tolkien insists that this view of the poem remains influential, and potently so; but he identifies in it a 'paradox' that has given *Beowulf* something of the flavour of an enigmatic poem. The paradox, he thinks, has to do with the disjunction between perceived defects in the theme and structure of the poem on the one hand, and the widely reiterated nobility, grandeur and genius of the poem on the other. After surveying some other critics, Tolkien declares: 'The riddle is still unsolved.' His solution (the thesis of his lecture: that the monsters are at the heart of it, not in the margins) is a good one, but—as with OE riddles more generally—perhaps not the only one. He goes on to discuss the nature of what he calls 'Northern' bravery: its unyieldingness. He quotes Ker again ('the Northern Gods have an exultant extravagance in their warfare which makes them more like

Titans than Olympians; only they are on the right side, though it is not the side that wins. The winning side is Chaos and Unreason but the gods, who are defeated, think that defeat no refutation.') He finishes by defining true heroism as unyielding will and courage made 'perfect because without hope'.

We are getting closer to the ethos of Anglo-Saxon life itself, which so inspired Tolkien and which is immanent in both *The Hobbit* and *The Lord of the Rings*. But to revert to the actual subject of this chapter—what has any of this to do with pockets?

Despite not being invented until the 1600s, pockets make a surprising appearance in *Beowulf*. About two-thirds of the way through the poem the titular hero recalls his fight against the monstrous Grendl. Here, for the first and only time in the poem, we hear about Grendl's enormous glove.

> He had this roomy 'glof',
> a strange accoutrement, intricately strung
> and hung at the ready, a rare patchwork
> of devilishly fitted dragon-skins ['*dracan fellum*'].
> I had done him no wrong, yet the raging demon
> wanted to cram me and many another
> into this bag—but it was not to be.

> (lines 2085b–90)[4]

A *glove*? It is a strange detail, so much so that translators often try and gloss it over, rendering the word as 'bag' or 'satchel'—the celebrated Seamus Heaney translation of the poem, which I have just quoted, actually renders 'glof' as 'pouch'. But 'glove' is most assuredly what the word means.

Here is something else: Andrew Orchard notes that it is not until Beowulf's retelling, here, that we readers learn 'the name of the Geat devoured by Grendl' in the original attack.[5] His name is Hondscio, which means—'glove' ('compare', Orchard suggests, 'modern German *Handschuh*'). So the glove is in a sense doubly pointed-up here. Why?

In fact, critics on the glove do not know quite what to make of it. An article by Earl R. Anderson points out various Latin analogues.[6] Some other editors and critics make reference to an Icelandic legend recorded by Snorri Sturluson—the god Thor is travelling towards the land of Giants and is finds shelter from darkness and thunder in a 'a very big hall' with a 'side chamber'. In the morning he discovers that he has been sleeping in the glove of the giant Skrymir; and that the thunder he thought he heard was actually the giant's snoring. (Orchard points out that the glove in *this* legend is 'evidently more of a mitten, since there are apparently no fingers to it, and the "side chamber" turns out to be the thumb'.) But does this illuminate the *Beowulf* passage? Skrymir's glove is clearly on a completely different scale to Grendl's, and simply drawing out parallels from myth does not explain the function of this reference in this specific text.

So, why a *glove*? I propose a reading of *Beowulf* that takes Grendl's glove to be no anomaly. What function does a glove serve except to cover a hand, to give it grip, either to keep it warm or otherwise to protect it? And *hands* occupy an extraordinarily significant place in the representational economy of *Beowulf* the poem.

Now, one simple explanation of the 'glof' might be simply to emphasise the might of the beast's arm. The idea would be: if his glove is large enough to fit entire men inside, his hand must be *gigantic*. This in turn only serves to emphasise Beowulf's own strength in defeating him. But actually it is the craft, rather than the sheer size, of the glof that gets stressed in the poem, the 'rare patchwork / of devilishly fitted dragon-skins'. This is an interesting detail. It is not stated unambiguously that Grendl made this glove himself, but it is surely as likely that he did as that he did not, for after all he has no servants or slaves to do the work on his behalf. Yet because Grendl is so consistently and emphatically bestialised in the rest of the poem this strikes an odd note. We think of him very much as more animal than human; but here we cannot avoid the suspicion that he is a maker—strictly speaking, we could call him Grendl Glover. Of course, the notion that Grendl is more beast than man is something suggested by other details in the poem. For instance, and apart from the giant glove, we never see him using tools. He does not, for instance, wield a sword; and it is part of the carefully balanced symbolic logic of the poem's universe that he cannot be defeated by a sword either. Beowulf's repudiation of weaponry appears at first to be as reckless as the monster's:

> The monster scorns
> in his reckless way to use weapons;
> therefore, to heighten Hygelac's fame

> and gladden his heart, I hereby renounce
> sword and the shelter of the broad shield,
> the heavy war-board: hand-to-hand
> is how it will be, a life-and-death fight.

(433–40)

But later we discover 'something that they [the Geatish warriors] could not have known at the time', namely 'that no blade on earth . . . could ever damage their demon opponent'. This is because 'he had conjured the harm from the cutting edge' (26): suggesting an ability to create magical charms again at odds with the notion of him as a mere beast.

So: if our assumption is that Grendl does not use a sword because he is too much the beast for such sophistication, the poem itself suggests otherwise. The glove, and his skill in magical charms, implies that the truth might be simpler. He does not use a sword because he does not need one. Over and again the poem stresses his deadly strength of hand:

> Greedy and grim he grabbed thirty men . . .

(121)

> No counsellor could ever expect
> Fair reparation from those rabid hands.
> All were endangered; you and old.

(158–8)

> He grabbed (*nam þa mid handa*, lit. 'clutched with his hand')
> and mauled a man on his bench . . .

(746)

> Venturing closer,
> His talon was raised to attack Beowulf . . .

(747–8)

The Danes have bolted their hall-door against this attacker, but nevertheless 'the iron-braced door / turned on its hinge when [Grendl's] hands touched it . . . he ripped open / the mouth of the building' (721–24). Strong! In Beowulf, of course, he meets his match in terms of strength-of-hand. Grendl grabbed thirty men, but Beowulf has 'the strength of thirty / in the grip of each hand' (379). Grendl attacks:

> He was bearing in
> with open claw when the alert hero's
> comeback and armlock forestalled him utterly.
> The captain of evil discovered himself
> in a handgrip harder than anything
> he had ever encountered in any man.
>
> (749–55)

The poet stresses the *manual* element of the conflict to an almost hyperbolic degree: 'he had never been clamped or cornered like this . . . [he] got a firm hold. Fingers were bursting . . . the latching power / in his fingers weakened . . . [Beowulf] kept him helplessly / locked in a handgrip'. It follows from this that it is precisely Grendl's hand that becomes the trophy of his defeat.

> Clear proof of this
> could be seen in the hand the hero displayed
> high up near the roof, the whole of Grendl's
> shoulder and arm, his awesome grasp.
>
> (833–36)

> . . . the awful proof
> of the hero's prowess, the splayed hand
> up under the eaves.
>
> (984–86)

In fact it is the monster's whole arm, ripped from its shoulder by Beowulf's strength: but it is the *hand* that is the element upon which the poem concentrates. Later Beowulf boasts that Grendl 'broke and ran. Yet he bought his freedom / at a high price, for he left his hand . . . ' (971–72); and then again later still: 'although he got away / to enjoy life's sweetness for a while longer, / his right hand stayed behind him in Heorot' (2096–99).

It has, in other words, something to do with hands. When Beowulf boasts that he will kill Grendl with his bare hands it is, in part, just that: a boast, a vaunt of strength. Clearly it requires greater strength, and closer quarters, to kill with bare hands than it does to kill with a weapon. But something more than that is going on. Using his hands signifies, for Beowulf, *agency*. Hrothgar praises the strength of Beowulf's father to his face (' . . . your father. / With his own hands he had killed Heatholaf . . . '). Beowulf himself recalls killing a huge sea monster: 'through my own hands, / the fury of battle had finished off the sea beast' (557–58). When he fights Grendl's mother his sword fails and he realises 'he would have to rely / on the might of his arm . . . [he] gripped her shoulder' (1537–38). And as an old man, Beowulf recalls killing 'Dayraven the Frank' in open battle:

> No sword blade sent him to his death,
> my bare hands stilled his heartbeats.

> (2506–07)

And he goes on with evident regret that he will not be able to challenge the dragon in the same manner:

> I would rather not
> use a weapon if I knew another way
> to grapple with the dragon and make good my boast
> as I did against Grendl is days gone by.

So he takes his sword, although in the event it does him no good. At the crucial moment in the battle it snaps, and the poet notes that Beowulf's hand *is simply too strong for his weapon*:

> When he wielded a sword
> No matter how blooded and hard-edged the blade,
> His hand was too strong, the stroke he dealt
> (I have heard) would ruin it.

> (2680–84)

It has to do with hands. What is happening here, over and above the sheer vaunt of physical strength, is the weighted construing of a particular triad that in turn determines the structures of power in the text. *Beowulf* is a poem about power in the first instance. The narrative, which concerns the physical power (and courage, but mostly power) of the hero is interleaved with passages that elaborate the logic of political power. The poet gives us advice from the start, on how to win and keep allies, on how not to alienate one's people. The authority of specific kings may be challenged in the poem, but authority itself (which is to say, power) is consistently respected.

Often the *Beowulf*-poet invokes the highest authority, God Almighty. Beneath God come kings, and beneath kings the king's men—the ordinary people such as you and I, do not figure in the poem at all, unless it is as the low thief who sneakily steals from the dragon and wakes him to rage near the end. Indeed, one of the core relationships in the poem is that between Hrothgar the King, 'protector of the Shieldings' and Beowulf, who for most of the poem is not a king. We might ask why the protector of the Shieldings does not, in fact, *protect* his Shieldings against Grendl; why, in other words, he requires an outsider, a Dane, to do that job for him. But to ask this question, of course, is to misunderstand the role of Kings. Kings do not fight hand-to-hand with monsters (Beowulf's combat with the dragon at the end of his life is a key exception, of course, and one to which I will come back). Kings send in their champions, or warriors, to do that sort of thing. That is what it means to be King.

To put it concisely: there are three ways of killing mentioned in *Beowulf*. Most directly, one may kill with one's bare hands. Then again, one may kill with a weapon: sword, knife or spear. Or, finally (and this is the mode of kings) one may kill with a *word*. Kings speak and others die; and they are able to do this because they have subjects who will wield swords, or their bare hands, to make those words come true. Beowulf in a figurative, but also more than figurative, sense *becomes* Hrothgar's hand. The King wills the blow, and Beowulf executes it.

This in turn implies that metaphorical or metonymic conception of the King as the whole kingdom, or as the kingdom as a sort of leviathan man. Beowulf's actual hand become a synecdoche for himself as a warrior, and in turn for the power that a king can muster; at the same time that Beowulf himself becomes a metaphorical 'hand' of the king himself.

Why are hands so prominent in this poem? There is something *honest* about the 'hand'. Hand-to-hand seems to be presented as a more straightforward, cleaner mode of conflict than swordfighting. It predominates *because* of its honesty, in a sense. This connects,

I think, with something that Heaney says about the tone of the poem in his introduction to his translation.

> I remembered the voice of the poem as being attractively direct, even though the diction was ornate and the narrative method something oblique. What I had always loved was a kind of four-squareness about the utterance, a feeling of living within a constantly indicative mood . . . (xxvii)

There is, in other words, a ready-to-hand-edness about the poem's tone. It is a poem that feels hand-worked, a poem whose occasional roughness of texture and construction seem to be the fingerprints left by the sculptor's or potter's hands in the medium he has worked. And it is a poem that celebrates not merely strength, but strength-of-hand.

Why would a warrior wear a glove? The dandy adornment of the body is presumably not to the point. Presumably the issue is, rather, one of protection. And here we come up against another notable oddity in the account of Beowulf's fight with Grendl's mother. Quite apart from Beowulf's improbable ability seemingly to breathe under water there is the counter-intuitive protection afforded him by his chain-mail.

> So she lunged and clutched and managed to catch him
> In her brutal grip; but his body for all that,
> remained unscathed: the mesh of the chain mail
> saved him on the outside.
>
> (1501–04)

But this is patently not right. Were Grendl-mama using her talons like swords, as she subsequently does ('her savage talons / failed to rip the web of his war-shirt') we could understand how chain mail would help prevent the blow cutting into the warrior's skin. But how can something as flexible as *chain-mail* help against a giant monster who is trying to *crush* the life out of you in a 'brutal grip'? Sheet metal might act as a rigid exoskleleton, but chain-mail cannot do this. So what is going on?

The protection chain mail offers is to do with the difficulty a weapon has in penetrating, not in tensile-strength. The warrior's own skin must be both flexible and strong, as well: and if hands are to become death-dealing then they will need to combine flexibility and rigidity. Beowulf's strange flexible-and-rigid chain mail merely enacts this essential quality of the warrior's own body, a transference of his strength onto his outward wear. Grendl's glove does something similar. It is an external emblem of the monstrous capacity for death that the creature's hand represents.

This is my point. The *manual* quality in the poem is precisely what endears it to so many readers and critics. *Beowulf* is a poem with which we, as readers, *grapple*; it admits us to a world that flatters our sense of the *strong touch*. It is a poem that we feel we can grasp, take in our hands and *feel*, not just admire in a distant or cerebral sense.

To put this another way: where later poetry sometimes reads as too polished, too (we might say) machine-tooled, *Beowulf* with its rough-edges and burly awkwardnesses, its inconsistencies and narrative jolts, feels like something *hand-made*. Its appeal was therefore always likely to increase after the cultural aesthetic shifted from admiring finish, polish and regularity as the eighteenth and nineteenth century tended to do, towards admiring individual craftwork the way we do today. Hand-made is now a term of approbation, after all; and all the little niggles and glitches in the product are things in which we symbolical invest our admiration, precisely because they represent the craftsman's touch. No longer to be explained away as 'not silk', the Hessian-cloth-texture of the poem is presented as the very ground of its appeal.

But this is the irony of the piece, of course. Because of all the works admitted to the canon of English literature *Beowulf* is the only one that was *not* hand-made, not produced *cum manis* onto manuscript. It was not *written*. Oral composition is the work of the spoken word and the memory, not the processes of hand-writing or hand-typing than nowadays characterise composition. But Grendl's glove, the magical and threatening hand-covering, is exactly the right emblem for the strong-manual, dextrous-manual and above all the intimate, connective, *hands-on* quality that the poem exhibits.

This brings us back to *The Hobbit*, the work of Tolkien's hand. Bilbo's pocket is a kind of glove. What it contains is a ring—an adornment for the finger of a hand. It used to puzzle me why Tolkien, a devout Catholic who regarded marriage as a holy sacrament and a source of profound, sacred joy for humanity, should have chosen a *wedding band* as the type of the greatest evil in the world. In the following chapter I attempt to answer that riddle.

7
The Riddle of the Ring

From the pocket to what is *in* the pocket. This riddle can be cast in the form of a straightforward question, although its answer is not so straightforward. Why a ring?

To unpack the question a little: why might Tolkien light upon a *finger-ring* to embody the central force of his symbolic conception, making it the most powerful and most dangerous artefact in his imaginary world? More: although each of the other magic rings (the three elven, the seven dwarvish and the nine mannish) carries a precious stone, the one ruling ring is a plain gold circle. Which is to say: it takes the form of a wedding band. We might want to argue that there is something strange in Tolkien, a devout Catholic with strong views on the sanctity and importance of marriage, himself happily married, taking a wedding ring as his supreme symbol of the corruptive power of evil in the world.

This statement needs immediate qualification. Of course the one ring is not a wedding band in any literal sense. Its resemblance is figurative and symbolic rather than literal. But to explore the way the ring, and rings in general, signify in *The Lord of the Rings* is to open up some intriguing aspects of what I take to be Tolkien's fundamentally sacramental imagination, which in turn illuminate the way this book works, as a great Catholic as well as a great Fantasy novel.

Immediate objections suggest themselves. Perhaps there is nothing especially remarkable about the use of a ring as the trigger or accelerant of Tolkien's large narrative. Some sort of item or treasure is frequently the focus (the 'mcguffin', as such narrative stratagems are dismissively called) of adventures in the Romance tradition. This might be an object over which characters fall out, or after which characters quest. One of Tolkien's key strategies, as many critics have noted, is to invert the conventions of such tales. *The Lord of the Rings* is a sort of quest narrative, but with the difference that the quest is to destroy rather than discover an item of precious treasure. Is it fair to ask whether there any deeper significance to the ring beyond its position as narrative facilitator? Perhaps there is nothing essential about the ring apart from this functionality. It is possible that Tolkien could equally well have built his novel around a golden chalice, or a golden torc, or a golden coin, or—for all we know—a golden ankh, dolphin or miniature football boot. But to put it in those sorts of terms (they are ridiculous choices in this context; but why *are* they ridiculous?) does at least highlight the *rightness* of Tolkien's actual choice. There is something intuitively appropriate about the ring. Why might that be?

One way to start answering such a question would be to look at the way the ring functions within the logic of Tolkien's story, as well as looking at the symbolic and subtextual resonances of his creation, to have some sense of why he placed this particular artefact at the heart of his imaginative conception.

Actually, when one starts to look at *The Lord of the Rings* 'through the ring', as it were, it starts to assume a degree of ubiquity. The 'fellowship of the ring', the nine companions who take the ring south, echo an Arthurian circle of knights (a round table). Mordor, the birth- and death-place of the ring, itself externalises a ring shape, surrounded on all sides by forbidding mountains. Actually this is only partly true: according to the map the ring of mountains protecting the land of shadow falls away to the East; although there are no indications of this in the novel—no suggestion that Frodo and Sam should trek East to enter Mordor through Eastern foothills, rather than clamber up the forbidding mountain ranges. In the *Silmarillion* the council place of the Valar is called 'the Ring of Doom'. In an earlier draft of the *Silmarillion* material, collected after Tolkien's death in the volume *Morgoth's Ring*, the ring of the title is the whole of Middle Earth, through which (and especially through the gold ore threaded within it) Morgoth's malignancy circulates. Only water is immune from his evil.

As architectural or geographical features, rings are interestingly ambiguous. A surrounding wall might figure as protection against a hostile exterior world; or it might equally well figure as confinement, a prison wall to prevent escape. Something of this semiological doubleness inflects Tolkien's treatment of 'rings' in his work, focused of course on the One Ring, with an almost uncanny balance. Arguably it also functions as a Tolkienian gloss upon the institution of marriage.

It is tempting, although rather fruitless, to list his possible sources, the many occurrences of magic rings in previous cultures of which Tolkien was certainly aware. For some commentators the parallels with Wagner's cycle of opera *Der Ring des Nibelungen* are striking, although Tolkien repudiated them.[1] Of course, Tolkien's denial does not mean that Wagner can be dismissed entirely out of hand. John Louis DiGaetani has argued that Wagner's influence is pervasive in early twentieth-century British literature, citing in particular Conrad, Lawrence, E. M. Forster, Woolf and Joyce. But as DiGaetani points out:

> Wagner's *Der Ring des Nibelungen* is most basically about the relationship between love and power. The ring itself, which will give infinite wealth and power to the person who possesses it, can achieve its power only if its bearer renounces love forever.[2]

This is not the dichotomy presented in *The Lord of the Rings*. Indeed, something of the reverse is true. The ring achieves some of its sinister, uncanny effect in the novel precisely by creating a weirdly intense *parody* of the love relationship. Gollum loves his ring as he might, under other circumstances, have loved a fellow being: he calls it his 'precious', he talks to it and so on. Of course, this 'love' is not presented as a positive force. It is too claustrophobically exclusive, too much a version of unhealthy narcissism, and it overrides all other duties of care, love and honour.

More relevant to Tolkien's purposes (we might assume) are the many references to rings as precious objects and tokens of trust and fidelity in Old English literature. From this perspective the ring is interesting primarily because it represents, as the phrase goes, 'portable property': valuable, displayable and easily transported. Gold rings are a good way for a Lord to reward his loyal followers. But there are problems here as well. A gold ring with an inset precious jewel would be a more valuable piece of portable property than a plain gold band; and yet, of course, in *Lord of the Rings* the reverse is the case—the plainer ring is the most powerful.

There are, as critics have noted, certain inconsistencies in the way the One Ring is portrayed in *The Lord of the Rings*. Sometimes it is inert; sometimes it seems to possess will and even agency. It can be 'wielded' only by someone with a strong will; but some of the strongest wills (Boromir's for instance) are overwhelmed without even direct contact. There is also a, presumably deliberate, vagueness as to what the ring might actually do in the wrong hands. Gollum possesses it for a very long time and does nothing more with it than use it as a means of becoming invisible. Yet the implication is that, on a properly skilled hand, it can wreak terrible damage. How? we wonder—does lightning lance forth from the beringed finger? Does it summon down atomic-bomb-like death on armies? Tolkien does not spell it out.

Tom Shippey identifies some other difficulties. Gandalf's conversation with Frodo in the second chapter of the first book, says Shippey, contains assertions concerning the ring which are 'at the heart of *The Lord of the Rings*' adding 'if they are not accepted, then the whole point of the story collapses'. He picks out three: firstly that 'the Ring is immensely powerful, in the right or the wrong hands'; secondly the ring is 'deadly dangerous to all its possessors: it will take them over, "devour" them, "possess" them'; thirdly, 'the Ring cannot simply be left unused, put aside, thrown away: it has to be destroyed'.[3] And some characters (Gollum, Boromir) are indeed corrupted, devoured and destroyed by the ring, consistent with these premises. But as Shippey notes there are many characters whom are untouched: including Sam (who hands the ring back to Frodo without demur); Aragon, Legolas, Gimli, Merry and Pippin who all appear indifferent to it. At the beginning of the story Gandalf tells Frodo that he 'could not "make" you' relinquish the ring 'except by force, which would break your mind' (*LotR*, 74). Yet at the very end of the book Gollum wrenches the ring from Frodo precisely by force, assaulting him and biting his finger off, and yet Frodo's mind remains unbroken. Shippey's solution to this is that 'all the doubts just mentioned can be cleared up by the use of one word, though it is a word never used in *Lord of the Rings*. The Ring is "addictive".' Like a drug to a contemporary drug-addict, the ring overwhelms the individual's power to 'just say no'.

There are problems, however, with the 'addictive' explanation. It seems, for instance, that Bilbo does not become 'addicted' to the Ring, even though he possesses it for decades, using it often. Boromir, on the other hand, does become 'addicted' despite never possessing it. Moreover, addiction does not address the notion that the forceable removal of the ring is described as something that will break Frodo's mind, and the later contradiction of this assertion. Rather, the imaginative logic of the novel suggests that a person with 'great Will' might master the Ring and wield it (although his or her intents would be perverted to evil); whereas a 'little' person would be unable to master it, and would instead become mastered *by* it (like Gollum). It is hard to reconcile this with the idea of an 'addictive' Ring; on the contrary, it tends to play up the idea of the Ring as an agent itself, with its own will against which the human characters must pitch their own.

The Ring is clearly 'to do' with Power. But more important than this rather nebulous fact is the point that the Ring is a *binding* agent, tying together all the other Rings of Power: a locus of connection ('One ring to bring them all and in the darkness bind them'). 'Bind' is an interesting word. It means several things. Most obviously it means to tie-together or tie-up, literally or metaphorically. It can also refer to marriage. It is etymologically connected with 'band': a 'wedding band' is so called precisely because it *binds*. The Ring binds itself to its bearer. It binds together, by magic charm and as a form of marriage, all the other rings. In other words the resemblance between this 'binding' Ring and the ordinary marriage band is more than mere superficial appearance. There is a form of marriage—binding, exclusive, life-devouring—at the heart of Tolkien's conception of the ring.

Nor is marriage an arbitrarily chosen trope. It is for Tolkien something more than just a contract of cohabitation between two people. It is a *magical* bond—magical in the strong, Catholic sense of the word. In other words, it is a sacrament. To be clear: I am suggesting that one answer to the question posed at the beginning of this chapter is that Tolkien chooses a Ring that resembles a marriage band precisely because, for a Catholic, the marriage ring is a sacramental icon. This is a crucial point, I think: because Tolkien conceives of his subcreated world in sacramental terms. I mentioned this briefly at the beginning of the present study; now is the time to go into it in a little more detail.[4]

The Latin 'sacramenta' is the translation used of the New Testament Greek μυστηριον (*musterion*, 'mystery'); and in Christian theology a sacrament is 'a visible sign of an invisible grace'. Catholics recognise seven sacraments: baptism, confirmation, penance, the Eucharist, priestly ordination, marriage and extreme unction (or 'the anointing of the sick' as the latter has, since Tolkien's time, been renamed). These rituals are symbolic of divine grace entering into the material realm, but in a crucial sense they are *more* than symbolic. According to Aquinas 'the Christian sacraments are ways in which God lives in us and in which we, in this life, live in God'.[5] The mystery of the sacraments is bound in with the mystery of the Incarnation. God, says Aquinas, was not obliged to incarnate himself in material form in order to confer his grace on humanity; but by choosing to do this he connected the spiritual world with the material world. St Augustine saw sacraments as a physical 'signum', or sign, of non-physical (which is to say, spiritual) truth—so, for instance, that the water of baptism symbolises the non-material spirit of God. Aquinas agreed that the sacraments were symbolic rites, but insisted that they were at the same time *more* than just symbolic.

> Aquinas firmly believes that God brings us to himself as creatures of flesh and blood. He thinks that, in the end, we are drawn into the life of God by someone like ourselves, by someone living a human life in our material world. And he believes this is where sacraments enter into the picture . . . The sacraments of the Church are physical signs and genuine causes of grace. They are symbols which make real what they symbolize.[6]

This, I think, helps gloss Tolkien's repeated insistence of animadversion against allegory. As I argue above, we do, I think, need to take seriously Tolkien's statement of 'cordial dislike' of allegory and acknowledge that *The Lord of the Rings* is poorly served by that sort of reductive reading. A better way to think of the novel is not as allegory but as a sub-creative materialisation—an incarnation, in a manner of speaking—of what Tolkien took to be certain spiritual realities.[7]

That *The Lord of the Rings* is a great work of Catholic literature, as well as a great work in the Fantasy tradition, has been argued by several critics.[8] I have already quoted the letter that Tolkien wrote to Father Robert Murray in 1953, describing his own work as 'fundamentally religious and Catholic'. And even without 'decoding' the novel as a religious allegory we can see that, naturally enough, many elements from Christian myth have shaped the imaginary world of Middle-earth. In particular the novels demonstrate a fascination with the Fall that introduces mortality to the world, and with ethical choice. Writing to Milton Waldman in 1951 Tolkien said that 'all this stuff is mainly concerned with Fall, Mortality and the Machine'.[9] It tells the story of self-sacrifice, and a saviour who travels the paths of the dead only to return in triumph; of the tremendous significance of the moral choices people are presented with, particularly of ordinary people caught up in extraordinary times.

Bernard Bergonzi, in his article 'The Decline and Fall of the Catholic Novel' argues that 'the English Catholic novel . . . did not dramatize Catholic theology *tout court*, for there is no such single entity, but a particular and extreme theological emphasis, where religious beliefs were caught up with literary attitudes and conventions'.[10] Assuming we wish to bracket *The Lord of the Rings* with the writers about which Bergonzi is here talking (Graham Greene and Evelyn Waugh predominantly) we might wish to go on and explore how 'particular and extreme' the theological emphasis of Tolkien's fantasy is. The particular element that articulates itself through the work is, I am suggesting, precisely this sacramental element.

One such element is the matter of free will. As Colin Manlove points out, one malign effect of the Ring is precisely to compromise Frodo's free will.

> Frodo has been 'chosen' for his task; by itself this is reasonable enough, for it would still leave him room to decide whether to take it up. But there are additional determining factors. Bilbo could voluntarily leave the Ring to Frodo because the Ring wanted to go to Frodo: as Gandalf says 'he would never have just forsaken it, or cast it aside. It was . . . the Ring itself that decided things. The Ring left *him*.' And since the Ring wants to be with Frodo, it is impossible for him to get rid of it as it was not for Bilbo: Gandalf tells him that he could not 'make' Frodo give it up 'except by force, which would break your mind'. Therefore, Frodo has to keep the Ring.[11]

Later in the novel, Manlove suggests, 'this core of necessity is hopefully overlain with an apparent act of will'. Frodo, reflecting on his 'evil fate' recalls that 'he had taken it on himself in his own sitting room in the far-off spring of another year'. According to Manlove, however: 'this is not true to the facts'. Certain difficulties do indeed present themselves. For example, how is it that Bilbo was able effectively to 'divorce' himself from the Ring? Manlove's answer (that the Ring wanted to leave) addresses the question on the terms of the localised rationalisation provided by the text rather than according to its symbolic logic. But does this mean that Bilbo somehow has more free will than Frodo? That cannot be: Catholicism does not say that free will is distributed amongst human beings like height or wealth, some with more and some less. We all have the freedom to choose good or evil; and it is a choice equally important to all of us.

One way of answering this question would be to say that Bilbo can divorce himself from the Ring where Frodo cannot because Bilbo's story (primarily *The Hobbit*) takes place within the ethical framework of Old Germanic culture; where Frodo's story in *The Lord of the Rings*—though set in the same fictive world—actually takes place within the different conceptual and ideological-theological climate of Tolkien's Catholic beliefs.

Free will in Christian theology means that we all have—at all times, whenever we make a choice—the freedom to choose to do good or evil. The fact that God (omnipotent, and knowing the future as He does) already knows all the choices we are ever going to make in our life does not diminish this freedom *as it presents itself to us*, in time, continuously. But marriage is something of a special case that divides Protestant and Catholic theologies. For a Protestant it is possible to choose divorce (which is to say; Protestants have the freedom, under certain circumstances, to choose to end their marriage). This is not a choice offered to Catholics. Of course, a Catholic might say, everybody who enters into a marriage does so, or *should* do so, of their own free will. That is to say, the proscription against divorce can be thought of as a way of saying merely that once a choice has been freely made it is then necessary to live with the consequences of that choice—which, if anything, places a higher value upon the notion of free will. Of course Catholics are perfectly capable of freely willing for themselves the evils of adultery, bigamy and so on. Marriage is no more a *practically* binding relationship for them than it is for a non-Catholic. But in Catholic belief it is a *spiritually* binding one.

Catholics who go through a form of divorce and begin relationships
with others are, their priest might say, only fooling themselves. In
the eyes of God they are still married.
Frodo's ambiguous position with respect to the Ring mirrors this
problematic. Once he accepts the Ring (although at that point he
knows no better: we wonder—if Frodo had known all the trouble
bound up with the Ring, would he have accepted it from Bilbo?)—
once he *has* accepted it, he is bound to it. He cannot divorce himself
from it. Only death can break the bond. In the novel this is realised
by the death of the Ring itself, which occurs at the moment of the
death of Gollum.

This may seem like a rather bleak, even carceral vision of marriage,
but it is not out of keeping with Tolkien's thoughts on the subject.
In a letter to his son from 1941 Tolkien wrote that women are
'instinctively monogamous' (qualifying the judgement with 'when
uncorrupt') but that men are not. Their fallen nature destroys the
possibility of a monogamous alignment between male bodies, minds
and soul.

He goes on:

> However, the essence of a *fallen* world is that the *best* cannot
> be attained by free enjoyment . . . but by denial, by suffering.
> Faithfulness in Christian marriage entails that: great mortifica-
> tion. For a Christian man there is *no escape*. Marriage may help to
> sanctify & direct to its proper object his sexual desires; its grace
> may help him in the struggle; but the struggle remains.[12]

This may seem a rather extreme way to construe marriage ('for a
Christian man there is *no escape* . . . '), especially when Tolkien ends
this same letter by commending his son to 'the one great thing to
love on Earth: the Blessed Sacrament'. There is, we might feel, something alarming in any free agent being so remorselessly bound to
anything.
At that time when he was still friendly with C. S. Lewis, Tolkien
wrote to offer an opinion upon Lewis's book *Christian Behaviour*
(1943), in which the argument is advanced that there ought to be
two forms of marriage: one a Christian commitment, lifelong and
binding; the other a purely secular State-sanctioned contract which
could be dissolved. Tolkien disapproved of this idea, insisting (the

words in square brackets mark Tolkien's revisions to the original draft of this letter) that

> *Christian Marriage*—monogamous, permanent [lifelong], rigidly 'faithful'—is in fact the truth about sexual behaviour for all humanity: this is the only road of total health [total human health] (including [with] sex in its proper place) for all [*all*] men and women.[13]

There is an interesting diremption between 'permanent' and 'lifelong' here. One of the pieces of prose not included in the *Silmarillion* is a fairly lengthy discussion entitled 'Of the Laws and Customs among the Eldar pertaining to Marriage and Other Matters Related Thereunto' (it is included in volume 10 of Christopher Tolkien's *History of Middle Earth, Morgoth's Ring*). Here we learn that the elves lived according to strict notions of married chastity:

> The Eldar wedded once only in life, and for love or at the least by free will upon either part. Even when in after days, as the histories reveal, many of the Eldar in Middle-earth became corrupted, and their hearts darkened by the shadow that lies upon Arda, seldom is any tale told of deeds of lust among them.[14]

There is one detail of quasi-Lewisian compromise: Tolkien adds a period of betrothal ('the betrothed gave silver rings one to another') that 'was bound to stand for one year at least, and it often stood for longer. During this time it could be revoked by a public return of the rings, the rings then being molten and not again used for a betrothal. Such was the law.' Should the betrothal lead to marriage the betrothed 'received back one from the other their silver rings (and treasured them); but they gave in exchange slender rings of gold, which were worn upon the index of the right hand.'[15]

All this business with the interchange of rings is very interesting. We might, in the light of it, want to read the One Ring as embodying a sort of malign anti-marriage, the photographic negative, as it were, of a blessed sacrament. The only major character in *The Lord of the Rings* whom Tolkien dramatises as a functioning member of a happy marriage is also the only character in the book wholly immune to the power of the ring: Tom Bombadil, who alone amongst all the major characters in the book has a wife. He asks Frodo for the ring, and Frodo 'handed it at once to Tom':

> It seemed for a moment to grow larger as it lay far a moment on his big brown-skinned hand. Then suddenly he put it to his eye and laughed. For a second the hobbits had a vision, both comical and alarming, of his bright blue eye gleaming through a circle of gold. Then Tom put the Ring around the end of his little finger and held it up to the candlelight. For a moment the hobbits noticed nothing strange about this. Then they gasped. There was no sign of Tom disappearing![16]

The point of this episode is to dramatise that the ring has no effect upon Tom (when Frodo later slips the ring on he becomes invisible to everybody except Bombadil). It is 'alarming' to see Tom's blue eye through the ring presumably because it recalls and inverts the red eye of Sauron. But my suggestion here is that the episode depends as much upon Tom's status as happily married man as to his slightly inchoate status as 'spirit of the land'. It is remarkable to think that Tom and Goldberry are the only functioning—which is to say, loving, sacramental—marriage in the whole of *Lord of the Rings*; or at least, they are until the ring is destroyed and marriage again becomes possible (and, for example, Sam can marry Rosie). Therefore is Tom immune to the malign power of the One Ring. Indeed, the hobbits' sojourn in Tom and Goldberry's house is figured as the symbolic equivalent of travelling through a wedding band: 'the hobbits stood upon the threshold, and a golden light was all about them . . . The four hobbits stepped over the wide stone threshold.'[17]

I am still, I hope, steering clear of the suggestion that we read *The Lord of the Rings* as an allegory of marriage; or even that it represents some sort of satire upon marriage as a oppressive power-trap. Rather Tolkien has taken 'marriage', in the broadest sense and with an understanding of marriage as a synecdochal sacrament for the connection between the material and the spiritual, as a structuring principle for his Fantasy. What is wedded in *The Lord of the Rings* is not so much 'a man and a woman' (let us say, Sam and Rosie; or Aragorn and Arwen). It is the possibility of the connection of a materially embodied reality to a form of divinity. But what saves this aesthetic conception from a banal piety is precisely the double-edged valences of the Ring. It is both attractive and alarming: the ring around us protects, but also hems us in. Marriage is a connection founded in love, but also a restriction on the polygamous nature of man ('Faithfulness in Christian marriage entails . . . great mortification'). It draws us and it makes us suffer, but it also connects us with the grace of a bountiful and exacting God. This is the appeal, and the cost, of the central project of *The Lord of the Rings*.

The ring is a riddle, and its solution unpacks deeper, more spiritually profound riddles. And here is Riddle 48 from the *Exeter Book*, one of the riddles that scholarship has failed, satisfactorily, to solve:

> I heard a radiant ring, with no tongue,
> intercede for me, though it spoke
> without argument or strident words.
> The silent treasure said in front of men
> 'Save me, helper of souls.'
> May men understand the mysterious saying
> of the red gold and, as the ring said,
> wisely entrust their salvation to God.

I am, in other words, suggesting that Tolkien's imaginative creation of a sacramental gold ring connects, in suggestively oblique ways, precisely with an Anglo-Saxon riddle that proposes such a magic circle as a link between men and God.

8
The Lord of the Rings and the Riddle of Writing

This book has followed a roundabout road from the riddles in general, to the riddles contained within *The Hobbit* through questions of hands and rings. These last two concerns come about in part because this novel is handiwork, and rings adorn hands. I have sometimes thought that crowns, by adorning heads, imply that it is our clever brains that make us special amongst the animals; but that Tolkien's preference for rings over crowns speaks, perhaps, to a deeper truth. A clever brain may be a very useful thing, but without the means to work cleverness into the world it is nothing. Maybe we overpraise ourselves, Saruman-like, for our powers of thinking. Maybe it is our clever *hands* that really separate us from the animals: dextrous, thumb-opposed, grasping, manipulating, shaping, making. Conceivably, a ring is, as it were, a crown for the hand.

Hands wear gloves, and rings, and do many things; but one particular thing hands do is *write*. And 'writing' is the whole of the larger horizon of Tolkien's achievement: his world is written into existence, before anything else can be said of it. Tolkien was a dedicated handwriter, whose own beautifully formed calligraphy, especially in the runic and Elvish scripts mentioned above, is a thing of beauty in its own right. Not that he was averse to more modern modes of 'writing'. Christopher Bretherton sent him a typed letter, apologising for not hand-writing his message. Tolkien replied (on 16 July 1964) 'I do not regard typing as a discourtesy. Anyway, I usually type, since my "hand" tends to start fair and rapidly fall away into picturesque inscrutability. Also I like typewriters; and my dream is of suddenly finding myself rich enough to have an electric typewriter built to my specifications, to type the Fëanorian script.'[1] For a writer supposedly opposed to modern technology and 'the machine' this love of type-writers might seem odd; unless we refer to that very unTolkienian authority Marx, and his distinction between tools and machines. A tool is an extension of the worker's body and therefore of his/her labour; a machine stands apart for the worker, and indeed turns the worker into an adjunct of itself, tending to alienate him/her from his/her labour. A typewriter is clearly a tool, rather than a machine.

And at any rate, writing by hand, whether with one tool (a pen) or another (a typewriter), has its own magic, and its own puzzles. And this is perhaps truer in *The Lord of the Rings* than any other thing Tolkien wrote. It may be worth out while to consider, in this context, the riddle of writing.

I shall begin to address that large riddle by focusing on a specific moment in *The Fellowship of the Ring*: the Moria chapter, when Frodo and his companions are driven beneath the Misty Mountains. There are evident parallels between the construction of *The Hobbit* and *The Lord of the Rings*, structurally speaking. In the former, Bilbo and his companions must cross the Misty Mountains to get where they are going, and do so beneath rather than over the peaks. In the latter the situation is exactly paralleled for Frodo and his companions. In both books the parties encounter orcs, and something larger and more evil: Gollum and the ring in the earlier novel, the Balrog and Gandalf's death in the latter.

But what I am particularly interested in for the moment is that it is in the Moria chapter, and only there (I note one exception below), that Tolkien's fellowship encounter written texts. Specifically the chapter includes two splendid examples of Tolkien's own gorgeous calligraphy, inset into the text. The first (and how I wish UK copy-right legislation permitted me to reproduce it) is the elvish writing inscribed onto the gate at Moria. The image is of two pillars, and beside them two trees, the branches of each tree intertwined with each pillar. In the space between them is a large star, just below the centre of the composition; above this is a crown, with a second larger crown above that topped by a constellation of seven smaller stars. Linking the two pillars, and arcing over these various elements, is a semi-circular arch, in which the elvish script is carefully written.

This of course is the occasion for one of the most memorable rid-dles in *The Lord of the Rings*, one that manages to trick even Gandalf.

The Elvish script says 'speak friend and enter'. Gandalf takes this to mean he must divine the magical password, and he tried a number of possible charm-words in vain. In fact the riddle has fooled him—he needs only do what he is told, speak 'friend' (*mellon*, in Elvish) and the door opens.

The second image is the less decorative. It is a rectangular plaque upon a tomb, on which is written, in angular dwarf-runes, the legend: BALIN SON OF FUNDIN LORD OF MORIA. These two images in the main body of the book, and the charts of various Elvish and Dwarfish alphabets in the book's appendices, stand testament to Tolkien's interest in fine calligraphy. But they also pose a question: why are there so few *written texts* in the world of the *Lord of the Rings*? There are lots of oral texts, for the novel is littered with interpolated songs and verses and riddles that have been memorised and repeated by various characters. But tabulating all the written texts mentioned does not give us very much:

1. *Moria-writing*: Namely the two texts already mentioned, together with the written record the Fellowship discover inside Moria. They attract attention by virtue of being so splendidly, visually rendered.
2. *Bilbo's book*: But this exists in the novel largely (until the very end) as unwritten; something Bilbo will get around to at some point. More, it exists in a complicated metatextual relationship with the novel we are reading, so I will put it on one side for a moment.
3. *The odd single rune*: Gandalf marks his fireworks with a G-rune, for instance; and scratches a 'G'-rune on a stone at Weathertop.
4. *One 'scroll'*: mentioned and quoted in the 'Council of Elrond' chapter, in which Isildur writes down what the ring looks like, records its inscription, and declares it is 'precious' to him. Which leads me, of course, to:
5. *The ring*: Sauron's ring has writing upon it, of course, although it is writing only visible when heated in Frodo's fire. The writing, reproduced in the novel, is in the elvish script; although the language is the 'black tongue' of Mordor. It identifies the ring as the 'one ring' that rules all the others. Now, obviously, this is writing of the profoundest and most penetrating significance for the novel. More, it is evil. It precedes, and determines, all the (actual) writing that constitutes Tolkien's novel. Can we say, taking things

a little further, that it in some sense *stains* written text with some malign mark or quality? The ring-writing itself, and Isildur's scroll, are permanent records of the wickedness of the ring in action, after all.

This might start us thinking about the way written marks can be misinterpreted. Strider and the hobbits do not understand Gandalf's 'G' rune at Weathertop. Gandalf himself misses the true meaning of the Moria-Gate inscription. Writing, perhaps, is a riddle in this sense: that it tends to mislead or wrongfoot us, to distract us from the answer.

But actually I want to argue a position almost the reverse of this. Gandalf's problem with the Moria-gate inscription is that he *over*-reads; he assumes a level of complexity that is not there. When he sees how straightforward the instruction is he laughs. Something similar is the case with 'the remains of a book' they find at the beginning of book 2, chapter 5. Initially it looks as though this, with an almost facetious literalness, is going to be 'difficult to decode', in this case because it is so materially damaged.

> '*We drove the orcs from the great gate and guard*—I think; the next word is blurred and burned: probably *room*—*we slew many in the bright*—I think *sun in the dale.*'

And so on. But in fact, the reading of this text reveals a near-fatal facility, a slippage between text and world. They read the words '*We cannot get out. The end comes, drums drums in the deep . . . they are coming*' and without intermission these words becomes their reality.

> There was a hurrying sound of many feet.
> 'They are coming!' cried Legolas.
> 'We cannot get out,' said Gimli. (*LotR*, 341)

In other words, the thing with written language is not that it is too obscure, or ambiguous, or slippery; but *on the contrary*, that *it is too plain*. It does exactly what it says (you speak 'friend' and enter). It bridges the gap between text and world too immediately, and renders itself real with a dangerous completion. This is at the heart of the power of the ring. The whole novel is a written-textual articulation of that fact.

Writing in this sense is prior; foundational. If we wanted to invoke Derrida, we could say: *Lord of the Rings* is a logocentric text. It is what you find when you excavate down, below the surface logic of the represented, past the oral traditions and remembered songs. Which is why Moria is the precisely the right place for these two fine calligraphic interpolations, and why no such writing (I mean: samples of actual Middle-earth calligraphy, inserted into the text) is found anywhere else in the novel, the ring excepted. The symbolic logic of Moria is: dig down deep enough, and you free a terrible, destructive evil. This evil is literalised as 'Balrog', a fiery agent of destruction. But the novel has already established the crucial fiery agent of destruction in the literal letters of the One Ring ('"I cannot read the fiery letters," said Frodo, in a quavery voice.') Oral literature connects you with a living tradition of other people; but written literature short-circuits community and conducts a spark of terrible danger directly into reality.

There is a larger irony here, and it is one that recalls the idiom of riddles themselves. Indeed, it is almost too obvious to need pointing out—a meta-textual observation about how this potential-for-evil danger of written language inflects a text that is itself embodied in written language. But rather than getting diverted into that, I want to say something, briefly, about a different sort of 'writing': the writing with moving images of cinema.

An even more immediate mode of linking audience to story than written script, of course, is the motion picture. It is a handicap, if only a small one, that this book on *The Hobbit* was written before the author had the opportunity to see the three films recently made out of this book. Certainly it would be hard to discuss *The Lord of the Rings* today without also discussing the trilogy of films, directed by Peter Jackson, that were made out of the books by New Line cinema. It is a trivial observation that 'films are not the same as books'—no film ever is, and actually I would say that Jackson did, by and large, a good job with an extremely difficult brief. There are moments when the divergence between written text and visual text is more marked, however. I do not mean the absence of Tom Bombadil, or the lack of any 'Scouring of the Shire': script-writing decisions made for at least arguably valid reasons. But to re-read—say—*The Two Towers*, after watching the second movie is an interesting experience.

Even at their best, motion picture adaptations of books (indeed *especially* the best examples of the form) are insidious and plaguey things, liable to overwrite one's memory of the source text. I had read *Lord of the Rings* many times before seeing the films, and have re-read the books since; and I find myself surprised by how different the emphasis is between this book and that film. There is the fact that the movie braided-together the stories of Frodo and Sam on the one hand, and Aragorn, Legolas and Gimli on the other, where Tolkien's novel is scrupulous about separating them out. But more to the point is the treatment of the latter. Broadly this amounts to (I mean, in Jackson's *Two Towers*): Aragorn, Legolas and Gimli pursuing the abducted hobbits; Pippin and Merry meeting ents, Aragorn, Legolas and Gimli meeting the Rohirrim, and finally *a lengthy climactic hour-long battle sequence at Helm's Deep*. To re-read the novel after seeing the film is to be struck by how localised and, in a way, low-key the Helm's Deep material is—just the one chapter—and how elongated and emphasised, by comparison, is all the stuff on Fangorn and the ents. As if Tolkien loves trees more than battles; where Hollywood loves battles more than trees.

Of course, put it like that, and it seems obvious: of *course* Tolkien loves trees more than battles! Of course Hollywood takes the exact contrary view! But I think something else is going on here; something that almost a riddle. This is the question concerning the referent of the title: *which* two towers? Tolkien himself is not entirely helpful as far as this riddle goes. 'The Two Towers', he conceded, warily, 'gets as near as possible to finding a title to cover the widely divergent Books 3 & 4; and can be left ambiguous.' Initially he planned to call Book III *The Treason of Isengard* and Book IV *The Journey of the Ringbearers*, or else *The Ring Goes East*. He had several possible suggestions for an overarching name for the two together, an arrangement forced upon him by the exigencies of postwar publishing and not one with which he was happy.

The riddle, then, is: which two towers? Tolkien's own illustration of the towers, and a note at the end of *The Fellowship of the Ring* suggests the towers are Minas Morgul and Orthanc. But in a letter to Rayner Unwin Tolkien instead specifies Orthanc and the Tower of Cirith Ungol. And as far as Tolkienian scholarship goes, a case has been made for pretty much any permutation of the five towers that appear in the story: the tower of Cirith Ungol, Orthanc, Minas Tirith, Barad-dûr and Minas Morgul. The motion picture, of course, plumps unambiguously for: Barad-dûr in Mordor and Orthanc in Isengard. I will come back to the towers in a moment.

I ask myself, as any critic ought, howsoever few actually do: does my proximity to this novel make it impossible for me to get the requisite critical distance upon it? Take for example, the matter of Gandalf's return from seeming death in the mines of Moria. This is a narrative development that seems to me (on my umpteenth, or perhaps umpty-first, reading) perfectly natural and logical. But I know some who did not know the story, and who, watching the movies for the first time, groaned mightily when Ian McEllen popped up again, thinking it a cheesy and ridiculous plot-twist.

Gandalf's return is not gratuitous, or out of context. Indeed, the whole of the third book (*Two Towers* 1) is *about* this—about, that is to say, rebirth. It is the return from death; or more precisely it is about the vivification of the inert. So on the one hand characters are presumed dead and then discovered alive: Merry and Pippin, for instance, as well as Gandalf himself. Of course the case with Gandalf is more than that the others thought him dead but actually he was alive. Gandalf actually does die, becomes a corpse, and then is reborn, 'sent back' in his word, although he does not vouchsafe by whom. What was it like being dead? That is a riddle worth answering. 'I lay staring upward while the stars wheeled over, and each day was as long as a life-age of the earth.'² 'Wandered', with its hint of 'wondered', is particularly nice.

Perhaps the most striking thing about his resurrection is that Gandalf comes back invulnerable. The last we see of Gandalf the Grey he is complaining that he is tired ('what an evil fortune! And I am already weary' (*LotR*, 348)). Now he appears to have almost limitless energy—when the four of them ride all day and all night across Rohan, Gandalf permits them only a couple of hours rest; and whilst Legolas and Gimli sleep the wizard stands, leaning on his staff and peering into the darkness. Not only does he not need sleep, he cannot be harmed by weapons. He tells his companions that 'none of you have any weapon that could hurt me'. This carries with it the suggestion that all Gandalf's subsequent battlefield heroics with Glamdring is a kind of play-acting: for he can no more be slain than could Milton's Satan. But this state of affairs *is* logical, according to the shape of Tolkien's imaginarium: Gandalf has been put on the same level vis-à-vis mortality as the Nazgul, who similarly cannot be killed in the normal course of things (although Saruman, it transpires, can).

A little later in the narrative, Gandalf performs a sort of Lazarus-act on Theoden. The king goes from being functionally dead, an inert and seemingly beyond-aged man to being a vigorous leader and warrior. Gandalf's return, and Theoden's rebirth, are two of the most significant events of *The Two Towers*; symbolic both of the turning of the tide against Sauron. And standing in some manner of typological relationship, extra-textually, to the resurrection of Christ.

Then there are the ents. Trees, whilst being, of course, alive, are more or less inert. The ents trope the coming to life of inert matter: the ents are the scenic, character and structural externalisation of Gandalf's return to life. They (ents, Gandalf) share a sense of the intense, beautiful slowness of everyday time—to quote again the words Gandalf uses to describe life from the perspective beyond life: 'each day was as long as a life-age of the earth'. Yet both act swiftly, and decisively, against evil. To put it in a nutshell: in this book, the inert comes alive. Tolkien's brilliant move with the ents, and much of the focus of this book, is the vivification of the insentient and unmoving.

This, then, is (I think) the real meaning of the two towers of the title. The reference is not to the architecture of the secondary world, but rather to *life and death themselves*. This book traverses the hinterland between the Tower of Life and the Tower of Death, the crisscrossing and unexpected reappearances that weird space enables. In brief, then, the first half of *The Two Towers* is a book artfully, and I think eloquently, passing from the tower of Death to the tower of Life. Gandalf, dead, revivifying; Theoden, a living corpse, returned to youth; Trees, rooted and insentient, transformed by Tolkien's imagination into roving, powerful ents. The second half of *The Two Towers*, in complementary fashion, traces the opposite trajectory; from Life to Death, or some ghastly state in between which is not yet dead but not quite life. It does not seem to me either irrelevant or random that the main characters of the first part of *The Two Towers* move, broadly, east to west; where Frodo, Sam and Gollum move, broadly, the opposite way, from west to east. One way of summing up this book would be to invoke Coleridge's famous but, I think, poorly understood phrase 'Nightmare Life-in-Death'. It is this that the book delineates. Gollum is a major figure in this section partly because he embodies this Coleridgean fate: a creature who has lived far beyond his natural span of life and is more profoundly damaged and miserable as a result than is easily described. But the theme of the book hits home most powerfully in Chapter II, 'the Passage of the Marshes'. This is introduced by a clever little glance back to *The Hobbit*'s riddles:

> Alive without breath
> as cold as death
> never thirsting, ever drinking;
> clad in mail, never clinking.

The original answer to this riddle ('fish') is supplemented, in this chapter of the later novel, by a *second*, much more eerie solution to this riddle. For Gollum's words perfectly describe the warriors ('they lie in all the pools,' says Frodo, dreamily: 'pale faces, deep deep under the dark water . . . grim faces and evil, and noble faces and sad / Many faces proud and fair, and weeds in their silver hair. But all foul, all rotting, all dead'). These cannot be actual corpses, as Sam points out; for they died an age ago. But whatever they are they turn the very landscape into a place in which some grisly remnant of life clings to death.

As with the warriors alive-without-breath beneath the waters of the Dead Marshes (and as with Gollum himself), so with Frodo. Stung by Shelob at the end of the book, and so mortified that Sam initially believes him a corpse; yet a poisoned body in which life still clings. Shelob, also ancient, is also more Death than Life. She smells of death. She has no care for the doings or structures of the living, except as food. The Nightmare of Life-in-Death is very different, indeed *profoundly* so, from Death-in-Life. The latter is natural; a ripeness; the grain of existence. The former is a kind of violation. This book understands that.

This is why, I would say, this is the right place (in Tolkien's pattern) for Faramir's account of the Numenoreans. This quasi-Atlantean civilisation is Tolkien's revisioning of Ancient Egypt, and an object lesson in pride punished. But the crucial details are the way the Numenoreans tried to cheat death, and created a population of ghastly mummy-like individuals as a result. The rulers created tombs that are more splendid and beautiful than the houses of the living, because they were in thrall to death and had turned their back on life.

The Return of the King carries through this elaboration of the theme of Death-in-Life/Life-in-Death. It opens, for instance—after settling Pippin in Minas Tirith—with a big-set piece scene in which the restless alive-in-death cluster around Aragorn, eager to be granted peace. The king in waiting walks the path of the dead and the dead come to him armed: 'pale banners like shreds of cloud, and spears like winter-thickets on a misty night' is how Legolas describes them, in a piercingly Hardyesque moment of lyrical phrasing. They are likened to winter because winter is what they are; Aragorn's magic is in turning them from an arrested, eternal winter into the sort of winter that passes on to make way for Spring. And as the book ends, it passes through Chapter 8 'The Houses of Healing' and the near-deathly-alive, wounded in the battle, are brought back to life, again by Aragorn's special magic. And in the middle we have the striking scene of Denethor's suicide. He has to die, in order for the rule of the Stewards to end and the rule of the King to begin. But suicide is a semiotically tangled from this novel's point of view, an act that shifts valence from pagan stoic heroism to Christian sin and damnable wickedness across the same divide that creatively divides Tolkien's own imagination. Certainly he does not want to parse self-murder as a nobly Roman action. Accordingly, erring perhaps too far on the other side, he forces it into the straight-jacket of over-coded pseudo-Christian moralising. Gandalf lectures Denethor sternly on the baleful pride and despair of such an action. 'Authority is not given to you, Steward of Gondor', he booms, 'to order the hour of your death'—presumably forgetting, in the moment, that he himself effectively threw himself into the chasm at Khazad-Dum in order to save his comrades. Or perhaps it is one law for wizards; another for Gondor. We might be tempted to think that a double standard. For in point of fact one of the general trajectories of this book is *precisely* that pseudo-samurai or Horatius-at-the-Bridge sacrifice of self. How else to describe Frodo and Sam going (as they think) into certain death? Or the Rohirrim galloping will-nil towards a massively larger army? Or Gandalf rejecting the truce terms and dooming (they all think) the entire army to destruction? But out of this death is snatched, eucatastrophically, life: victory—the trope of Christian sacrifice, redemption and the final solution of the mystery life-in-death that generates life *from* death.

The riddle of writing, in Tolkien, is somehow the riddle of death. To be wise is good; but to be too wise, and especially to revel pridefully in one's wisdom, like Saruman, is not good. And to be all wise— for again I bring the argument back to the sayings of the all-wise, the

Alvíssmál—is death. I wonder if Tolkien was attracted to the story of Thor and the too-clever dwarf because it suggests that knowing *all* the answers is actually the loser; that knowing all the answers is a kind of petrification. Alvíss' pride can be intuited from the smug range of his knowledge; but it leads directly to a kind of petrified death-in-life. To read from 'riddles' in the narrow sense, to religious mysteries in the larger: Alvíss hoped for union with a god, to marry (that crucial sacrament) a god's daughter, but he was not worthy. Religious mysteries do not exist in order to be trivially 'solved'; the individual who blithely claims to *know* all the riddles of faith, God, life and death is at the least fooling his/herself, and at the worst runs the risk of leading people astray. The answer to the biggest riddles of life, we might think, is neither in book-learning nor in knowing more generally. It is in loving.

9
The Volsung Riddle: Character in Tolkien

Some years ago I had the pleasure of interviewing Brian Aldiss at the Cheltenham literary festival. I say interview; Aldiss, an old pro of the festival-and-interview circuit, effectively monologued, very entertainingly, for an hour and a half. I enjoyed it enormously. During the course of a wide-ranging discussion, he touched on the success of Tolkien and the Peter Jackson *Lord of the Rings* movies then being in the cinemas. Aldiss said that he had a relatively low opinion of the novel, chiefly because it had, in his words, 'no characters' in it; or (he added) to be more precise it had only *one* character—Gollum. What he meant, of course, was that of all the figures appearing in the novel, only Gollum shows the complexity we have come to associate with 'character' in the modern sense; the sense of an internal dynamic or conflict. The remaining figures, we might think, are types rather than characters: defined by a governing humour—the king-in-disguise heroism of Aragorn; the stoic unwavering loyalty of Sam Gamgee—that may be subject to temptation (as Boromir is tempted by the thought of possessing the ring) but is otherwise linearly and straightforwardly conceived. This is not a flaw in Tolkien's aesthetic, I think. If his concept of 'character' is more static than many other twentieth-century writers, that reflects both his and the novel's immersion in Dark Age and Medieval culture, whose literature is much more widely supplied with types than characters in the modern sense—and also, perhaps, his own Christian beliefs. If one considers human personality the outward manifestation of an eternal, God-given soul, then one may be less likely to see it as radically mutable.

This in turn is part of a much larger discussion about the representation of 'character' in modern literature. Without wishing to digress too egregiously, I shall sketch a couple of points relevant to what I want to argue here. In its earliest forms, the novel tended to take 'character' as a fixed quantity; as did earlier prose and verse romances. A character might be heroic, or villainous, brave or quixotic; but that character would remain that way throughout the story. This changes, broadly speaking, at the end of the eighteenth-century with the invention of a new mode of novelistic storytelling, the *Bildungsroman* or 'novel of personal growth and development'. This is a somewhat contested point, but I am here following Franco Moretti's influential thesis that the *Bildungsroman*, as a novelistic form, was more-or-less invented out of whole cloth in the later eighteenth century following the success of Goethe's *Willhelm Meister* novels. This helped create the climate into which a new set of stories could be written, tracing the growth and personal development of their titular protagonist.[1] A thumbnail definition of a *Bildungsroman* might be: a story in which the main character grows and changes, such that by the end of the novel s/he is in some radical sense a different person to the one they were at the beginning. Jane Austen's *Emma* (1815) is an example of such a novel: Emma Woodhouse is recognisably the same woman at the end of that novel as at the beginning, but the emotional and psychological force of the book lies in the way it traces her growing self-awareness and maturity, becoming altogether a less shallow, thoughtless individual. By contrast Samuel Richardson's earlier *Pamela* (1740), a phenomenal bestseller in its day, cannot be described as a *Bildungsroman*. Its central character, Pamela Andrews, is a virtuous, simple, happy and chaste serving maid. During the course of the novel she is pursued by her master Mr B., who wishes to seduce her. She resists him, is abducted, nearly raped, forced to live under a series of appalling psychological and physical stresses. Eventually Mr B. relents, and marries her. At the end of the novel she is exactly the same virtuous, simple, happy, chaste woman she was at the beginning. To say so is not to denigrate Richardson's writing, actually. On the contrary, his point is precisely the dramatic demonstration of virtue triumphing. To say that such a treatment rings false by our contemporary standards of psychological verisimilitude is, in a sense, to make an anachronistic criticism. Certainly our present-day understanding of 'character' is that prolonged, severe trauma will distort it, even after the stress is removed, marking it post-traumatically; that prolonged suffering tends to warp a person's character. Indeed, the success of 'the *Bildungsroman*' as a mode of novel-writing was so widespread that it has now, generally speaking, been simply incorporated into what we expect of novelistic characterisation. We take it for granted that the characters in our novels will grow and change, will go (in that hideous Hollywood-screenwriter phrase) 'on a journey' psychologically speaking. Each must manifest 'a character arc'. Moretti points out that it is in the nineteenth century that literature suddenly becomes fascinated with telling the stories of children growing up, from *David Copperfield* and *The Mill on the Floss* through to Joyce's *Portrait of the Artist* and Proust. The relatively new focus on childhood and adolescence is what we might expect from a mode such as *Bildungsroman*. After all, it is when we are children and adolescents that our 'character' is most malleable, changing and developing over the process we call 'growing up'. Indeed Moretti notes that it is after this that Shakespeare's Hamlet—of all pre-Romantic characters the most internally conflicted—becomes conventionally thought of as, in essence, a teenager. In a connected move, 'adolescence' itself started to become thought of as a Hamletian time, marked by moodiness, a fondness for dressing in black, quarrelling with one's parents, obsessing over the opposite sex and indulging in angst-y thoughts about life, death and the universe. Moretti notes that Shakespeare's play actually specifies Hamlet's age at 30, something many who know the play by reputation only may find surprising. Similarly, it is not coincidence that Tolkien's hobbits grow accordingly at a strangely decelerated pace, not reaching maturity until 33.

I shall come back to Hamlet in a moment. For now, I am trying to tease out some of the riddles of 'characterisation' as they appear in Tolkien's work. To that end I am going to discuss a lesser-known piece of Tolkienian writing.

In the mid to late 1930s, at around the time he was working on *The Hobbit*, Tolkien was also pondering the story of Volsungs. More to the point he was attempting to solve what he took to be one of the large-scale riddles of this body of myth; and to that end he wrote, apparently for his own satisfaction (certainly he did not try to publish it during his own lifetime), a modern English poem in a scrupulously imitated pastiche of Anglo-Saxon alliterative verse.

This was later edited for publication by his son Christopher as *Sigurd and Gudrún*: 170 pages of heroic poetry, attended by 200 pages of detailed editorial commentary. It is possible that you are already familiar with the story of the Volsungs and the Niblungs; perhaps from the original Sagas, or from the *Prose Edda*—or perhaps in one or other modern retelling. The most celebrated of these are both later nineteenth century. Englishman William Morris's *The Story of Sigurd the Volsung* (1876) was once a fairly famous poem, and one Tolkien certainly knew. Most famous of all is Wagner's operatic recasting of the legends, *Der Ring des Nibelungen* (1869–74). But it is a complicated legend that involves a whole chunk of story, and it seems to me that Tolkien addresses it *as* a riddle, in the larger sense. Accordingly I am going to summarise it here; for it is not really possible to talk about the poem without reference to the legend Tolkien is retelling, and these legends perhaps are not as well known as they might be.

The story starts, as the best ones do, with an enormous pile of treasure. The Norse god Odin has been imprisoned by an individual called Hreidmar. It so happens that Hreidmar and his sons can take the form of animals, if they choose; and Odin has been imprisoned because he previously killed Hreidmar's son Otr (in the form of an otter). To get free again, Odin ransoms himself with a hoard of treasure that he, in turn, takes from the dwarf Andvari. The dwarf is naturally enough unhappy about having to relinquish his gold, and begs Odin's middleman (Loki) to be allowed to keep one ring. Denied this, he curses the whole hoard, and the ring especially. Hreidmar gets his gold, though, and Odin goes free.

That, in effect, is the backstory. Tolkien's focus is not so much on these supernatural beings as the mortal dynasty of the Volsungs; but it is worth touching on what happens to this gold in the meantime. Hreidmar's remaining sons, Regin and Fafnir, desire it, and kill their father to get it. Regin demands his share, but Fafnir wants to keep it all to himself, so he puts on a 'Helm of Terror' to scare his brother away. Fafnir then takes the form of a terrible dragon, and curls up on his pile of gold in a lair, which is, as we all know, how dragons like to enjoy their wealth.

It is at this point that Odin's grandson, Volsung, enters the story. He has eleven children, and we are particularly concerned here with his son and daughter Sigmund and Signy. Signy marries a neighbouring king, Siggeir of the Gauts. But Siggeir is a bad sort. He betrays the alliance and chains up all ten sons of Volsung in the forest to be eaten by wolves. Only Sigmund survives that unpleasant fate, and he takes his vengeance on nasty Siggeir with the help of a son conceived upon his sister Signy, wife of his enemy and Queen of the Gauts. The Gauts are slaughtered, but Signy chooses to die with her husband, which, since she hates him, is a rather puzzling decision.

Sigmund returns to his land and rules as king, and here (a) his incestuously conceived son is killed, and (b) he marries again and fathers Sigurd. Since Sigmund dies in battle before his son is born, and since his mother also dies, Sigurd is raised in the forest by Regin (from the backstory). Now we get onto more familiar, Wagnerian story-territory. Sigurd grows up to be the greatest warrior in the world. Regin decides to use him to get his hands on the treasure hoarded by his dragon-brother, sending him to do what Regin is too weak or cowardly to do himself: kill Fafnir. Regin intends, after Sigurd has managed this, to eat the dragon's heart—thus gaining supernatural wisdom—and afterwards to dispose of Sigurd. And indeed Sigurd does kill the dragon. On Regin's instruction he cuts out and cooks the dragon's heart for him. But the fat spits and burns Sigurd's hand. When he instinctively puts this wound to his mouth Sigurd tastes the dragon and acquires the ability to understand the birds. They tell him of Regin's evil plan and Sigurd quickly kills him with his sword.

The treasure is now Sigurd's. What next? Well, some birds tell Sigurd that the most beautiful woman in the world, the celebrated Brynhild, is lying on a mountaintop, surrounded by a wall of fire, waiting for the mightiest warrior in the world to brave the flames and claim her. So off Sigurd goes, leaps the fire and wakes Brynhild with a kiss. The two fall in love, and swear oaths of fidelity to one another. This takes us up to the end of Wagner's opera *Siegfried*, Siegfried being the German form of Sigurd's name.

Now Gudrún enters the tale. She is the daughter of king Gjúki and his sorceress-queen Grímhild. When Sigurd goes to stay with them (now we are into the story of Wagner's *Götterdämmerung*) Grímhild decides he would make a good husband for her daughter. That he is in love with, and sworn to, Brynhild is clearly an obstacle, but Grímhild gets around this by giving him a memory-erasing magic potion. I say memory-erasing, although presumably the only portion of Sigurd's memory that gets erased is the bit about having met and fallen in love with Brynhild. Anyway, under the influence of this potion Sigurd agrees to marry Gudrún. Since this makes Brynhild once again marriageable material, Grímhild decides that her son, Gudrún's brother Gunnar, can marry her. The problem here is that Gunnar is not the mightiest warrior in the world (that is Sigurd) and so can not broach the wall of fire to get to her. But by means of another handy magic potion, Grímhild gives Sigurd the outward appearance of Gunnar. He then, obligingly enough, rides off and claims Brynhild on Gunnar's behalf. Brynhild is, as you might expect, a bit confused by this, but goes along with it; and Sigurd-in-the-likeness-of-Gunnar seals the deal by giving Brynhild the cursed ring from Andvari's hoard.

Brynhild, coming to the court of Gjúki as Gunnar's betrothed, is naturally distressed to find Sigurd already in residence, and pledged to Gudrún. Things get, narratively, a little confused at this point. You might think Gunnar would be grateful to Sigurd for taking on his form and braving the wall of fire to win him the world's most beautiful woman. But instead he decides he is going to kill him, and although he is too squeamish, or scared, to do so directly, he persuades his half-brother Gotthorn to stab Sigurd in his sleep. (According to the legend the dying Sigurd hurls his sword at Gotthorn and cuts him in half.) When grief-stricken Brynhild goes off to throw herself onto Sigurd's funeral pyre, everyone seems happy to see her go, which again seems odd given the trouble they all went to get her in the first place. In Tolkien's version they say: 'Crooked came she forth / from cursed womb / to man's evil / and our mighty woe.'[2]

That is the end of the story of Sigurd and Brynhild. The remainder is Gudrún's story. Griefstruck at this turn of events, she is nevertheless married off to 'Atli' (Atilla the Hun) in a dynastic treaty-style wedding. But Atli has heard of the huge hoard of gold. He wants it; and when he invites Gudrún's brothers Gunnar and Högni—the two men in the world who know where the treasure is—to a mighty feast, he is actually planning to torture them into revealing its location. Gunnar and Högni come with their war band, and there is a big fight at Atli's court, with a good deal of hewing, smiting and slaying. Eventually the Huns capture both brothers. Gunnar promises to tell Atli where the treasure is, provided he brings him his brother Högni's heart, cut out of his breast. Atli cuts out a slave's heart and tries to pass it off as Högni's (although why he should wish to spare Högni is far from clear); but the heart trembles with fear when it is presented to Gunnar, so he knows it can not be Högni's. So finally Atli chops out Högni's actual heart. It doesn't tremble, so Gunnar knows his brother really is dead. Then he refuses to tell Atli what he wants to know (even though he promised to); and, wrathful, Atli throws him in a pit of snakes.

Naturally upset by the deaths of her brothers, Gudrún decides on revenge. She and Atli are parents to two children, the rather sweetly-named Erp and Eitill. Sweetness is not their fate though: Gudrún kills them, makes their skulls into cups, liquifies their flesh, serves it in the skull-goblets and feeds it to her husband. After Atli has supped she tells him what she has just done. The horrified man takes to his bed without even pausing to punish Gudrún for her crime. Gudrún creeps in later that night and knifes him to death. Then she burns the palace down, wanders in the woods for a while forlorn, and finally drowns herself in the ocean. That is the end.

This is the story Tolkien decided, probably in the early 1930s, to retell in verse. He did so, in Christopher Tolkien's opinion, in part to come up with solutions to the various problems, the narrative chicanes and oddities of motivation the original presents the reader, amongst which are: why does Sigurd leave after winning Brynhild the first time? Why not marry her straight away? Why, since she is already betrothed to Sigurd, does Brynhild agree to marry Gunnar? Sure, he breaches the wall of fire (it was actually Sigurd in his likeness, though Brynhild does not know that) but not only does she not want to marry him, she has already sworn herself to somebody else. After he wins Brynhild why does Gunnar decide to kill Sigurd? And having done so, why does he let Brynhild immolate herself? And finally, after traveling together to Atli's court, and fighting side by side against Hunnish treachery, why does Gunnar demand the heart of his beloved brother Högni? *The Legend of Sigurd and Gudrún* offers answers to most of these questions, although sometimes a little obscurely. In part this is a function of the poem's extreme terseness. Events are compressed, elided or even omitted altogether, such that going through *Sigurd and Gudrún* feels like reading the epitome of a longer poem.

The main lacuna in the Volsung story is accidental. The earliest version of the tale is today preserved in a document called the *Codex Regius*, now kept in Copenhagen. It is in two parts: after the first thirty-two leaves, or pages, a passage has been lost, perhaps eight pages long. Tolkien thought these eight pages, containing a significant chunk of 'the Long Lay of Sigurd' had been deliberately stolen. Without it we have two separate stories. Story A takes the conventional, satisfying form of the hero overcoming the monster and getting the girl: Sigurd slays Fafnir, and wins the beautiful Brynhild. That, we might think, looks like a very serviceable Happily Ever After. But wait, here is Story B: Brynhild will only marry the bravest warrior in the world. She loves Sigurd, who fits that bill. But Sigurd is betrothed to Gudrún; and Brynhild is won instead by Gunnar. The braided wires of these four lovers' destinies go into the black box of the story and come out the other side with Sigurd murdered in his sleep, a grieving Brynhild throwing herself on his funeral pyre, and Gudrún heartbroken.

Now, the big question (the missing section of *Codex Regius*) is how we get from Story A to Story B. But the black box portion of Story B is a problem too. As far as that goes, Tolkien jotted down 'notes . . . on his interpretation of the tangled and contradictory narratives that constitute the tragedy of Sigurd and Brynhild, Gunnar and Gudrún', written, in Christopher Tolkien notes, 'very rapidly in soft pencil, and difficult to read'. Tolkien's sequence of events, rather clearer in his notes than in his actual poem, is: Brynhild finds out about the deception (that it was not Gunnar, but Sigmund-in-the-likeness-of-Gunnar, that won her) and is 'mortally wounded' in her pride; so wounded, indeed, that she decides not only to kill Sigurd, but to 'avenge herself upon Gunnar' for his part in the deception. Accordingly she 'lies terribly against Sigurd and herself', and tells Gunnar that when Sigurd—in Gunnar's form—rode through the flames, he had sex with her. This, not being part of the deal, outrages Gunnar. He has Sigurd killed; but once this is accomplished Brynhild comes out with the truth, so revealing that Gunnar has unjustly slain his sword-brother and widowed his sister. It all makes sense, although according to a rather stiffly limitedly consecutive logic of human motivation. But it does not address the bigger problem of how Brynhild is still behind the wall of flame waiting to be claimed *after* Sigurd has already ridden the wall of flame and claimed her *in his own name*. How, in other words, do we get from Story A to Story B? How can Sigurd, having once sworn himself to Brynhild, then go on to swear himself to Gudrún?

There are two possible answers to this question. One of them is simple and psychologically interesting. The other is implausible, awkward and much less interesting, psychologically speaking; but because it preserves a sense of Sigurd's 'noble heroism' it is the one Morris, Wagner and Tolkien follow. This second explanation has already been mentioned: Sigurd unwittingly drinks a magic potion that makes him forget his first love. But it does not have to be that way. There is a much simpler and more satisfying explanation available to us. Why does Sigurd act this way? Because *especially where matters of love and sexual desire are concerned, men's oaths are not necessarily to be trusted.* Now this solution to the 'riddle' has the advantage not only of being—to put it simply—true as far as the world-at-large is concerned. It also turns Sigurd from a type into a character. It stops him being an improbable epitome of manly virtue, and presents him instead as genuine, resonant and three-dimensional—shifts him from being a static icon from myth. Turns him, in other words, from an antique statue into a modern individual.

But I know of no version of the story that spins things this way. Our investment in Sigurd's dull Heroic Nobleness and absolutely unimpeachable honour is, perhaps, too profound. And something of the same marionette-like logic rusts Tolkien's Brynhild too: her only motivation her own wounded pride, her method dependent upon an assumption of absolute truthfulness.

This is where the comparison with *Hamlet* comes in. The story that Shakespeare worked into his celebrated play is an ancient one, and found in many cultures. In the sources that Shakespeare used it is fairly straightforward. Hamlet is the king's son. His father is killed by his uncle in a palace *putsch*. There is nothing secret about this palace revolution—it is an open *coup d'état*. To consolidate his power the usurper executes key figures of the old guard. Hamlet, as the old king's son and heir, is evidently at danger of death, and to avoid this he lights on a clever plan. He pretends insanity, hoping that his uncle will consider him harmlessly beneath contempt as a madman. The ruse works, and Hamlet is able, under the disguise of madness, to kill his father's murderer.

Now what is crucial here is the way Shakespeare *adapts* this story. In his version Hamlet is still the son of a royal father killed by his uncle in a palace *putsch*. But the *coup d'état* is secret; Claudius murders Old Hamlet in his garden and everyone thinks the old king died of natural causes in his sleep. Claudius's succession to the throne is regarded as legitimate. Moreover, one of the first things Claudius does in Shakespeare's play is announce to the whole court that young Hamlet is next in line to the throne, effectively adopting him as his son. So rather than facing his imminent death, Hamlet finds himself royal heir and a prince of the realm. He has no need to protect his life by pretending to be mad.

He pretends to be mad anyway.

Why? In Shakespeare's play it is hard to say exactly; or more precisely it is hard to say why in the terms of the play's *sources*, because those sources treat characters as logical and rational agents. If characters in those sorts of stories do a certain thing or act in a certain way, there must be a straightforward reason why. Shakespeare's Hamlet is a much more profound piece of characterisation. The play precisely requires us to try and puzzle out *why* Hamlet acts the way he does. To what extent is his madness play-acting, and how far has grief forced an actual irrationality to the surface in his behaviour? Shakespeare understood what Freud, centuries later, was to build a career elaborating: that often our motives are hidden even from ourselves; that our subjectivity is made up as much of the irrational as the rational (of the unconscious as the conscious). That, moreover, this is particularly true with respect to traumatic events such as bereavement; and it is equally so with regard to repressed and taboo desires. Even Hamlet does not really understand why he gets so very furious with his mother in her bedroom. He rationalises his rage as a commitment to public chastity, especially for the over-forties, but that is not the *real* reason he gets so murderously het-up. Where sex is concerned it can be hard for us to untangle our motives.

Shakespeare turns Hamlet from a scheming two-dimensional character into an immensely complex, nuanced three-dimensional individual. Indeed, Shakespeare's Hamlet is one of the first properly modern figures in world literature. This, indeed, is in large part why this play enjoys the titanic reputation it does. Medieval literature has its fair share of colourful and engaging characters (and much more than a fair share of blank ciphers and cardboard heroes); but there is no one in it like Hamlet; and *we* are much more like Hamlet than we are like Chaucer's knight.

How does this relate to Tolkien? *Sigurd and Gudrún* is an exercise in conscious archaism not just in subject matter, and not just in poetic form and idiom. It treats its characters in flat, archaic ways. It did not have to do so. What makes *The Lord of the Rings* much more than an exercise in reheating old mythology under an invented nomenclature and geography is the way its main conceit parses a much more interesting and much more contemporary dilemma. Of course some of Tolkien's players are as brightly coloured and as stiffly static as any from the *Edda*—Aragorn, say; or Elrond. But at the heart of the narrative are three figures that are as modern, in their way, as Hamlet: Frodo, Sam, and above all, Gollum. Frodo is, as a character, acted upon by various forces—his sense of duty, his awareness of a kind of family belatedness, his love of home and his draw to the excitements of otherness; and all these things are written over, in complex ways, by his increasing dependence on the ring. Sam appears to be a more straightforward individual: deeply attached to his home, loyal to his master, yet fascinated by the un-Shire-like glamour of the elves. But out of his three-way internal struggle the story renders a kind of stubbornness of purpose, and heroism, that is all the more effective for being pitched at so ordinary a level. Gollum, as Aldiss noted, is the most interesting of all. His possession of the ring is of longer duration, and his addiction to it more deeply rooted, than any other character we encounter in Tolkien's storytelling (with the possible exception of Sauron himself). Yet Gollum's character has not been flattened or homogenised by his ring possession. In a sense he is a kind of anti-Sam, as stubborn and purposeful (in his way) as the hobbit, devious where Sam is straightforward, wicked where Sam is virtuous. And despite all this his character is as much a mode of apprehending pity as it is part of the ethical binarism of the larger narrative. With Gollum the unimaginable and sustained pressure of evil upon an ordinary soul has resulted in a kind of bizarre eversion, a forcing of what is inside out, such that Gollum's odd little mannerisms, his habit of referring to himself in the third person, his toddler-like verbal tics and evasions, his self-pity and the remnants of his sense of duty and courtesy—all these things enact a kind of excavation of character (in the modern sense) itself.

In other words, what makes *The Lord of the Rings* particularly valuable as fantasy is the way it bridges old Anglo-Saxon fascinations with heroism, doom and catastrophe with modern fascinations with guilt, desire, power, compromise and the hidden springs of psychological life. And although there is nothing so nuanced, or complex in *Sigurd and Gudrún*, it is a revealing text so far as Tolkien's understanding of characterisation is concerned.

* * *

Does Bilbo change during the course of *The Hobbit*? We might say that for Tolkien personality—character, behaviour, subjectivity—is determined by soul. We are not automata, merely performing our programming; for we have 'free will'. But saying so is not to concede, from a traditionalist Catholic point of view like Tolkien's, that human subjectivity is in a state of continual and radical flux. People may change a little, but they do not change much, and in the mass they hardly change at all. 'Free will' is, as it were, a horizontal freedom: we may choose to do good or evil, to live in accordance with our Creator's will or to seek to thwart it. But we do not have the vertical freedom implied by '*Bildungsroman*': to change in any radical sense, since the 'we' entailed in such a change is determined not by brain chemistry, genetics or environment but by an eternal spirit donated by God. We may choose to act in one way or another, but we may not choose to be other than who we are.

The changes to Bilbo's 'character' in *The Hobbit*, in other words, are external. He becomes a little less sedentary, a little less stay-at-home, a little less bourgeois.[3] As a function of this he becomes less timid and less existentially myopic; but these are figured not as alterations to his subjectivity so much as the uncovering of more heroic values that were always present. Adventures are more than diverting ways of passing the time; they are opportunities for us to test ourselves, to bring out aspects of ourselves that have been hidden.

Another way of saying this would be to suggest that there is an *inertia* in Tolkien's conception of how 'character' works. To say so is not necessarily to denigrate his writerly approach to the question; for too much fluidity and flux in the representation of a character is as distorting as too immovable a rigidity. Moreover, this inertia cuts both ways. We might suggest that an individual who has been traumatised may suffer, but can be healed. For Tolkien, it appears, this is not so. Frodo's experiences carrying the ring through *The Lord of the Rings* mark him in ways that cannot be expunged by a happy ending followed by decades of contented, uneventful living. Even Sam, who only had the ring for a short space of time, is indelibly traumatised by it. The novel suggests only one remedy: that both characters leave Middle-earth altogether, and travel to a magical westward realm. There is another reason, of course, why Tolkien conceives of 'character' in this way; and to discuss it I return, yet again, to the *Exeter Book*. Writing to his son Christopher (8 January 1944), Tolkien copies out three lines of Anglo-Saxon verse:

> Longað þonne þy læs þe   him con leoþa worn,
> oþþe mid hondum con hearpan gretan;
> hafaþ him his gliwes giefe,   þe him god sealed.[4]

He adds, translating the passage:

> From the *Exeter Book*. Less doth yearning trouble him who knoweth many songs, or with his hands can touch the harp: his possession is his gift of 'glee' (= music and/or verse) which God gave him. How these old words smite one out of the dark antiquity! Longað! All down the ages men (of our kind, most awarely) have felt it, not necessarily caused by sorrow, or the hard world, but sharpened by it.[5]

'Longað þe him'; 'this man languishes'; 'longing defined this man'. This is at the heart of Tolkien's sense of character: longing defines us. It is longing that makes us what we are. Not *Bildungsroman*, derived from the German word *Bildung* (meaning 'growth' or 'education') but *Longingsroman* is what Tolkien writes.

10
The Enigma of Genre Fantasy

> The problem with Realism is that it is almost inevitably superficial. But the problem with the metaphorical modes of fiction, Science Fiction, Fantasy, 'magic realism' and the like, is almost that they are *too deep*.
>
> (Pierre Delalande)

I do not intend, in this chapter, to try and generate an itinerary of every author who has been influenced by Tolkien or written a sub-Tolkien Fantasy novel: this book does not have the space to encompass such a survey. Indeed, a lifetime is too short (and eternity barely long enough) for such a task, for post-Tolkien fantasy has proved astonishingly fertile, and most of its texts are very lengthy. Nor do I intend here to attempt a discussion of the various subgenres post-Tolkienian fantasy is sometimes divided into by fans: Heroic Fantasy, Sword and Sorcery, Gritty Fantasy, Urban Fantasy, Weird fiction and the like. Some fans, and some critics too, spend a great deal of time upon such taxonomies. But it seems to me that taxonomy itself is a poor way of apprehending what it is about Fantasy that has made it so successful. Quasi-structuralist attempts to fit the larger body of Fantastic literature into a grid miss the point of the mode—which is, of course, the desire to escape the grid altogether.

I do not say so wholly to dismiss taxonomic studies of the form. Of course, there is pleasure to be had in spotting similarities and parallels between things, and grander totalising pleasure in disposing of a large body of diverse individual texts into a small number of pigeonholes. The pleasure, to put it bluntly, has to do with control; and when it is applied to the world (as Linnaeus did) there is some point to it, for the world, for most human history, has been hostile and even dangerous. But when it is applied to SFF it misses the crucial thing that draws us to these texts in the first place: not the illusion of control (power), but the sense of *transport*. Broadly speaking, this is what is distinctive about the appeal of Fantasy texts to fans of Fantasy. The technical vocabulary of criticism, by talking about 'novums' and 'estrangement' and 'structural fabulation', although they are talking about this thing, do not sound as if they are, which may be a distraction. Closer to the money-shot is the descriptor 'Fantasy' itself: a word which has a spread of meanings, not all of them negative or merely escapist in connotation. Why 'fantasy', then? Or, perhaps it would be better to say: what is behind the desire for fantasy?

Again, speaking very broadly, readers of Fantasy pick up their favourite books because those books give them something missing from the world as it actually is—and missing, too, from artistic representations of the way the world actually is; or 'realism' as it is sometimes called. We might call this thing 'enchantment', a sense of magic. Readers of SF are in search of something similar in their preferred genre: a newness that the actual world lacks, except that it is too easy to imagine that this newness inheres in one or other prop or physical item (a time machine, a ray gun, a spaceship). But this is to reduce SF to gadgets. This is not the right way of thinking about the problem, however, for the world itself has no lack of gadgets—is, indeed, rather over-supplied with gadgets. Better to talk in terms of 'sense of wonder', provided we realise that this in practice is a slightly less rebarbatively awe-inspiring quality than the eighteenth-century 'Sublime'. It might, in fact, be best to think in terms of 'cool' if that did not carry with it the odour of imprecision. Heroic Fantasy, we know, takes as its setting a pre-industrial world, in which some of the conveniences according to modern humanity by machines fall within the purview of magic, whilst others are dispensed with altogether. The former strategy enables escapist fantasy about the empowerment of magical skill; but the latter strategy also enables escapism, by giving the readers access to an earthier, more authentic, more empowered, more physical existence than they have trapped as pale wageslaves by the webs of Civilisation and Its Discontents.

Now, the standard defence of escapism goes something like this: 'what's *wrong* with escapism? Who is it that opposes escape? Jailers!' It's an incomplete logic, although there is a grit of truth in it. If you are a parent, and your teenage child spends eight hours a day upon their bed in heroin-induced lassitude as a strategy of escaping the anomie of modern teenagerdom, you do not need the soul of a jailer to want him, her, to stop. Art is about modes of engagement with the world, not modes of avoiding it.

Escapism is not a very good word, actually, for the positive psychological qualities its defenders want to defend; it is less a question of breaking one's bars and running away (running wither, we might ask?); and more of keeping alive the facility for imaginative *play*, which only a fool would deny is core to any healthy psychological makeup. Kids are good at play, and have an unexamined wisdom about it; adults, sometimes, forget how vital it is. What is wrong with Art that insists too severely on pressing people's faces too insistently against the miseries of actual existence is not that we should not have to confront Darfur or Iraq, poverty or oppression; it is that such art rarely gives us the imaginative wriggle room to think of how things might be improved, or challenged, or even accepted. Imaginative wiggle room, on the other hand, is something SF-Fantasy is very good at.

An art that simply depresses is liable to be an ineffective art because it will tend to disable rather than enable imaginative engagement. Fantasy carries us away. We want it to: that is why we go to it in the first place. As to why we get such pleasure in being carried away (get such pleasure, not to put a finer point on it, by focusing on what the world is missing, on its lack) . . . this is a large question and one with which this study must be largely concerned. But to begin with it is worth dwelling momentarily on this trope of 'carrying away'.

The difference between a metaphor and a simile is a matter of semantic nicety that some people find hard to articulate. This is perhaps because there is not really a difference; the two words are used more or less interchangeably in many contexts. But I like to insist upon a difference for all that: simile, as the word suggests, is a way of talking about something by comparing it to something that is similar: 'Achilles is courageous, like a lion' focuses our attention on the point of likeness. The word *metaphor*, as rhetoricians remind us, means a carrying over, a passage of meaning from one thing to another thing.

This might sound like hairsplitting, but there is a difference here, and it seems to me one that opens a chasm of signification that speaks directly to the desire at the heart of SFF. 'Achilles is a lion' metaphorically carries across from one thing to a completely different thing. Because, crucially, Achilles is *not* a lion—there are a wealth of ways in which Achilles and a lion are different. To say 'Achilles is metaphorically a lion' is in one part to bring out a point of simile (in this one respect—his courage—Achilles is a lion) but it is always, inevitably, to do much more: it is to generate (in Samuel Delany's words) an imaginative surplus, a spectral hybrid of beast–human. This imaginative surplus is what carries us away, and metaphor is its vehicle. That is partly what I mean when I talk about SFF as being in crucial ways a metaphorical literature: one that seeks to represent the world without reproducing it.

'Desire' then is, I am suggesting, at the heart of SFF's appeal; and I am saying something else—I am saying that, whilst desire is also at the heart of the structuralist, systematizing urge, it is a desire radically opposed to the desire we call Fantasy. Fantasy, in a healthful, ludic, rejuvenating way, is precisely about escaping the grid. It is about the imaginative and affective surplus, the overspill. Indeed, I am tempted to say, because this is the case, the desire of Fantasy (let us qualify it a little: of the *best* Fantasy—and without wanting to sound circular, I would suggest that this is in fact by way of identifying what it is about those texts that makes them the best) comprehends the excessive nature of desire itself.

It tells us nothing about the reason so many people fall in love with (the phrase is not hyperbolic) *The Hobbit* and *The Lord of the Rings*, to say that it is 'a portal-quest fantasy'. That is indeed a feature of the text, and one it shares with many other texts; but most of these others texts are not enchanting—we do not fall in love with them) in the way we do with Tolkien. Actually *The Lord of the Rings* is a book precisely about desire, and what is so canny in its delineation of the operation of that desire is the way it dramatises it as simultaneously transporting and isolating; it excavates, we might say, our instinctive understanding that desire is captivating in a wonderful *as well as an enslaving sense*. It is a striking thing, in this respect, that nobody doubts the intense desirability of the ring at the heart of the narrative, even though, in Tolkien's rendering, it is never made explicit what it is the ring actually *does*. It has something to do with power, we are told; and the person who has the ring will be able to wield power—tyrannically—although at the same time the various people who have the ring in the book (Gollum, Frodo, Sam) seem to derive no social or practical empowerment. Indeed, on the contrary: the efficacy of the artefact seems pointedly antisocial: it can make them disappear, it can remove them completely from the social body.

There is a moment early in the first film of Jackson's trilogy where Sauron is shown wielding the ring. He sweeps his arm on the battle-field, and sending scores of warriors flying into the air is a rare lapse of representational sophistication in a film-trilogy otherwise, I would say, sensitive to the point of the text. Certainly, subsequently Jackson abandons such literal-mindedness, and is much better about finding visual analogues for the ring's appeal. Because this is the whole point. The ring does not work in this text as some kind active mcguffin. It is not a *gadget*. Rather the ring *construes desire itself*, and in doing so makes manifests its intense, destructive desirability, precisely *as absence*. It is something not there, a little hollow, a badge of literal invisibility, something associated with the dark in subterranean caverns or the inaccessibility of riverbeds. The ring is lack, and it is part of Tolkien's brilliance to understand so thoroughly that lack is the currency of desire.

Actually, and to digress momentarily, I am not sure this is what Tolkien thought he was doing; I think he *thought* of his ring in terms of lack because he meant the ring to symbolise evil, and for his Boethian/Acquinian theological perspective on the world evil is absence: the world itself, as God, is necessarily good except insofar as it has been eroded or perverted by evil. But that does not alter what I am saying, I think. There are reasons why *The Lord of the Rings* has had the global impact it has, that its myriad imitators have not. Tolkien's novel construes desire (readerly desire) because it understands desire.

Adam Phillips has some interesting things to say about masturbation which, strange as it might seem, are relevant here. Philips starts by quoting Leo Bersani:

> Bersani once said in an interview that the reason most people feel guilty about masturbation is because they fear that masturbation is the truth about sex; that the truth about sex is that we would rather do it on out own, or that, indeed, we are doing it on our

own even when we seem to all intents and purposes to be doing it with other people. The desire that apparently leads us towards other people can lead us away from them. Or we might feel that what we call desire is evoked by details, by signs, by gestures; that we fall for a smile or a tone of voice or a way of walking or a lifestyle, and not exactly for what we have learned to call a whole person; and that this evocation, this stirring of desire, releases us rather more into our own deliriums of fear and longing than into realistic apprehension of the supposed object of desire. There is nothing at once more isolating and oceanic than falling for someone. Lacan formulated the 'objet petit a' to show us that the promise of satisfaction always reminds us of a lack . . . and that this lack, disclosed by our longings, sends a depth charge into our histories.[1]

It would be almost fatuous to note that the ring, in *Lord of the Rings*, is an *objet petit a*; fatuous, really only because it is so extraordinarily obvious that this is what the ring is. But it is another phrase from that little passage that leaps out at me in the context of understanding the desire behind SF and Fantasy: 'there is nothing at once more isolating and oceanic than falling for someone'. That is right, I think, as an account of what it is like to fall in love with someone. More than that, though, those two words, 'isolating and oceanic', seem to me wonderfully apt as a way of approaching how the best fantasy wins us.

The core of Tolkien's book, then, is its apprehension, through its concrete realisation, its worldbuilding and backhistory and characterisation and so on, of the radical undesirability of desire; or the desirability of the undesirable. The point is that the phrasal superposition of desire and undesired only looks like a paradox. Actually it is an articulation of something much more significant. Philips again:

Anna Freud once said that in your dreams you can have your eggs cooked any way you want them, but you can't eat them. The implication is clear: magic is satisfying but reality is nourishing . . . Indeed, we could reverse Anna Freud's formulation and say that when it comes to sexuality it is the fact that you can't eat the eggs that makes them so satisfying. The fact that, as Freud remarked, desire is always in excess of the object's capacity to satisfy it is the point not the problem; it is the tribute the solitary desiring individual pays to reality. This is a problem only if you are a literalist rather than the ironist of your own desire. It's not that reality is disappointing, it's that desire is excessive. It's not that we lack things, it's just that there are things we want.

In this passage I am tempted to replace 'dreams' with 'Fantasies', and to extend the observation to those novelistic excrescences of fantasy life booksellers label under that term. And I am tempted to suggest that 'sex', here, connects with the fundamentally libidinous energies that flow through our love for these narratives.

There is one further point I want to make, to do with 'escape'. A reason why people look down upon Fantasy is that they see it as evading moral and social responsibilities more realist modes of art press upon their readers. If a contemporary of Dickens read about the extreme poverty of Jo the Crossing Sweeper, he or she was being confronted with an emotionally engaging example of a real social phenomenon. Dickens' humour and sentimentality were both designed to engage his readers in the problems of the world. We do not read about the (it seems weird even putting it in these terms, but you see what I mean) *extreme poverty* of Gollum in the same way. Gollum is extremely poor, in a material sense; I could believe that Smaug is a victim of Dragonism, his evident intelligence and many talents overlooked by those who are too prejudiced to see beyond the scales; I daresay many of the rank and file soldiers in the orc army come from broken homes, and had little opportunity for advancement except joining the military. But it would be ludicrous to read the books this way, because they frame their ideological concerns not linearly but metaphorically.

This, however, is, in the popular idiom, a feature, not a bug. One reason Tolkien's imaginary realm has proved so successful is precisely its structural non-specificity. What I mean is: Tolkien treats material that has deep roots in, and deep appeal to, various cultural traditions; but he does so in a way—as fictionalised worldbuilding rather than denominated myth—that drains away much of the poisonous nationalist, racist and belligerent associations those traditions have accumulated over the centuries. A thumbnail history would go like this: in the late nineteenth and early twentieth centuries, Wagner's *Ring* melodramas spoke to a great many people about a particular northern-European cultural identity; about a group of linked, potent emotional attachments to history, landscape, to the numinous and the divine, to matters of heroism and everyday life. I am trying not to sound sneery as I say this (I mean melodrama in the strict sense of the word), because these things did, and do, matter intensely and genuinely to many people. But there is a reason, a room-filling elephant of a reason, why *Der Ring des Nibelungen* no longer has this general resonance. It is because the cultural reservoir from which it draws much of its power also supplied cultural capital to the worst regime ever to take charge in Germany, and therefore lubricated the most catastrophically destructive war ever to be waged in the world. In saying this I am not, of course, blaming Wagner for the Nazis. Indeed, the endless debates about Wagner's own ideological 'purity' ('was Wagner an anti-semite?' Short answer: yes. Long answer: yes, *like just about every other gentile in nineteenth century Europe*) seem to me to miss the point. The restless churning through this question happens because we are desperate to acquit Wagner so that we can enjoy his music with a clean conscience. We ask the question, get the uncomfortable answer, and ask it again. In our guts resides the queasy comprehension that Wagner *can not* be acquitted. Politics can not be neatly separated out from the *Ring* cycle, leaving only a washed-and-scrubbed sequence of pretty orchestral tone poems behind. I love the *Ring* cycle, and listen to it regularly; but I would never try to deny that it is political all the way through, down to its very marrow. It is, to be precise, about the notion that history and myth are in some sense the same thing—a very dangerous notion indeed.

Tolkien's story is not the same as the *Ring* cycle; his 'ring' (as he crossly reminded correspondents) not the same as Alberich's ring. But a considerable amount of the heft and force of *Lord of the Rings* derives from the way Tolkien draws on the same broader cultural, mythic, northern-European heritage. What saves *Lord of the Rings* is that it is not about Germany, or about England; or to be more precise, that it is about England and Germany only secondarily, in an eloquently oblique (a cynic might say: in a *plausibly deniable*) manner. Tolkien found a way of articulating the same deep-rooted cultural concerns in a way that avoids being poisoned by the cultural specificity of European Fascism. I offer these thoughts not as a value judgement of his fiction, so much as an explanation for why *Lord of the Rings* has done so extraordinarily well—resonated so powerfully with so many people—in the postwar period. It rushed in to fill the gap that more culturally specific art had supplied before that kind of art was discredited by the 1940s.

This is part of the appeal, but also of the strength, of Fantasy as a modern phenomenon. We prefer stories of Marvel superheroes to actual stories of 'crime fighters' (policemen, soldiers and so on) because we have lost faith in the latter, or more precisely lost faith that the latter can ever exhibit the kind of perfect heroism we want our stories to articulate. Hogwarts, being fictional, can apprehend something very important—school—without being tangled in the messy specificity of actual real-world schooling. A sequence of novels set in Eton would be noisome; although that is, in effect, what Rowling has written. The twentieth century has cured us of our attachment to a certain kind of ideology-text; and the cure we have chosen is: worldbuilt fiction. I could add lots of other examples, from West Wing to Westeros. But I have probably said enough.

* * *

I said at the beginning of this chapter that I intended to dodge what would be the onerous duty of listing all the figures who have written novels in the Tolkienian mode. But I do want to add, as a pendant, an observation about one writer of post-Tolkien fantasy, because she happens to be so very good—and because a *riddle* relevant to our purposes here is fashioned in her greatest novel. I am talking about Ursula Le Guin.

Le Guin's *Earthsea* series, beginning with *The Wizard of Earthsea* (1968) is not only amongst the finest examples of post-Tolkien fantasy, it is explicitly and directly influenced by Tolkien himself. Le Guin creates a world of myriad islands located in a huge, perhaps endless, ocean. Each island has, in addition to its regular inhabitants, a resident wizard, and these individuals (all male) are trained at a wizard university in the central island of Roke.

The Wizard of Earthsea tells of the early life of Earthsea's greatest wizard, Ged; and the story is continued in Le Guin's several sequels, *The Tombs of Atuan* (1972), *The Farthest Shore* (1974), *Tehanu* (1990) and *The Other Wind* (2002). One of the things Le Guin borrows from Tolkien is his nominalism—which is to say, his belief that the world is 'named' into existence, and that words and languages therefore have profound power. In Le Guin's books, this is manifested by the convention that, where people from various cultures and various geographical locations speak various languages, there is underlying everything a 'true speech' that directly names reality. Magic is performed by invoking objects in this ur-language. To be more precise, the distinction is made early on in *The Wizard of Earthsea* between two kinds of magic, 'true magic' and 'illusion'. The latter is a trick easily played, but the object conjured has the appearance but not the substance of reality. 'Why do wizards get hungry then?' one character asks Ged. 'When it comes to suppertime at sea, why not say, *Meat-pie* and the meat-pie appears and you eat it?' 'Well', Ged replies: 'we could do so. But we don't much wish to eat our words, as they say. Meat-pie is only a word after all . . . we can make it odorous, and savorous, and even filling, but it remains a word. If fools the stomach and gives no strength to the hungry man.'[2] What is called in the book 'true magic', however, is the power to step outside the simulacra of 'only words'. To know an object's *true* name is to have actual power over it. Wizards, accordingly, frame their charms in the Old Speech.

The riddle of Earthsea has to do with this nominalist belief in the apprehending power of language. What (the riddle says) is Earthsea? We must look to the Old Speech, which Le Guin's Ged starts to learn first at the Wizard University. The novel vouchsafes us a few examples of the true tongue. We discover, for instance, that the true word for 'rock' is *tolk*—this refers to 'the dry land on which men live'. The word for 'sea' in the true speech, on the other hand, is *inien*. So the answer to the riddle can be found, neatly enough, by translating it into Le Guin's true-tongue. What is Earth-sea? It is *tolk-inien*. The riddle is: what is Earthsea? Le Guin is far from the only writer of Fantasy who acknowledges that her creations are *Tolkinien*, of course.

11
. . . And Back Again?

C. S. Lewis opens his study of the Psalms by declaring his relative incompetence for the task.

> It often happens that two schoolboys can solve difficulties in their work for one another better than the master can. When you took the problem to a master, as we all remember, he was very likely to explain what you understood already, to add a great deal of information which you didn't want, and say nothing at all about the thing that was puzzling you. I have watched this from both sides of the net; for when, as a teacher myself, I have tried to answer questions brought me by pupils, I have sometimes, after a minute, seen that expression settle down on their faces that assured me that they were suffering exactly the same frustration which I had suffered from my teachers. The fellow-pupil can help more than the master because he knows less. The difficulty we want him to explain is one he has recently met. The expert met it so long ago he has forgotten. He sees the whole subject, by now, in a different light that he cannot conceive what is really troubling the pupil; he sees a dozen other difficulties which ought to be troubling him but aren't.
>
> (C. S. Lewis, *Reflections on the Psalms* (Houghton Mifflin 1958), 1)

'The fellow-pupil can help more than the master because he knows less' looks like a riddling kind of observation, but in fact it touches on something important about riddles. In some of the riddles of *The Hobbit* we are given the answer; but others (what *is* a burrahobbit? What *does* Good Morning mean?) we are not. But having the answer is less important than engaging with the process of thinking them through.

In the fourth chapter of the present study I took up John Rateliff's suggestion that, as far as the enigmata that Gollum and Bilbo swap between them, 'these riddles predate the book'.[1] It is possible to imagine Tolkien (of course this is mere speculation) setting out at some point in the 30s to compose nine riddles, some adapted from existing sources, some invented from whole cloth, by way of constructing an acrostic meta-riddle to which the answer is, precisely, a famous riddle contest between a god and a dwarf, the *Alvíssmál*. If Tolkien engaged in this riddling game, he did not include the answer in *The Hobbit* itself. But perhaps he felt he did not need to.

To pick up the thread from that fourth chapter: what might have drawn Tolkien to the *Alvíssmál*? It is, obviously, a riddle-contest; and there is something nicely symmetrical in coding a riddle contest so that the riddles in it make reference to another riddle contest.[2] But I wonder if there is something more. Recall that the story of the *Alvíssmál* is that the dwarf Alvíss has come to Thor's house claiming that he was promised the god's daughter in marriage. Thor tells the dwarf he may have the girl if he can answer all of the god's riddles. This Alvíss does, drawing on a genuinely impressive knowledge-base—not for nothing does his name mean 'all-wise'. But he has been tricked; like Gandalf with the trolls, Thor has distracted him long enough for the sun to come up and petrify him.

Why might Tolkien be drawn to this particular riddle contest? Why might he have repurposed his nine riddles for *The Hobbit*? What is at stake in the contest between Gollum and Bilbo is not a divine marriage, but a plain gold band with magical properties. In Chapter 7 I explored the similarities between this (malign) gold ring and the example of the (good) wedding band, also magical in a religiously sacramental sense. Gollum, like Alvíss, can answer all the riddles Bilbo throws at him; save only the last one. But his knowledge does not save him.

Alvíss the dwarf is clever, but—despite his name—he is not *wise*. Indeed, his proud delight in his own cleverness and knowledge prevent him from seeing that he is being tricked. This in turn is an important distinction in Tolkien's work. Saruman is very clever, and very knowledgeable, but he is not wise. Gandalf knows less, and is sometimes baffled, but he possesses wisdom. Tolkien understands that it is better to be wise than clever. In this he is true to his religious beliefs; for one of the valences of Christ's instruction that we 'become as little children' (Matthew 18:3) is the greatness of untutored faith over mere adult cleverness. And like C. S. Lewis's schoolchildren, it is better for us to turn out hearts to the mysteries of life together than passively to take on board the intellectual knowledge of adults. *The Hobbit* is a book that lives in the heart before it exists in the head, howsoever ingeniously that head—in this case, mine—addresses the riddle: *what is a hobbit?*

* * *

What, then, is the solution? What is the answer to the riddle of *The Hobbit?* The intention, in framing the question this way, is not intend to suggest that there could be only one answer, only one way of decoding this beautifully entertaining, suggestive, playful novel. It is, rather, a matter of wondering to what extent it is possible to think of the novel *as* a riddle. It seems to present a straightforward adventure story; but the meat of the whole is much more debatable.

Bilbo the hobbit is a respectable, solid, middle-class fellow; familiarly English, and indeed (in the author's own words) the sort of man who belongs to a community that is 'more or less a Warwickshire village of about the period of the Diamond Jubilee'. The hobbit, in other words, has the background and values of Tolkien himself, and the stature of Tolkien's own youth—I mean, Bilbo, as an adult, is about as tall as Tolkien himself was as a child on the verge of adolescence. But Bilbo is more than this. He is pitched out of his comfortable, parochial hole, and forced to travel to a far country to fight a war. Something similar happened to Tolkien himself. John Garth's study of Tolkien's own experiences in World War One is cautiously suggestive:

> It would be misleading to suggest that *The Hobbit* is Tolkien's wartime experience in disguise; yet it is easy to see how some of his memories must have invigorated this take of an ennobling rite of passage past the fearful jaws of death. The middle-class hero is thrown in with proud but stolid companions . . . the company approaches the end of their quest across a desolation, a once green land with now 'neither bush nor tree, and only broken and blackened stumps to speak of ones long vanished.' Scenes of sudden, violent ruin

ensue . . . we visit the camps of the sick and wounded and listen to wranglings over matters of command and strategy.[3]

It does not hazard anything too revolutionary to suggest that a 'hobbit' is, in a sense, a bit of Tolkien's own youth—of his own home. What about the word, 'hobbit'? Tolkien provides one etymology for it in the appendices with which *The Lord of the Rings* concludes:

> Hobbit is an invention. In the Westron the word used, when this people was referred to at all, was *banakil* 'halfling'. But at this date the folk of the shire and of Bree used the word *kuduk*, which was not found elsewhere. Meriadoc, however, actually records that the King of Rohan used the word *kûd-dûkan* 'hole-dweller'. Since, as has been noted, the Hobbits had once spoken a language closely related to that of the Rohirrim, it seems likely that *kuduk* was a worn-down form of *kûd-dûkan*. The latter I have translated, for reasons explained, by *holbytla*; and *hobbit* provides a word that might be a worn-down form of *holbylta* [i.e. 'hole builder'] if that name had occurred in our own ancient language.[4]

Tom Shippey discusses this invented etymology and suggests a different one:

> *Hol*, of course, means hole. A 'bottle', even now in some English place-names, means a dwelling, and Old English *bytlian* means to dwell, to live in. Holbytla then, = 'hole-dweller, hole-liver'. 'In a hole in the ground there lived a hole-liver.' What could be more obvious than that?[5]

So, 'hole-builder' and 'hole-dweller' are two possible cod-etymological roots for the word hobbit. I want to suggest a third.

Tolkien considered himself wholly English, but he was well aware that he bore a German surname. He knew too what his name meant— I mean, the semantic content of the elements of his name. The 'tol' part of 'Tolkien' means 'foolish, stupid, rash' (*Tölpel* is modern German for 'fool'). The 'kien' part is a version of the German word *Kühn* which means 'brave' or 'bold'. Indeed, Tolkien himself played on the meaning of his own name: he wrote a character called 'John Jethro Rashbold', a version of Tolkien himself, into his 'The Notion

Club Papers' (published posthumously in *Sauron Defeated*). 'Rashbold'
is one way of articulating the—to Tolkien, pleasing—oxymoron of his
surname. Another might be 'Dull-keen', which has the advantage of
retaining much of the sound of the original. 'Dull', another linguistic
descendent from the Old High German *tol*, 'foolish', originally meant
'foolish' or 'stupid', and later came to be applied to edges and blades,
meaning blunt. 'Keen' is, in a way, more interesting. Originally this
word meant 'sharp', as in sharp-witted, clever, skilled—and of course
it still means *literally* sharp, having a sharp edge, for we still talk of
a 'keen blade', just as Chaucer talked of 'a knyfe as a rasour kene' in
1385. But 'keen' also means eager, bold, brave. Indeed, the OED thinks
the latter 'sharp' meaning precedes the 'brave' one ('this ON sense
['sharp'] is the original one, the connecting link with the other ['bold,
brave'] being the idea of "skilled in war" "expert in battle".')
    Foolish-sharp. Dull-keen. Tolkien. In Old Norse (a language in
which Tolkien was, of course, expert) the word for 'sharp' or 'keen'
is: *bitr*. The modern English word 'bitter' retains a spectral sense of
this; for something is bitter, originally—like a bitter wind, or a bitterly
cold morning—because it *bites*; because it is sharp, because it is *keen*.[6]
Similarly the Old English *bîtan* means 'biting, cutting, sharp'. *Hob*, on
the other hand, means originally 'rustic', 'homely', 'clownish'. Spenser
calls the simple-minded rustic peasant in his pastoral poem *The
Shepheard's Calender* (1579) 'Hobinall' with this meaning in mind; and
clumsy, awkward, absurd fellows were called 'hobbledehoys' well into
the nineteenth century. The dullness of the 'hob' is of a rural, homely
sort; but it is a dullness for all that. And it would be as oxymoronic as
linking 'dull' and 'keen' to put the two forms together into: *hob-bitr*.
    It seems to me that this particular riddling answer ('what is a hob-
bit?' 'he is dull-keen'—that is, 'he is Tolkien') accords with the larger
logic of the tale. We connect to the story through the ordinariness
of Bilbo; and Bilbo's experiences are Tolkienian. More, this manner
of etymological decoding, the reading through of modern words and
names to get at their aboriginal significances, was meat and drink to
Tolkien. To ask 'what is a hobbit?' is to ask both 'what does the word
hobbit mean?' and to ask 'what is the hobbit "about"? What does it
signify in the largest sense?' The answer to both questions is: *hob-bitr*
is cognate with *Tol-kien*.

* * *

Here is a related speculation. Amongst other things, hobbits are humpty-dumpty. I do not mean that they are eggs (although, to go right back to the beginning of this book: 'a box without hinges key or lid / yet golden treasure inside is hid' describes Bilbo pretty well, provided only we read the 'treasure' not as actually descriptive of yolk but metaphorically descriptive of the courage and endurance our hero discovers locked away within himself). No, I mean an earlier meaning of the term: for, to quote the *OED* again, a 'humpty-dumpty' is 'a short, dumpy person'; and means, as an adjective, 'short and fat'. Nowadays 'humpty dumpty' is most likely to make us think of the famous nursery rhyme; but as we have been exploring in this book, nursery rhymes are very often riddles. Indeed, to quote from Iona and Peter Opie's *Oxford Dictionary of Nursery Rhymes*, the very familiarity of this verse tends to occlude it.

> Humpty Dumpty sat on a wall,
> Humpty Dumpty had a great fall.
> All the king's horses,
> And all the king's men,
> Couldn't put Humpty together again.

'Humpty Dumpty has become so popular a nursery figure and is pictured so frequently that few people today think of the verse as containing a riddle.' Of course it does: it is just that the solution—'egg'—is, as the Opies note, 'known to everyone'.[7] Alternate answers to the riddle have been proposed: Richard III is one, on account of his hump-back and his defeat at the Battle of Bosworth. Another popular answer is a large cannon, allegedly so-called, used during the English Civil War. In the spirit of Tolkien's own *Lord of the Rings* appendices I would like to suggest another solution to this familiar riddle, and it goes like this: etymologically 'humpty' is distantly related, via the forms 'Humphrey' and 'Humbert', to 'hobbity'. Describing somebody as 'hombetty' or 'hobbety' was to call them short and stout; and the early medieval Romance *Ringe* describes its hero as 'ane hubbity-duppety fellowe yclepit Fraodo, þat wiþ greete heorte did þi Ringe of powre destrowe'.[8]

* * *

At the end of the novel, Balin reports that the new prosperity at Laketown means 'they are making songs which say the rivers run with gold'. 'Rivers run with gold' is a riddle to which the answer is: 'sunset', when the setting sun turns the waterways golden with its light. And sunset is the appropriate note on which to end any novel, just as dawn (we recall the first meeting in *The Hobbit* between its titular hero and Gandalf: '"Good morning!" said Bilbo') is the appropriate note on which to begin one. Indeed, it is worth going back for a moment to the little-noticed riddle with which *The Hobbit* opens:

> 'Good morning!' said Bilbo, and he meant it. . . .
>
> 'What do you mean?' [Gandalf] said. 'Do you wish me a good morning, or mean that it is a good morning whether I want it or not, or that you feel good this morning, or that it is a morning to be good on?'

Bilbo's answer ('all of them at once!') is not really a very satisfactory answer to what is, in fact, a rather profound question. How do our words mean? How—for instance—do those strings of words, bound between boards, that we call books manage to generate specific reactions, images and emotions in the minds of readers? Gandalf suggests four ways of understanding words—his example is 'good morning', but his approach can be expanded to include any and all verbal communications. He suggests that we can interpret words intersubjectively, descriptively, personally or ethically. The first case is subjunctive, in the sense that when I say something I am expressing an unfulfilled wish or condition about your state of being. The second and third are indicative, descriptions either of outer reality or inner mood. The fourth is the least idiomatic of all. To greet somebody with 'good morning' and thereby to mean 'I wish you to take the opportunity of *this* morning to do good, not evil, in the world' would be a strange way of proceeding. Which is to say, addressing somebody as 'good morning' is not usually a riddle, and even if we take it as one it is poorly answered by saying 'Intersubjective! Descriptive! Personal! Ethical!' But all these things apply to the novel. The novel (the novel called *The Hobbit* for example) establishes a specific relationship with its reader—indeed the narrator of *The Hobbit* actually addresses the reader directly at various places in the text. The novel describes the world through which its character move, and the state of minds of those characters themselves. And most importantly of all, for Tolkien and writers like him, novels have a moral imperative. It is the business of novels to make the world better, not worse; to give people paradigms for good behaviour not wicked. To show that even ordinary people can, if they persevere and tap their reservoirs of bravery and duty, prevail against crushing circumstances. That they can be heroes.

The Old English for Good Morning would be *Gód Morwe* (Chaucer's Miller says brightly 'Hayl, maister Nicholay! Good Morwe!'); or else *godne dæie* ('good day'). Indeed, the word 'morn' is the occasion for one of those interesting mini-essays with which the *OED* is so well supplied. The OE is 'morgen'; the ON 'myrginn'.

> The affinities outside Teut. are doubtful. Some refer the word to the pre-Teut. root **merk-* to be dark; but the absence of consonant-ablaut, as well as the inappropriateness of the sense, seems to render this view less probable than the alternative hypothesis that the root is **mergh-*, represented by the Lith. *mirgu*, to twinkle, *margas* parti-coloured. (OED 9:1086)

Also relevant is the entry on 'Morrow', a word (now archaic) that comes via the ME 'morwe' or 'moru', both shortened forms of *morwen*, 'the morn'. Morning as 'the time of darkness', in the sense that it is the time when darkness dwindles, 'darkloss', does not seem so farfetched to me. But like the anonymous *OED* etymologist, I am rather struck as the morning as twinkletime, howsoever twee that makes me. And perhaps there is a deeper riddle here. It looks counterintuitive to think of 'morning' as *the time of dwindling*, because we think of dawn as the opposite of this: the time when the sunlight grows stronger, and the day begins. But in a larger sense we are all always dwindling, and time is chasing away. The strong streak of plangent beauty that runs through both *The Hobbit* and (especially) *The Lord of the Rings* has to do the inevitable passing away of the old times. It is this above all that makes both novels *Losingsromans*. Even the immortal elves diminish, and go into the west; mortals fade and die, ages pass, and whole ways of life trace out an elegiac diminuendo. It was Tolkien's sense of himself as untimely, as born into an inhospitable modernity of machines, haste and noise, that informed his acute sense of both the poignancy and the beauty of this sense of dwindling. It is simultaneously dull *and* keen, both an infuriating stubbornness in the grain of existence (*hob*) and something that sharply pierces through mere appearance to reveal a keenly shining truth beyond the veil of life (*bitr*). It gives his novels a plangency that raise them far above the usual Fantasy fare, and it—Tolkien's unique vision, his sense of himself as both a mortal man, doomed to die, and a spirit promised hidden, mysterious glory—addresses, in the most profound sense, the riddle that is *The Hobbit*.

Notes

Introduction

1. I can think of almost no exceptions to this convention, actually—I mean, crime novels that do not include the solution to their own riddle—except amongst the postmodern experimentalists of novel writing. For example, there is Roberto Bolaño's masterful *2666* (2004); a profound meditation upon crime and mystery that deliberately withholds the satisfactions of solution and closure.
2. F. E. Hardy, *The Later Years of Thomas Hardy, 1892–1928* (1930), 54. Jules Renard's *Journal* for 1906 contains a similar, though more exasperated, reaction to the notion that the universe is a riddle: 'our dream dashes itself against the great mystery like a wasp against a window pane. Less merciful than man, God never opens the window'; ('Notre rêve se heurte au mystère comme la guêpe à la vitre. Moins pitoyable que l'homme, *Dieu* n'ouvre jamais la croisée'; Léon Guichard and Gilbert Sigaux (eds), *Jules Renard, Journal 1887–1910* (Paris: Gallimard 1982), 1067).
3. Tom Shippey, *The Road to Middle Earth: How J. R. R. Tolkien Created A New Mythology* (2nd edition; London: HarperCollins 1992), xv. Ellipses in original. Shippey goes on to, as it were, 'solve' the riddle of Tolkien's polite expression of thanks and admiration: 'the Professor's letter had invisible italics in it, which I now supply. "I am in agreement with *nearly* all that you say, and I only regret that I have not the time to talk more about your paper: especially about design as it appears *or may be found* in a large *finished* work, and the *actual* events or experiences as seen or felt by the *waking* mind *in the course of actual composition*".' One advantage of the politeness-language of Old Western Man is that it enables the speaker to express a genuine ambiguity, neither falsely praising nor discourteously dispraising, in a way that is creatively riddling rather than hypocritically dissembling.
4. W. P. Ker, *The Dark Ages* (Oxford 1904), 64–5.
5. 'I thought of you when some Kipling surfaced at Christmas dinner—"The Egg Shell". My aunt recited it, "a nice piece of nonsense," only for my ex-Naval dad to point out that it wasn't nonsense at all, but a resonant description of naval warfare in WW1, the Whitehead being a torpedo. I found it interesting how one person's metaphor, or nonsense, could be another's highly specific depiction.' Roger Peppe, private correspondence.
6. Paul O'Prey (ed.), *Robert Graves: Selected Poems* (London: Penguin 1986), 154.
7. Humphrey Carpenter (ed.), *The Letters of J. R. R. Tolkien* (London: HarperCollins 1995), 353. Tolkien attended the lectures Graves gave during his stint as Oxford Professor of Poetry in 1964, finding them 'ludicrously bad'.

8. The omitted stanzas and other variants are recorded in Alan Jacobs (ed.), *Auden: For the Time Being: A Christmas Oratorio* (Princeton: Princeton University Press 2013).
9. Tolkien, *The Lord of the Rings* (1954–55; 1 Vol. edition; London: HarperCollins 2012), 11.
10. It was a dislike he repeated in several places, although sometimes in more qualified form. In a letter to Milton Waldman (probably written in 1951) he wrote 'I dislike Allegory—the conscious and intentional allegory—yet any attempt to explain the purport of myth or fairytale must use allegorical language.' An earlier letter to Stanley Unwin (31 July 1947), responding to Stanley's son Rayner's report on the first book of *The Lord of the Rings*, tempered anxiety that the book not be treated as an allegory—'do not let Rayner suspect "Allegory" . . . the actors are individuals'—with a very general concession: 'of course, Allegory and Story converge, meeting somewhere in Truth. So that the only perfectly consistent allegory is real life' (Carpenter, *Letters*, 145, 121).
11. Søren Kierkegaard, *Philosophical Fragments or A Fragment of Philosophy* (trans. David F. Swenson; Princeton: Princeton University Press 1962), 46.
12. Patrick J. Murphy, *Unriddling the Exeter Riddles* (Philadelphia: Pennsylvania University Press 2011), 7.

1   The Anglo-Saxon Riddleworld

1. S. A. J. Bradley, *Anglo-Saxon Poetry* (London: Dent, Everyman 1982), 367–8.
2. *The Elder Edda: A Selection* (trans. Paul B. Taylor and W. H. Auden; Introduction by Peter H. Salus and Paul B. Taylor; London: Faber and Faber 1969), 20, 22. The volume's dedication is: 'for J. R. R. Tolkien'.
3. Carolyne Larrington, *A Store of Common Sense: Gnomic Theme and Style in Old Icelandic and Old English Wisdom Poetry* (Oxford: Clarendon Press 1993), 86.
4. Sigmund Freud, *The Future of an Illusion* (trans. W. D. Robson-Scott; London: Hogarth Press 1927), 16.
5. Bruce Mitchell and Fred C. Robinson, *A Guide to Old English* (1986); quoted in John M. Hill, *The Anglo-Saxon Warrior Ethic: Reconstructing Lordship in Early English Literature* (Gainesville: University of Florida Press 2000), 8.
6. The translation is by Gavin Bone, *Anglo-Saxon Poetry* (Oxford 1943).
7. W. P. Ker, *The Dark Ages* (Oxford 1904), 44.
8. Humphrey Carpenter (ed.), *The Letters of J. R. R. Tolkien* (1985; London: HarperCollins 1995), 172.
9. Della Hook's *Trees in Anglo-Saxon England: Literature, Lore and Landscape* (Woodbridge: Boydell and Brewer 2010) exhaustively explores the many ways trees figured 'life, death and rebirth' in Anglo-Saxon culture.
10. 'Ents had interested Tolkien since he first wrote on Roman roads in 1924 and identified them with the orþanc enta geweorc, the "skilful work of ents" mentioned in the poem *Maxims II*. Anglo-Saxons believed

in ents . . . what were they? Clearly they were very large, great builders, and clearly they didn't exist any more. From such hints Tolkien created his fable of a race running down to extinction' (Tom Shippey, *The Road to Middle-Earth: How J. R. R. Tolkien Created a New Mythology* (2nd edn; London: HarperCollins 1992), 119). My reading is rather different to Shippey's. After all, Tolkien's ents have no interest in making roads.

11. Similarly, the charm that protects Macbeth against 'man of woman born' ought surely to have been proof against Macduff. From his mother's womb untimely ripped he may have been, but Caesarian section is still a mode of birth, and from a woman too. I once published a story in which Macbeth lives on for centuries, until twenty-second century reforestation expands the extent of Burnham Wood to encompass Macbeth's castle, and a robot is finally able to kill him. This may strike you as a limiting pedantic literalism, of the sort that did not encumber Shakespeare's imagination, and I would not disagree with you. But the point I am making is that there is a similarly concrete, precise streak in Tolkien's imagination too.

12. Daisy Elizabeth Martin-Clarke, *Culture in Early Anglo-Saxon England* (1947; Johns Hopkins University Press Reprints 1979), 33.

13. Maria Artamonova, 'Writing for an Anglo-Saxon Audience in the Twentieth Century: J. R. R. Tolkien's Old English Chronicles', in David Clark and Nicholas Perkins (eds), *Anglo-Saxon Culture and the Modern Imagination* (Cambridge: D. S. Brewer 2000), 86.

2 Cynewulf and the *Exeter Book*

1. Gwendolyn Morgan, 'Religious and Allegorical Verse', in Laura C. Lambdin and Robert T. Lambdin (eds), *A Companion to Old and Middle English Literature* (Westport, CT: Greenwood Press 2002), 26–36; 32.

2. Gregory K. Jember, *The Old English Riddles: A New Translation* (Denver, CO: Society for New Language Study 1972).

3. A. J. Hawkes, 'Symbolic Lives: the Visual Evidence', in John Hines (ed.), *The Anglo-Saxons from the Migration Period to the Eighth Century* (Woodbridge: Boydell and Brewer 1997), 339.

4. Frederick Tupper (ed.), *The Riddles of the Exeter Book* (Boston: 1910), lxxix. Reviewing this volume in the same year, R. W. Chambers commented: 'in the meantime Professor Tupper has become convinced that the so-called First Riddle, which in his edition he passed over as "demanding no place here," is in reality an enigma which conceals the name of Cynewulf, and so shows us who is the author of the Riddles. The lot of a convert is seldom an easy one, and Professor Tupper has been involved in a good deal of controversy, which is by no means over yet.' I dwell on this as indicative of the sorts of debates about the *Exeter Book* riddles that were being aired amongst scholars during Tolkien's own youthful study of the topic.

5. Humphrey Carpenter (ed.), *The Letters of J. R. R. Tolkien* (London: HarperCollins 1995), 385.

6. Carpenter (ed.), *Letters*, 148.

7. In a letter to his son of 7–8 November 1944 Tolkien described a vision he had whilst praying at mass: 'I perceived or thought of the Light of God and in it suspended one small mote (or millions of motes to only one of which was my small mind directed), glittering white because of the individual ray from the Light which both held and lit it . . . And the ray was the Guardian Angel of the mote: not a thing interposed between God and the creature, but God's very attention itself, personalized. And I do not mean "personified", by a mere figure of speech according to the tendencies of human language, but a real (finite) person' (Carpenter (ed.), *Letters*, 99). His vision folds the theology of incarnation into a mystic vision of God as light.

8. Kevin Crossley-Holland, *The Exeter Book of Riddles* (London: Penguin; revised edn 1993), 3.

9. Carpenter (ed.), *Letters*, 347.

10. Carpenter (ed.), *Letters*, 343.

11. Crossley-Holland, *Exeter Book of Riddles*, 85–6. He adds: 'the Anglo-Saxons' love and fear of the sea is conveyed as well in these lines as anywhere in Old English literature'.

12. 'Roverandom', in Tolkien, *Tales from the Perilous Realm* (London: HarperCollins 2008), 37, 83.

13. This is Carolyne Larrington's translation, minimally adapted, from *The Poetic Edda* (Oxford: Oxford University Press 1996), 13.

14. To be clear—my proposed answers are: Jörmungandr; (F) Astitocalon; Niðhöggr (or perhaps Y Ddraig Goch).

15. Carpenter (ed.), *Letters*, 134, 389. 'Brightman' is the theological scholar F. E. Brightman (1856–1932).

16. See Ann Harleman Stewart, 'Kenning and Riddle in Old English', *Papers on Language and Literature* 15 (1979), 115–36.

17. *Old English Poems and Riddles* (translated with an Introduction by Chris McCully; Manchester: Carcanet 2008), 27.

18. McCully, *Old English Poems and Riddles*, 45.

19. Two Robin Chapman Stacey essays say a great deal more on this intriguing matter: 'Instructional Riddles in Welsh Law' (in Joseph Falaky Nagy and Leslie Ellen Jones (eds), *Heroic Poets and Poetic Heroes in Celtic Tradition: A Festschrift for Patrick K. Ford* (Dublin: Four Courts Press 2005), 336–43) and 'Speaking in Riddles' (in Próinséas Ní Chatháin (ed.), *Ireland and Europe in the Early Middle Ages: Texts and Transmission* (Dublin: Four Courts Press 2002), 243–8).

20. Fergus Kelly, 'An Old-Irish Text on Court Procedure', *Peritia* 5 (1986), 74–106.

21. Christopher Guy Yocum, 'Wisdom Literature in Early Ireland' (2010), 24: http://homepages.inf.ed.ac.uk/v1cyocum/wisdom-literature.pdf.

22. Robin Chapman Stacey, *Dark Speech: the Performance of Law in Early Ireland* (Philadelphia: University of Pennsylvania Press 2007), 152. Radner is quoted from: J. N. Radner, 'The Significance of the Threefold Death in Celtic Tradition', in P. K. Ford (ed.), *Celtic Folklore and Christianity: Studies in Memory of William W. Heist* (Los Angeles: McNally and Loftin 1983), 180–99; 185.

23. Tom Shippey, who edited and translated this poem in 1976, calls it 'the best riddle-contest in Old English, and most like the Old Norse ones from the *Eldar Edda* and *The Saga of King Heidrek'*.

24. Dieter Bitterli, *Say What I Am Called: the Old English Riddles of the Exeter Book* (Toronto: University of Toronto Press 2009), 112.

25. *The Saga of King Heidrek the Wise* (translated from the Icelandic with Introduction, Notes and Appendixes by Christopher Tolkien; Cheltenham: Thomas Nelson and Sons 1960). The translations of the riddles that follow in this chapter are my own.

26. Robin Chapman Stacey, *Dark Speech*, 153.

27. Tom Shippey, *J. R. R. Tolkien: Author of the Century* (London: HarperCollins 2000), 173.

28. This is quoted from the website *Europrogocontestovision*.

29. 'Suntory launches calcium-enriched water': http://www.nutraingredients.com/Consumer-Trends/Suntory-launches-calcium-enriched-water.org

30. French writer Pierre Delalande, who is cited in the epigraph to the preface of the present volume, responded to 'Riddle 69' with a little rhyme of his own, 'O', composed in English:

> Sometimes we sound the consonant;
> Sometimes we mark its loss;
> The water-becomes-a-bone riddle
> When *eau* becomes an *os*.

31. Patrick J. Murphy, *Unriddling the Exeter Riddles* (Philadelphia: University of Pennsylvania Press 2011), 77; 26. Murphy also points up AD 4th-century rhetorician Donatus's 'definition of riddling as revealing the *occultum similitudinem rerum*, the hidden similarity of things' (26; quoting Donatus, *Ars Grammatica*, 3:6).

3   Riddles in the Dark

1. For a detailed discussion of the riddles, see Douglas Anderson's impressively comprehensive *The Annotated Hobbit* (London: Unwin Hyman 1988).

2. Snorri Sturluson, *The Prose Edda* (translated by Jesse Byock; London: Penguin 2005), 40.

3. To go off at a slight tangent, we might want to make the argument that this section of the *Prose Edda* records a riddle to which the answer was originally not a fetter for holding a wolf, but a *horse*—a steed as swift, quiet and strong as all the items listed. The '-nir' suffix in 'Gleipnir' means 'horse' (compare 'Sleipnir', "swift-horse", Odin's eight-legged mount, or Slungnir, King Adil's horse. *Gleipnir* would mean something like 'gripping horse', or 'steady-footed horse'.

4. This and the following two remedies are quoted from T. Anderson, 'Dental treatment in Anglo-Saxon England', *British Dental Journal* 197 (2004), 273–4.

5. Vafthruthnismal (*Poetic Edda*), stanzas 11–12. Translated by Craig Williamson in *A Feast of Creatures: Anglo-Saxon Riddle-Songs* (Philadelphia: University of Pennsylvania Press 2011), 15.
6. John D. Rateliff, *The History of the Hobbit: Mr Baggins* (London: HarperCollins 2007), 169.
7. 'Gnomic Verses', in Gavin Bone, *Anglo-Saxon Poetry* (Oxford 1943), 49.
8. Tom Shippey, *J. R. R. Tolkien: Author of the Century* (London: HarperCollins 2000), 24.
9. Douglas Anderson, *The Annotated Hobbit* (London: Unwin Hyman 1988).
10. Humphrey Carpenter (ed.), *The Letters of J. R. R. Tolkien* (London: HarperCollins 1995), 32.
11. Carpenter (ed.), *Letters*, 123.
12. Kevin Crossley-Holland, *The Exeter Book of Riddles* (London: Penguin; revised edn 1993), 31.
13. Douglas Wilhelm Harder, 'Timeline and Chronology for *The Hobbit*', https://ece.uwaterloo.ca/~dwharder/Personal/Hobbit
14. Counting the Preface (which begins 'This is a story of long ago') *The Hobbit* is disposed into 15+5 sections.

4 The Riddles of the All-Wise

1. Noting that Gollum 'does not hiss at all when reciting his riddles; they are anomalous to his normal habits of speech', John Rateliff speculates whether this fact indicates that 'these riddles predate the book' (John D. Rateliff, *The History of the Hobbit: Mr Baggins* (London: HarperCollins 2007), 106–7). Though it cannot be proved, it is certainly possible that Tolkien drafted all the riddles before he began writing *The Hobbit*.
2. James Carey's translation; James Carey and John T. Koch (eds), *The Celtic Heroic Age: Literary Sources for Ancient Celtic Europe and Early Ireland and Wales* (Malden, MA: Celtic Studies Publications 1994), 265.
3. Robert Graves, *The White Goddess* (amended and enlarged edition; London: Faber and Faber 1961), 13. Graves's huge, idiosyncratic book is explicitly an attempt to 'unriddle' the puzzles of myth and poetry. 'A historical grammar of poetic myth has never previously been attempted', he claims in the book's Preface, 'and to write it conscientiously I have had to face such "puzzling questions, though not beyond all conjecture" as Sir Thomas Browne instances in his *Hydriotaphia*: "what song the sirens sang, or what name Achilles assumed when he hid amongst the women".' Graves goes on to list some of the mythological riddles the book addresses, predominantly two lengthy riddling texts attributed to the Welsh bard Taliesin, but also encompassing the number of the beast in the Biblical *Revelation of Saint John* (Graves treats the number, written in Latin, as an acrostic riddle), and a variety of English poems.
4. This is from Brian Jacques' popular children's fantasy, *Redwall* (London: Hutchinson 1986). The answer, of course, is 'BARREL'.
5. Alan Garner's *Thursbitch* (London: Vintage 2004), 1.

6. If we go beyond poetry we can add the Abbot of Aldheim and later Bishop of Malmesbury, best known as a a writer of theological prose, but a man who also riddled. 'He also delighted in elaborate forms of word-play embodied in riddles, an amusement that proved consistently popular to the Anglo-Saxons in the vernacular as well as in Latin', H. R. Lyon, *Anglo-Saxon England and the Norman Conquest* (2nd edn; Harlow: Longman 1991), 281.

7. Tolkien's runes, unlike his various 'elvish' alphabets, are based on actual Anglo-Saxon runic script, although some letters are reversed, assigned different phonetic qualities and otherwise adapted. 'Tolkien used the Anglo-Saxon runic symbols and variations, reversals and inversions for the alphabet called Cirth or Angerthas, meaning runes, or, more literally, "engraved" letters. The forms of Tolkien's adapted runes signify linguistic sound relationships. An extra stroke is added to the voiced sound where there are pairs of voiced and unvoiced sounds' (Ruth S. Noel, *The Languages of Tolkien's Middle Earth* (Boston: Houghton Mifflin 1974), 43).

8. Ralph W. V. Elliot, *Runes: an Introduction* (Manchester: Manchester University Press 1980), 43.

9. Ralph W. V. Elliott, 'Cynewulf's Runes in *Juliana* and *Fates of the Apostles*', in Robert E. Bjork (ed.), *Cynewulf: Basic Readings* (London: Routledge 1996), 294. Elliot's thesis is that the disruption of the order of letters in Cynewulf's name reflects his spiritual disarrangement as a mortal sinner before God's perfect grace.

10. The word for 'fish' in Tolkien's Eldar or Sindar Elvish languages is nowhere recorded, but it would not surprise me if it began with an 's'. Elvish is well supplied with sinuous 's' words that pertain to the same semantic field, including *sîr*, river; *sir* 'flowing' and *súrinen* 'winding'.

11. Noel, *Languages of Tolkien*, 50.

12. 'The word *Alb* meaning lofty in the Celtic language; on which account the Alps, Apennines, Mount Albis, &c, got their names' (Godfrey Higgins, *The Celtic Druids* (1827), 394). The Scots Gaelic name for Scotland, 'Alba', means 'the mountainous country'.

13. Translated by Carolyne Larrington, *The Poetic Edda* (Oxford: Oxford University Press 1996), 110.

14. The 'staf' part of the word may be cognate with the modern English word 'staff'; and it is not a stretch to imagine that a kenning for a stalk of grain might be a word that compares it to a kind of staff. Perhaps the parallel with the ocean comes from not the individual stalk of grain, but rather a whole field. You will have seen, as I have, the wind moving over a full-grown field of wheat or barley and making the surface ripple like a sea.

15. Australian poet Peter Porter's 1989 lyric 'A Chagall Postcard' (from *Possible Worlds*) comes close to riddling this:

> Is this the nature of all truth,
> The blazing god, the bride aloof,
> The riddle cutting like a tooth,
> The dwarf that crows?

The god has seen the standing grain,
The bride is shrouded by her train,
The mystery is strung with pain,
A cold wind blows.

To compare this version of Porter's poem with the words Porter actually wrote (Porter, *Possible Worlds* (Oxford: Oxford University Press 1989), 17) is to grasp the slipperiness of specific vocabulary in the debatable realm both of riddles and discussion of riddles.

16. Jonathan Wilcox, 'Mock-Riddles in Old English: Exeter Riddles 86 and 19', *Studies in Philology* 93 (1996), 180–7.
17. It is perfectly possible to connect this belief to Tolkien's own Christian faith. After all the fish, IXTHUS, is a key Christian trope; any believer in Christ would have no difficulty in seeing him as, metaphorically, ringing the cosmos.
18. Corey Olsen, *Exploring J. R. R. Tolkien's* The Hobbit (Boston: Houghton Mifflin 2012), 106.

5   The Puzzle of the Two *Hobbits*

1. Tolkien, 'On Fairy Stories', in *Tree and Leaf* (London: Allen & Unwin 1964), 25.
2. Tolkien, *Unfinished Tales* (ed. Christopher Tolkien; London: Allen & Unwin 1980), 322.
3. Tolkien, *Unfinished Tales*, 325.

6   The Riddle of Bilbo's Pocket

1. According to pleasingly alliterative trio V. Cumming, C. W. Cunnington and E. Cunnington (*The Dictionary of Fashion History* (Oxford: Berg 2010), 86) the earliest recognisable 'interior' pocket dates from the sixteenth century. It was known originally as a French pocket: 'the earliest form of horizontal slit pocket with the opening covered by a flap'.
2. Patrick Rothfuss, *The Name of the Wind* (New York: Daw 2006), 427.
3. *Beowulf* (ed. A. J. Wyatt; Cambridge: Cambridge University Press 1914), i.
4. This is Seamus Heaney's translation: *Beowulf* (London: Faber and Faber 1999), p. 67. Heaney's translation is used throughout this chapter.
5. Andrew Orchard, *Critical Companion to Beowulf* (Cambridge: D. S. Brewer 2003), 121–2.
6. Earl R. Anderson, 'Grendl's *glof* (*Beowulf* 2085b–88) and Various Latin Analogues', *Mediaevalia* 8 (1982) 1–8.

7   The Riddle of the Ring

1. Tolkien was angered by a Swedish translator's assumption that 'the Ring is in a certain way "der Nibelungen Ring"'. He wrote to Allen & Unwin on

23 February 1961, that 'both rings were round and there the resemblance ceases' and adding that 'the "Nibelung" traditions . . . [have] nothing whatsoever to do with *The Lord of the Rings'* (Humphrey Carpenter (ed.), *The Letters of J. R. R. Tolkien* (1985; London: HarperCollins 1995), 306–7).

2. John Louis DiGaetani, *Richard Wagner and the Modern British Novel* (London: Associated University Presses 1978), 78.

3. Tom Shippey, *The Road to Middle-Earth: How J. R. R. Tolkien Created a New Mythology* (2nd edn; London: HarperCollins 1992), 126.

4. Relatively few critical studies have addressed the novel in these terms, although one exception is Stratford Caldecott's *Secret Fire: the Spiritual Vision of J. R. R. Tolkien* (London: Darton, Longman and Todd 2003). Caldecott quotes from the Catholic catechism (para 1147: 'God speaks to man through the visible creation') and argues that 'a sense of divine providence, of things meaning more than we know, of coincidences needing to be understood, is of course one of the strongest and most lasting impressions one receives from *Lord of the Rings'* (63). Caldecott has a different reading of the Ring to mine, however; seeing it as 'the archetypal "Machine" ' which 'exemplifies the dark magic of the corrupted will' (60).

5. Brian Davies, *Aquinas: an Introduction* (London: Continuum 2002), 210.

6. Davies, *Aquinas*, 215–18.

7. 'The theological significance of the sacraments lies in: (1) the exhibition of the principle of Incarnation. By the embodiment of spiritual reality in material form an appropriate counterpart of the union of God with man in the Person of Christ is made patent (2) Their expression of the objectivity of God's action on the human soul . . . (3) As ordinances mediated through the Church, their essentially social structure' (*The Oxford Dictionary of the Christian Church*, ed. F. L. Cross (3rd edn, ed. E. A. Livingstone; Oxford 1997), 1435). Sacraments work *ex opere operato*, which is to say it is the Grace itself, and not the person administrating them, that validates them. A sacrament administered by a priest is not invalidated should it transpire that the particular priest was married, a murderer or mad.

8. See for instance Shippey's *Road to Middle-Earth*, 177–84.

9. Carpenter (ed.), *Letters*, 145.

10. Bernard Bergonzi, 'The Decline and Fall of the Catholic Novel', in *The Myth of Modernism and the Twentieth Century* (Brighton: Harvester Press 1986), 175.

11. Colin Manlove, *Modern Fantasy: Five Studies* (Cambridge: Cambridge University Press 1975), 176.

12. Carpenter (ed.), *Letters*, 51.

13. Carpenter (ed.), *Letters*, 60. Italics in original.

14. Tolkien, *Morgoth's Ring*, ed. Christopher Tolkien; *The History of Middle Earth, Vol. 10* (London: HarperCollins 1994), 210.

15. Something similar was the case with hobbits as well: 'As far as I know hobbits were universally monogamous (indeed they very seldom married a second time, even if wife or husband died very young)', (letter to A. C. Nunn, drafted probably late 1958–early 1959; Carpenter (ed.), *Letters*, 293).

16. Tolkien, *The Lord of the Rings* (1954–55; 1 Vol. edn, London: HarperCollins 2012), 130.
17. Tolkien, *Lord of the Rings*, 120. Tolkien stresses the sense of Tom's house as a safe circle through which the Hobbits pass. They enjoy their only contented nights' sleep in Tom's beds. His house has windows 'at either end . . . one looking east and the other looking west' (*LotR*, 126). It is repeatedly described as suffused with golden light.

8   *The Lord of the Rings* and the Riddle of Writing

1. Humphrey Carpenter, *The Letters of J. R. R. Tolkien* (London: HarperCollins 1995), 344. The letter goes on to note 'I typed out *The Hobbit*.'
2. Tolkien, *The Lord the Rings* (1954–55; 1 Vol. edn, London: HarperCollins 2012), 524.

9   The Volsung Riddle: Character in Tolkien

1. Franco Moretti, *The Way of the World: the Bildungsroman in European Culture* (London: Verso 1987).
2. Tolkien, *Sigurd and Gudrún*, ed. Christopher Tolkien (London: HarperCollins 2009), 176–7.
3. Tom Shippey has an excellent discussion on the linguistic and semantic connections between 'bourgeois', 'borough' and 'burglar' as they pertain to Hobbits in his *Tolkien: the Author of the Century* (London: HarperCollins 2002).
4. George Philip Krapp and Elliot van Kirk (eds), *The Anglo-Saxon Poetic Records* (New York: Columbia University Press, 6 vols 1931–53), 3: *The Exeter* Book, 156.
5. Humphrey Carpenter (ed.), *The Letters of J. R. R. Tolkien* (London: Harper Collins 1995), 66.

10   The Enigma of Genre Fantasy

1. Adam Phillips, *Side Effects* (London: Penguin 2006), 59. The passage quoted a little further on is from 65.
2. Ursula Le Guin, *A Wizard of Earthsea* (1968; London: Gollancz 1971), 191.

11   . . . And Back Again?

1. John D. Rateliff, *The History of the Hobbit: Mr Baggins* (London: HarperCollins 2007), 107.
2. Another reason Tolkien may have been drawn to the *Alvíssmál* is linguistic. As Charlie Anderson notes, 'the Poetic Edda poem *Alvissmal* is fascinating, because it gives glimpses into the dialects / languages of these beings.

For example, the human *himinn* ("sky") is *hlyrnir* to the Aesir, *vindofni* to the Vanir, *uppheimto* the Jotnar, *fagraræfr* to the Elves and *drjupansal* to the Dwarves. Tolkien . . . lived and breathed the sources of Anglo-Saxon and Germanic myth, which are related to Norse myth. As a professional linguist, Tolkien must have seen that some translations of *Alvissmal*, for example Bellows' (1936), failed to show that the different dialects / languages might be unintelligible, and that the common language between the Aesir and the Dwarves was the language of humans', Anderson, 'Norse Mythology, Fantasy and *Lord of the Rings*': http://wbrondtkamffer.com/tag/j-r-r-tolkien (30 October 2012).

3. John Garth, *Tolkien and the Great War: the Threshold of Middle Earth* (London: HarperCollins 2003), 307–8.

4. Tolkien, *The Lord of the Rings* (1954–55; 1 Vol. edition; London: HarperCollins 2012), 1172. Might *kûd-dûkan* carry some echo of Tolkien's classical education? The Greek κυδ- is the root of words meaning 'renown, glory, esteem'; το δυικαν is Greek for 'the dual number'. Perhaps the Hobbits are 'twice renowned' in the sense that they appear in both *The Hobbit* and *The Lord of the Rings*.

5. Tom Shippey, *J. R .R. Tolkien: Author of the Century* (London: HarperCollins 2000), 46. Shippey also speculates that 'hobbit' may owe something to the word 'rabbit.'

6. The Old Norse Saga *King Heidrek the Wise*—which I talk about above, on account of its lengthy riddle context—begins with King Garðaríki, Heidrek's father, obtaining from the dwarfs the magic sword Tyrfingr, 'hét ok allra var bitrast', 'of all swords the sharpest'. 'Bitrast' might be translated 'bitterest', provide we keep this etymological sense of the meaning of 'bitter' alive.

7. Iona and Peter Opie's *Oxford Dictionary of Nursery Rhymes* (2nd edn; Oxford: Clarendon Press 1971), 215. Opie goes on to quote Lewis Carroll: ' "It is very provoking to be called an egg—very" as Humpty admits in *Through the Looking Glass*, but such common knowledge cannot be gainsaid.'

8. 'E. G. Withycombe (*Oxford Dictionary of Christian Names*) also associates a human being with the name [Humpty-Dumpty], suggesting that it echoes the pet forms of *Humphrey* which were *Dumphry* and *Dump*.' Opies, *Oxford Dictionary of Nursery Rhymes*, 215. Both 'hombetty' or 'hobbety' are variants noted in the *OED*. There is, of course, no actual medieval Romance entitled *Ringe*.

Bibliography

Works by Tolkien

Carpenter, Humphrey (ed.), *The Letters of J. R. R. Tolkien* (1985; London: HarperCollins 1995)

Tolkien, J. R. R., *The Hobbit* (1937; London: HarperCollins 2012)

——, *The Lord of the Rings* (1954–55; 1 vol. edition; London: HarperCollins 2012)

——, *Tree and Leaf* (London: Allen & Unwin 1964)

——, *Unfinished Tales* (ed. Christopher Tolkien; London: Allen & Unwin 1980)

——, *Morgoth's Ring* (ed. Christopher Tolkien; *The History of Middle Earth, vol. 10*: London: HarperCollins 1994)

——, *The Children of Húrin* (ed. Christopher Tolkien; London: HarperCollins 2006)

——, *Sigurd and Gudrún* (ed. Christopher Tolkien; London: HarperCollins 2009)

——, *Tales from the Perilous Realm* (London:HarperCollins, 2008)

Other works

Beowulf (ed. A. J. Wyatt; Cambridge: Cambridge University Press 1914)

The Elder Edda: A Selection (trans. Paul B. Taylor and W. H. Auden; Introduction by Peter H. Salus and Paul B. Taylor; London: Faber and Faber 1969)

The Poetic Edda (trans. Carolyne Larrington; Oxford: Oxford University Press 1996)

The Saga of King Heidrek the Wise (translated from the Icelandic with Introduction, Notes and Appendixes by Christopher Tolkien; Cheltenham: Thomas Nelson and Sons, 1960)

Anderson, Charlie, 'Norse Mythology, Fantasy and *Lord of the Rings*': http://wbrondtkamffer.com/tag/j-r-r-tolkien (30 October 2012)

Anderson, Douglas (ed.), *The Annotated Hobbit* (London: Unwin Hyman 1988)

Anderson, Earl R., 'Grendl's *glof* (*Beowulf* 2085b–88) and Various Latin Analogues', *Mediaevalia* 8 (1982) 1–8

Artamonova, Maria, 'Writing for an Anglo-Saxon Audience in the Twentieth Century: J. R. R. Tolkien's Old English Chronicles', in David Clark and Nicholas Perkins (eds), *Anglo-Saxon Culture and the Modern Imagination* (Cambridge: D. S. Brewer 2000), 71–88

Bates, Brian, *The Real Middle-Earth: Magic and Mystery in the Dark Ages* (London: Pan Books 2002)

Bergonzi, Bernard, 'The Decline and Fall of the Catholic Novel', in *The Myth of Modernism and the Twentieth Century* (Brighton: Harvester Press 1986), 172–87

Bitterli, Dieter, *Say What I Am Called: the Old English Riddles of the Exeter Book* (Toronto: University of Toronto Press 2009)

Bone, Gavin, *Anglo-Saxon Poetry* (Oxford 1943)

Bradley, S. A. J., *Anglo-Saxon Poetry* (London: Dent, Everyman 1982)

Brown, Devin, *The Christian World of The Hobbit* (Nashville, TN: Abingdon Press 2012)

Caldecott, Stratford, *Secret Fire: the Spiritual Vision of J. R. R. Tolkien* (London: Darton, Longman and Todd 2003)

Carey, James, and John T. Koch (eds), *The Celtic Heroic Age: Literary Sources for Ancient Celtic Europe and Early Ireland and Wales* (Malden, MA: Celtic Studies Publications 1994)

Carter, Lin, *Tolkien: a Look Behind the Lord of the Rings* (1969; updated edn, London: Gollancz 2003)

Cross, F. L. (ed.), *The Oxford Dictionary of the Christian Church* (3rd edition; Oxford: Oxford University Press 1997)

Crossley-Holland, Kevin, *The Exeter Book of Riddles* (London: Penguin; revised edn 1993)

Cumming, Valerie, C. W. Cunnington, and E. Cunnington (eds), *The Dictionary of Fashion History* (Oxford: Berg 2010)

Davies, Brian, *Aquinas: an Introduction* (London: Continuum 2002)

Delalande, Pierre, *Le Livre de Neant* (Paris: Inexistant 2012)

DiGaetani, John Louis, *Richard Wagner and the Modern British Novel* (London: Associated University Presses 1978)

Elliot, Ralph Warren Victor, *Runes: an Introduction* (Manchester: Manchester University Press 1980), 43

——, 'Cynewulf's Runes in *Juliana* and *Fates of the Apostles*', in Robert E. Bjork (ed.), *Cynewulf: Basic Readings* (London: Routledge 1996)

Garth, John, *Tolkien and the Great War: the Threshold of Middle Earth* (London: HarperCollins 2003)

Graves, Robert, *The Crowning Privilege: Collected Essays on Poetry* (London: Doubleday 1960)

——, *The White Goddess* (amended and enlarged edition; London: Faber and Faber 1961)

Gummere, Francis, *The Popular Ballad* (1907; Dover Publications 1959)

Hawkes, A. J., 'Symbolic Lives: the Visual Evidence', in John Hines (ed.), *The Anglo-Saxons from the Migration Period to the Eighth Century* (Woodbridge: Boydell and Brewer, 1997), 311–44

Heanry, Seamus (trans.), *Beowulf* (London: Faber and Faber 1999)

Hill, John M., *The Anglo-Saxon Warrior Ethic: Reconstructing Lordship in Early English Literature* (Gainesville: University of Florida Press 2000)

Jacobs, Alan (ed.), *Auden: For the Time Being: A Christmas Oratorio* (Princeton: Princeton University Press 2013)

Jember, Gregory K., *The Old English Riddles: a New Translation* (Denver, CO: Society for New Language Study, 1972)

Ker, W. P., *The Dark Ages* (Oxford 1904)

Kierkegaard, Søren, *Philosophical Fragments or A Fragment of Philosophy* (trans. David F. Swenson; Princeton: Princeton University Press 1962)

Lewis, C. S., *Reflections on the Psalms* (Boston: Houghton Mifflin 1958)

Lyon, H. R., *Anglo-Saxon England and the Norman Conquest* (2nd edn; Longman 1991)

Manlove, Colin, *Modern Fantasy: Five Studies* (Cambridge: Cambridge University Press 1975)

McCully, Chris, *Old English Poems and Riddles* (Manchester: Carcanet 2008)

Milbank, Alison, 'The Riddle and the Gift: the Hobbit at Christmas', *ABC Religion and Ethics* (24 December 2012): http://www.abc.net.au/religion/articles/2012/12/24/3660152.htm

Morgan, Gwendolyn, 'Religious and Allegorical Verse', in Laura C. Lambdin and Robert T. Lambdin (eds), *A Companion to Old and Middle English Literature* (Westport, CT: Greenwood Press, 2002), 26–36

Moseley, Charles, *J. R .R. Tolkien* (Tavistock: Northcote House/British Council 1997)

Murphy, Patrick J., *Unriddling the Exeter Riddles* (Philadelphia: University of Pennsylvania Press 2011)

Noel, Ruth S., *The Languages of Tolkien's Middle Earth* (Boston: Houghton Mifflin 1974)

Olsen, Corey, *Exploring J. R. R. Tolkien's The Hobbit* (Boston: Houghton Mifflin 2012)

Opie, Peter, and Iona Opie, *Oxford Dictionary of Nursery Rhymes* (2nd edn; Oxford: Clarendon Press 1971)

O'Prey, Paul (ed.), *Robert Graves: Selected Poems* (London: Penguin 1986)

Orchard, Andrew, *Critical Companion to Beowulf* (Cambridge: D. S. Brewer 2003)

OED: The Oxford English Dictionary (2nd edn; Oxford: Oxford University Press 1989)

Pearce, Joseph, *Tolkien: Man and Myth* (London: HarperCollins 1998)

Phillips, Adam, *Side Effects* (London: Penguin 2006)

Porter, Peter, 'A Chagall Postcard', *Possible Worlds* (Oxford: Oxford University Press 1989), 17

Radner, J. N., 'The Significance of the Threefold Death in Celtic Tradition', in P. K. Ford (ed.), *Celtic Folklore and Christianity: Studies in Memory of William W. Heist* (Los Angeles: McNally and Loftin 1983), 180–99

Rateliff, John D., *The History of the Hobbit: Mr Baggins* (London: HarperCollins 2007)

Rothfuss, Patrick, *The Name of the Wind* (New York: Daw 2006)

Shippey, Tom, *The Road to Middle-Earth: how J. R. R. Tolkien Created a New Mythology* (2nd edn; London: HarperCollins 1992)

——, *J. R. R. Tolkien: Author of the Century* (London: HarperCollins 2002)

Stacey, Robin Chapman, 'Speaking in Riddles', in Próinséas Ní Chatháin (ed.), *Ireland and Europe in the Early Middle Ages: Texts and Transmission* (Dublin: Four Courts Press 2002), 243–8

——, 'Instructional Riddles in Welsh Law', in Joseph Falaky Nagy and Leslie Ellen Jones (eds), *Heroic Poets and Poetic Heroes in Celtic Tradition: A Festschrift for Patrick K. Ford* (Dublin: Four Courts Press 2005), 336–43

——, *Dark Speech: the Performance of Law in Early Ireland* (Philadelphia: University of Pennsylvania Press, 2007)

Stewart, Ann Harleman, 'Kenning and Riddle in Old English', *Papers on Language and Literature* 15 (1979), 115–36

Sturluson, Snorri, *The Prose Edda* (trans. Jesse Byock; London: Penguin 2005)

Tupper, Frederick (ed.), *The Riddles of the Exeter Book* (Boston: 1910)

Wilcox, Jonathan, 'Mock-Riddles in Old English: Exeter Riddles 86 and 19', *Studies in Philology* 93 (1996), 180–7

Index

Printed and bound by CPI Group (UK) Ltd, Croydon, CR0 4YY